IN SEARCH OF T... ...CULPTURE

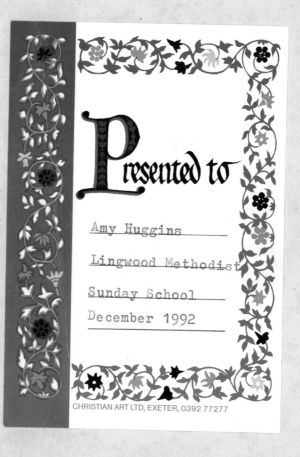

Presented to

Amy Huggins

Lingwood Methodist

Sunday School

December 1992

CHRISTIAN ART LTD, EXETER, 0392 77277

IN SEARCH OF
The GOLDEN
SCEPTRE

Stories of the Realm: 2

PHIL ALLCOCK

Phoenix

Front cover design by Vic Mitchell

British Library Cataloguing in Publication Data

Allcock, Phil
  In search of the golden sceptre
  I. Title
  823.914 [J]

  ISBN 0–86065–907–0

Phoenix is an imprint of Kingsway Publications Ltd,
1 St Anne's Road,
Eastbourne, E Sussex BN21 3UN.
Typeset by J&L Composition Ltd, Filey,
North Yorkshire.
Printed in England by Clays Ltd, St Ives plc.

Dedicated to my brother and sister-in-law, Paul and Di, and to my nephews, Tim, Jonathan and Christopher.
Your support, love and prayers have been—and continue to be—invaluable.

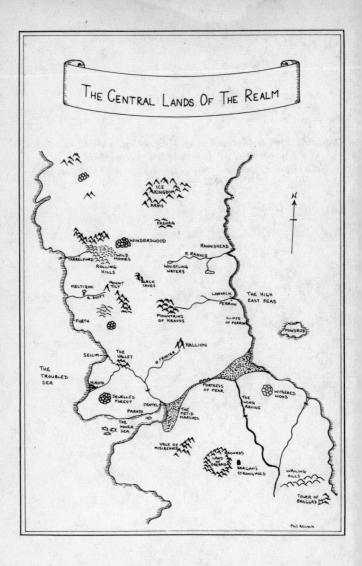

THE CENTRAL LANDS OF THE REALM

N

ICE KINGDOM
ARDIS
FASHAG
WINDERSWOOD
RANNISHEAD
WILD MOORS
TARRELFORD
ROLLING HILLS
R. RANNIS
WHISTLING WATERS
MELTIZOC
MOUNT TILT
BLACK CAVES
R. SWIFT
LANWICK
PERRON
THE HIGH EAST SEAS
FURTH
MOUNTAINS OF KRAVOS
CLIFFS OF PERRON
HINDROD
SELLIM
THE VALLEY
HALLION
R. FROSTER
THE TROUBLED SEA
KIROTH
JEWELLED FOREST
PARATH
JENTEL
FORTRESS OF FEAR
WITHERED WOOD
THE INNER SEA
THE FETID MARSHES
THE LONG RAVINE
VALE OF MISCREANCE
RONADD
LAND OF DREAMS
DARGAN'S STRONGHOLD
WAILING HILLS
TOWER OF BRAGGAD

Phil Allcock

Stories of the Realm

This is the second book in the trilogy of Stories of the Realm, recounting the tale of Taz-i-tor, the Golden Sceptre of Elsinoth.

The first book, *The Will of Dargan*, told how Kess and Linnil, the Quiet Ones, leave their secluded valley home to learn more about the Realm and about the dangers facing it. They set off to find Meltizoc the Wise, but on their way they meet Valor, a Mountain Guard. Valor tells them of an act of treachery that could indeed endanger the land—the theft of the Golden Sceptre of Elsinoth (Toroth) the Mighty, creator of the Realm.

The Sceptre has been stolen by its Keeper, Carnak. Valor is seeking to avenge the death of his father, who was killed by the fleeing Carnak. However, Carnak is under the spell of the evil Dargan, and he escapes to the Southlands, making his way eventually to the Dark Master's stronghold. Dargan wants the Sceptre because Elsinoth has breathed into it the essence of free will—the open choice that all people are given, between good and evil. Dargan is determined to bring the Sceptre's powers under his own control, so that he can force all the people of the Realm to follow *his* will.

Meanwhile, on Meltizoc's instructions, Kess, Linnil and Valor seek the help of the Crafters. After many adventures, they find Vallel and Vosphel, the golden-haired Water Crafter sisters; Hesteron, the tall and aloof Air Crafter; and Gatera, the huge Land Crafter. They are also joined by Merric, a wandering minstrel; and Rrum, a rock man they rescue from the Black Caves.

The group travels to the beautiful vale of Hallion for a meeting led by Tolledon, Guardian of the Realm. A twofold plan is devised for the recapture of the Sceptre. Firstly, an army will be assembled from the peoples of the Northlands, and will lay siege to the Fortress of Fear, which guards the only land route to the south. The fortress is occupied by Dargan's Zorgs, including the brutish Gur'brak and his minion Bar'drash. The army's main function, however, is to distract Dargan's attention from the small company of ten travellers who—as the second part of the plan—will travel to the Southlands by sea in a bid to regain the Sceptre.

The company sets sail across the Inner Sea under the leadership of Tolledon's son, Athennar, but they are attacked by a Scorbid, and Vosphel dies from its sting. Athennar's resolve to recover the Sceptre is strengthened, but he also wants to find his cousin Zendos, who has kidnapped the woman he loves, Melinya. Zendos is now Dargan's sorcerer, and he attacks the company when they reach the Southlands. The friends are scattered.

Linnil and Kess are captured by Zorgs but are rescued by Rrum, Sash (a black leopard befriended by Athennar) and a group of rock people. Meanwhile, the rest of the company travel through the Land of Dreams, where Hesteron and Vallel are saved from death by the gentle Mentars.

Athennar, Merric, Valor and Gatera travel on to Dargan's stronghold, but are trapped and imprisoned by Zendos. After great difficulties, their friends rescue them and, together again, the company finds Dargan's Throne Room.

Meanwhile, two groups of elves from the Northlands army try to find a route across the marsh that surrounds the Fortress of Fear. They are attacked by the vicious, mind-sucking Tarks, and several of their number are killed. However, they cross the marsh, and the Northern army captures the fortress after a fierce battle.

In Dargan's Throne Room, the nine friends find the Golden Sceptre, and Valor holds it aloft in triumph. The company then turns to leave. ...

1

Captured!

In the heart of Dargan's stronghold, the nine friends laughed and almost sang with joy; at last they had won back the Golden Sceptre! But they could not afford to stand and stare at it … they must escape quickly—now, while the way was still open to them.

The commanding figure of Athennar led the way towards the door.

Valor, one fist clenched in triumph, the other curled round the Sceptre, followed close behind. The others clustered around him, and the huge shape of Gatera joined Rrum at the back of the group.

The giant Land Crafter glanced around once more as they moved towards the door. Then he shuddered to a halt.

'The Eye!' he roared. He had noticed a wooden mask hanging behind the throne, and now lumbered back towards it. In one of the eye sockets glistened an oval green stone. 'We must destroy it!' he growled in explanation, 'or Dargan may use it to follow us!' Snatching the mask, he plucked out the Eye, threw it to the floor, and smashed it into fragments with the hilt of his sword.

At the same moment, a voice of pain screamed from beyond one of the walls of the room. A door creaked open, and a grotesque tapestry fluttered briefly before being pushed aside.

A cloaked figure with white hair, streaked with black, staggered into the room, clutching his left eye. The white pupil of his other eye gleamed with hatred as he caught sight of the companions, and he straightened and fixed them all with a cold glare.

'Dargan!' said Athennar, his teeth clenched.

Valor rushed forward with sword drawn. In his haste, he forgot that he was still holding the Sceptre.

'Stop!' commanded Dargan icily.

Valor halted. Although he was contorted with rage, he found he was completely immobilised. The others, too, stood helplessly frozen as Dargan's chilly stare turned into a sneer.

'Now you will pay for your insolence with your lives!' he said. Keeping watch on his captives, he roared impatiently, 'Zendos!' His face paled with the effort of will he needed to keep the whole company under his control. Although one eye had obviously been damaged by Gatera's action, both still gleamed with hatred.

The oaken doors opened, and Zendos the sorcerer strode through. He inhaled sharply as he caught sight of the paralysed company.

'Yes,' snarled Dargan. 'Your incompetence exceeds even your self-importance! You were supposed to have this rabble under your control!'

'I—I didn't realise there were more of them nearby. I thought—'

'You have done too much thinking already. This time you will just obey! Now fetch the Sceptre!' Dargan's eyes remained fixed on the travellers, but his voice was filled with even more venom than usual.

Zendos glared at the Dark Master. After a moment's hesitation, he crossed the room and

wrested the staff from Valor's grasp. Running his
hand thoughtfully along it, he paused and looked
back at Dargan.

'Bring it here!' snapped Dargan.

The sorcerer glared at his master. 'I am tired of
being your pawn,' he growled. 'It is time that I took
what should be mine.'

'You fool!' Dargan grated. 'You dare to defy me? I
taught you all you know. Now give me the Sceptre!'
His eyes flashed at the sorceror.

Zendos stood his ground rebelliously, glowering at
his master, but suddenly he winced with pain. 'No!' he
shrieked. His body convulsed and his face reddened
as he struggled to regain control. For a moment it
seemed that he would be successful. A hard light of
concentration shone in his eyes, and he started to
turn away. But then a sudden surge of the Dark
Master's power caught him, snapping his will. His
arm shot out involuntarily, throwing the Sceptre
across the floor to Dargan's feet. He collapsed on the
floor with a gasp of pain.

Meanwhile, Kess had been struggling. Fear and
hatred of the evil of the Dark Master battled inside his
mind. He had watched in a dream as Valor had
rushed forward and then halted. As Dargan's eyes
had swept across him, his own muscles had frozen,
too, although he was still able to see the battle
between the Dark Master and Zendos.

To Kess' surprise, he now felt a new emotion
stirring within—pity: he actually felt sorry for the two
combatants as they tested their wills against each
other. Recognising the hatred and lust for power that
consumed them both, he realised that long ago they
must have forsaken any hint of compassion. He knew
they would never be open to the power of love and
friendship that he had experienced with his company
of friends.

Even as these thoughts crossed his mind, some feeling returned to his body. Zendos and Dargan were still locked, will against will. He tried to ease his muscles slightly, and to his surprise found that he could move his arms freely. All the others, however, seemed immobile, except for Linnil, who was cautiously beginning to move her head.

Kess' mind raced. What could he do? He was no warrior—no cold-blooded slayer! Yet he knew that if Dargan defeated Zendos they would all be killed anyway.

The staff! he thought desperately. If only he could get hold of it and escape, Dargan would follow him, and his friends might have a chance to get away. Perhaps he could even break the staff and destroy its power.

No sooner had he thought this than Zendos fell, throwing the Sceptre towards Dargan. Seeing his chance, Kess rushed across the floor towards the staff, but tripped over a flagstone and fell, winded. As he looked up, Linnil rushed past him towards the Sceptre.

She was too late. Dargan grabbed the staff as Linnil's hand shot out to take it. Moving with surprising speed, he thrust the Sceptre through his belt and dragged Linnil in front of him. Then he drew a knife, which he held at her throat. Kess saw all this in a daze of pain and surprise.

'I have no more time to waste on you fools!' Dargan snarled. He backed towards the tapestry, keeping a close eye on Zendos, who was showing signs of recovery. Then, sweeping the tapestry back, he disappeared with the slam of a door. All was still.

'Linnil!' shouted Kess. He scrambled to his feet and raced after them, tearing down the tapestry in his desperation. The door beyond was locked! He hammered on it, kicked and cried out, but to no avail.

Meanwhile, mobility returned to the others. No longer were they bound by Dargan's will. Athennar ran to where Kess stood pounding on the locked door. 'It's all right—we'll find a way to open it,' he promised.

'Not so fast!' came a cold voice. Zendos staggered to his feet. 'Dargan may have beaten me now, but I will find him again. Meanwhile, cousin Athennar, I will avenge myself on you!' Pulling a small tube from his sleeve, he put it to his mouth, his face contorting as he pointed it at Athennar. A strange hum came from the tube, quickly followed by a concentrated pellet of sound—almost visible in the shock wave it produced as it zipped through the air.

Athennar ducked, and the wave hit the wall of the room and reverberated, drumming in their heads. Large chunks of masonry crumbled from the wall.

Zendos waved the tube in anger. 'This time you will not escape!' he shouted, before putting it back to his mouth. But even as he did so, the snarling form of Sash, the black leopard, smashed into him, sending him reeling to the floor. The blast from the tube hit the ceiling, which cracked, shifted, and started falling in large lumps. One block hit Zendos, and he crumpled.

'Well done, Sash!' shouted Athennar, springing towards the sorcerer; but Gatera blocked his way.

'I have to find out what he's done with Melinya!' Athennar yelled.

'It's no use—we've got to get out of here! The whole place is collapsing!' Gatera pulled him away. 'The door to Dargan's room!' he shouted to the others.

The convulsions within the Throne Room had twisted the frame that held the locked door, so Gatera shoved it open and lumbered through, followed quickly by Kess and the others. Behind them, the ceiling of the Throne Room rained down.

Beyond the door was a candlelit office, packed with scrolls and strange devices. Skeletal birds' heads decorated the furniture, and giant pitchers held multi-coloured liquids.

Kess barely took all these in. He was already looking for another exit. Then he saw it—in a dark alcove. 'Over here!' he called, running across to the opening. A cool draught of air came through it, and steps spiralled upwards. He took them two at a time, not waiting to see if anyone was following, but they were awkward and steep, and in his haste he twice nearly fell. Barely slowing, he soon saw light coming around a twist of the spiral. As he rounded it, he saw that the steps finished at an open trapdoor.

Forgetting all caution, he stepped through the trapdoor and found himself in one of the tower rooms. A door stood to his right. Tugging at it, he was almost knocked back by a gust of wind as the door opened. It led on to a long catwalk above a courtyard. Down below, several Zorgs were running around in wild panic, but Kess ignored them. A little way ahead of him, mounting a large, winged creature, was Dargan. In front of the Dark Master, draped over the Tark, was the slumped form of Linnil.

'Linnil!' Kess screamed desperately. He raced along the walkway, but the Tark took off effortlessly, bearing its burden up into the air, then out over the grim landscape beyond.

'Linnil!' he wailed again.

2

Doubt and Uncertainty

Kess peered forlornly out of the small window that overlooked a courtyard in the Fortress of Fear, and thought back over the events of the past few days. After using ropes to escape from Dargan's stronghold—Sash had somehow found her own way out—the company had made their way disconsolately back to Rronadd. Rrum's parents had greeted them warmly: the Rrokki had been busy, having intercepted and defeated some Zorgs that were on their way to reinforce the troops at the Fortress of Fear. Then they had heard that the Zorgs at the fortress had also been defeated, by the army from the Northlands.

Cheered slightly by the news, Athennar had led the company northwards, leaving Gatera and Rrum behind at Rronadd. After five days' travel, they had arrived at the Fortress of Fear.

Now Kess was alone again. Athennar was somewhere taking council with Hinno; Merric had disappeared, alone with his flute; Valor was renewing acquaintances with his Mountain Guard friends; and Vallel and Hesteron were no doubt walking or talking together somewhere. But his own seclusion only heightened his awareness of Linnil's absence. Once again, as he had every day since her capture, he wondered where she was and if she was safe. If only he had …

There was a knock on the door of his room. Kess called out a gruff 'Come in!' without bothering to turn around. A moment later he felt a hand on his shoulder.

'I feel the loss as well. Be sure, we will find her again. We must!'

Kess turned gratefully to Merric, who appraised him with obvious concern. 'I just hope she is safe—I'm afraid of what Dargan might do to her.'

Merric nodded in understanding. Suddenly his fist slammed down on the window ledge in frustration. 'If only I could have reached him—stopped him.'

'That's what I keep thinking—"If only". But we can't change what's happened.' Kess grimaced. 'When are we meeting to plan what we do next?'

'This afternoon. Apparently Tolledon and his company should arrive from Hallion shortly; they have been seen a league from here.'

Kess sighed. He felt so different from the country youth who had rashly embarked on this drawn-out adventure. So much had happened, and they had all travelled so far—but to what gain? Would Tolledon and Meltizoc be able to help?

What of the future? he thought. *Will we be able to find Linnil? Will Tolledon even allow such a venture?*

Tolledon cleared his throat and gazed at the other people in the small chamber. They were all dejected and weary. Athennar was more gaunt than ever, and seemed to carry a heavy burden in his soul.

The company had given their accounts of all that had happened. Now Meltizoc was speaking to the assembled group. 'And what happened to the impulsive young man who wanted to conquer everything by strength?'

Valor spoke quietly, despite his discomfort. 'I have learned that there are different kinds of strength,' he said.

'You have, nonetheless, played a valiant role,' interrupted Tolledon, 'and our thanks go to you and the rest of the company.'

'There is something I don't understand,' Hinno's elvish voice suddenly piped up. 'Why didn't Dargan's spell, or whatever it was, work on Kess and Linnil?'

'I think I know the answer,' replied Meltizoc slowly. 'Dargan's powers feed off evil, however small—including anger and hatred. From what he has said, Kess felt sorry for him—as perhaps did Linnil also. At that moment, Dargan had nothing to control—a little like grasping something that disappears. It took your selflessness, Kess, to defeat his evil.' The wise man looked kindly at Kess.

'Except that he wasn't defeated!' Kess blurted. 'We failed, and now he's got Linnil!'

Tolledon intervened. 'You must not regard it as a failure,' he said. 'You were not to blame for what happened. You got nearer to Dargan than anyone else could have done.'

'It's not finished yet,' said Athennar firmly. Tolledon looked at him, surprised by the interruption.

Athennar continued, 'We can still succeed. Dargan obviously hasn't mastered the staff yet—and now he has left the security of his stronghold. It will take him even longer to settle down and find out how to use its powers. Meanwhile, he has Linnil. We have no choice but to seek him again—and this time we will not fail!'

Kess looked at him gratefully, even though he did not share Athennar's confidence.

Tolledon looked thoughtful. 'You are right, my son, when you say we have no choice. Once Dargan can bend the Sceptre to his own will, it will herald the end of the Realm as we have known it. Athennar, if you and Hinno stay behind, we will discuss this matter further. The rest of you would probably like some fresh air.' He smiled. 'Thank you all. We have not lost yet!'

Merric, Hesteron, Vallel and Valor joined Kess in his room after the meeting. Kess felt comforted by their presence; even though they all seemed drained.

Hesteron slumped wearily into a chair. 'Sometimes it takes a long time and great courage to accomplish anything,' he commented.

Vallel smiled. 'We can help each other. Somehow I think we still all have our parts to play before this saga ends.'

'And my path will lie with you,' Merric told Kess. 'Troubadours rarely make vows, but this I promise on my oath: we will rescue Linnil from Dargan's grasp. I do not know how, but somehow we will. It will not be easy, though.'

'And I am with you, too!' chipped in Valor. 'I must still avenge my father by finding Carnak—wherever he is!'

Kess looked around his group of friends and smiled. Who could doubt such sincerity and loyalty? At last he felt that there was just a chance that they might succeed. Tolledon's recent words still rang in his mind: 'We have not lost yet!'

3
The Tower of Braggad

The wooden bridge swayed erratically in the wind that funnelled down the ravine. Its old timbers creaked and groaned, as they had done for years. The tired, stained ropes that formed the skeleton for the wooden bodywork were still strong enough, however, to take the weight of an occasional traveller who braved the only passage across the deep chasm.

A hooded, hunched figure brooded at one end of the bridge. After a few moments, he produced a knife from the depths of his black cloak. It was blunt, but a few moments' sawing cut through the ropes where they were attached to the stanchion. Quickly moving to the other post, he cut the remaining ropes. The bridge fell clattering, waving a brief farewell in the wind before smashing into the opposite cliff.

Satisfied, Dargan moved slowly away, chuckling darkly. A stray shaft of cold light illuminated the pale face beneath the hood and glinted off the chilling black eyes. As he approached the sombrely coloured, shuffling Tark that awaited him, he again began to brood over his plans. Absent-mindedly he stroked the slim, delicately carved staff that was tucked through his belt. Soon he would be able to start working on it again to unleash the secret of its powers. It tantalised his every waking moment, teasing him, taunting him.

He had been so near to unlocking the Sceptre's mysteries; so close to being able to rechannel its strengths for his own ends. But those interfering elves and men had foiled him. He frowned, the white pupils constricting slightly, like shrinking icebergs in an ocean of black.

Those meddlesome fools! he thought. He had been careless in underestimating them. He had also been careless in assigning Zendos to deal with them. Zendos had failed. Perhaps he had perished in the Throne Room: Dargan had heard it collapsing as he dragged Linnil away. Well, the incompetent sorcerer deserved such a fate! Some of those others, however, had managed to survive—he had seen them as he mounted Targul, who had so fortuitously arrived at the stronghold in time. Dargan had gloated as the Tark climbed into the sky, and had watched the figures gathering on the battlements until they were specks on a distant landscape.

He could almost imagine their curses floating up to him. Not only had he wrested the Golden Sceptre back from them, he had also captured one of their number—a pretty one at that!

He looked now at the auburn-haired young woman slumped on the ground by the Tark. What was it that one of the intruders had shrieked out as the Tark had launched itself upwards? *Linnil?* He wondered briefly who she was and why she had been involved in their futile mission to recapture the staff of Elsinoth. No matter! She was under his power now. He had focused his will on her to mount the steps leading out of his chamber, and when they had reached the battlements he had subdued her completely. She had been in a state of semi-consciousness ever since. That suited his purposes, and he rubbed his hands together in silent satisfaction.

Having destroyed the bridge, he would continue the journey to the Tower of Braggad, his home in the east for many years until he had moved to the stronghold by the Land of Dreams. When he reached his destination he would again start to try and unravel the mysteries of the staff. He was confident that it wouldn't take long, despite the loss of many useful books and artefacts left behind in the ruins of his former stronghold. The girl would have the privilege of being one of the first to experience his new powers. Then her friends would regret ever having dared to defy him.

He reached the sagging form of the young woman. Another bitter chuckle forced its way from his throat. Grabbing her roughly, he slung her again over the back of the waiting Tark. The creature was surprisingly strong despite its shrivelled body. However, the burden of carrying two humans for such a long distance was undoubtedly taking its toll. The dual green slits that served as eyes stared unblinkingly at Dargan as he mounted.

So the thing is tired! Well, by now it should be rested sufficiently to proceed. He had promised to supply it with a juicy slave from the caverns beneath the tower. When he had left the place, no doubt the slaves had thought themselves free of his influence. In a final act of cruelty, however, he had imprisoned them in the network of caves below the castle. They had access to food growing deep in the caverns and could get water from the underground lake. At the time, Dargan had thought that was suitable punishment—they would retain life while knowing they could never escape.

Now, however, it seemed like foresight; he would have a ready supply of slaves who would carry out his

every whim on his return. Some would form the basis
of new experiments. The wretched creatures would
wish they had died rather than lived, only to come
once more under his control. Yes, their current
imprisonment was just a taste of the troubles he
intended to inflict upon them when his time came!

He motioned the Tark to start the journey. Lazily
and reluctantly, the creature flapped its enormous
wings and rose slowly into the cheerless sky.

Linnil was confused. Colourless images superimposed
themselves upon her mind. Vague memories jostled
one another, but remained unclear. She felt a con-
striction on her thoughts, as if they had all been neatly
wrapped up and couldn't come into sharp relief again
until the cord tying them had been loosened. Struggling, she tried to crystallise them. She could just
remember who she was, and could dimly recall a voice
desperately calling her name. Focusing on that voice,
she strived to imagine its owner. Several times she
thought she had grasped a picture of the one she
sought, only to feel it slip away again out of reach.

'So, you're a fighter, are you? Good!' came a cold,
mocking voice.

She felt the mental bonds loosen.

'I suppose it does no harm to let you glimpse your
surroundings,' the voice continued in gloating tones.

The images began to clear and gain colour.
Refusing to release hold of the desperate cry,
however, she finally remembered—Kess! They had
been in a grim place—a big room. She had rushed
forward—for what? The Sceptre! But she had failed.
Instead, she had been captured by ....

The full realisation hit her. The chilling voice she
had just heard was Dargan's, and she was his prisoner.
But where were they? She felt a rough wind tugging

at her, and she seemed to be swaying slightly. Slowly she opened her eyes. At first she thought her mind had failed to register—although the wind had tried to batten her eyelids closed again, she had forced them to stay open, but all she could see was a cold, grey, featureless void. Then she became aware of a deep olive green patch of colour ahead of her; one that moved. She shrank back involuntarily as she glimpsed part of one eyeslit. This must be a Tark! She couldn't remember mounting it, but she had heard enough about the creatures to recognise it. As she moved, she felt a tight grip around her waist. Looking round, her eyes met Dargan's black gaze. She felt like screaming, but was unable to. His eyes bored into her, making her feel vulnerable, dirty and naked. Rapidly averting her gaze, she closed her eyes.

After a moment she opened them again. The same grey scene appeared ahead. Her eyes started streaming as she tried to look into the wind. To protect them, she concentrated her gaze downwards. Her stomach lurched. Far down below she saw the tiny shapes of boulders and trees. She shivered and wobbled, falling into a slight swoon. As she did so, she felt the bond tightening again, and everything faded back into a vision of chaos.

Dargan gave a grunt of satisfaction as the Tark landed. Everything seemed to be as he had left it. The cold brown rock slopes leading up to the castle gate of his old home were as harsh and unwelcoming as he had remembered—just how he liked them. Dismounting, he pulled the woman after him. He propped her against a crag and walked to the front of the Tark. Putting his hands on either side of its head, he looked with familiarity into the yellowish green slits. He had a glimpse of the creature's weariness, but was jolted to gain the knowledge of the defeat of his troops at the Fortress of Fear. His distrust of those stupid Zorgs had been confirmed. Ah well, he no longer needed the fortress. For a while, it had served its purpose as a raiding base, and as a defence for the Southlands. The northern army was welcome to it now. Their victory would be short-lived.

He withdrew his hands. 'Thank you, Targul. You must be tired. Go to the courtyard, and when I have found a slave, I will send him to you—or perhaps even two of them. You deserve a feast!'

The Tark gave an almost imperceptible nod and rose into the sky. It flew casually over the battlements and into the courtyard.

Dargan remained outside the door for a while. He had deliberately asked the creature to set them down here. Pulling Linnil to her feet, he prodded her into a stumbling walk. He retained a loose hold on her mind so that he could guide her faltering footsteps. Her glazed eyes looked ahead uncomprehendingly.

Suddenly he felt very tired. All this mind control sapped his own already drained energy. It would be different when he had the resources of the Sceptre to draw upon. He shook his head. Soon he would be able to relax and then, when rested, restart his experimental probing.

They moved forward to the giant doors guarding the main tower of the small castle; the Tower of Braggad. This was the key part of the building; the rest of the area was just a crude facade. The tower reared like a great bear from the side of the moun-tain. Crenellations led away from it to a smaller tower, also against the side of the peak. The small courtyard and keep were hunched into a natural cleft of the mountain, impregnable from the rear.

One of the tower's doors was open and hanging

askew from its great hinges. Ushering the girl
through, he glanced briefly at the damage to the
door. He would soon get a working party of slaves to
repair it. The room they had just entered was sparsely
furnished, with an old chest sitting forlornly against a
wall. The bottom of a spiral staircase spilled out into
the room, worn and old like the rest of the building.
Dargan ignored it, moved to the chest, and slid it
away from the wall. A heavily bolted trapdoor came
into view. He drew back the bolts and pulled the door
upwards. A dark, yawning hole greeted him.
Reaching down, he found a box of torches and lit one
with his firestick.

A slight groan came from behind him. The woman
was becoming a nuisance. He released the mental
bonds a little more so that she could find her own way
about. She stood dazed for a moment, looking stupidly around her, then she opened her mouth to
shout. Bending his will again so that she couldn't
speak, he pointed to the hole. Her feet dragged
themselves unwillingly in that direction. She
descended into the darkness and Dargan followed
her, pulling the trap door shut behind him. Grasping
a lever—attached through a slot in the floor to a
corner of the chest in the room above—he heaved.
The chest slid back into position, hiding the door
from prying eyes. The Dark Master gave a grunt of
satisfaction and motioned his prisoner on into the
mysterious gloom that awaited them beyond the
flickering torchlight.

4
News from the Southlands

The gloomy, overcast sky seemed to send down tendrils of misery that wormed their way into his every thought. Kess was tired of this despair. Occasionally his mood would lighten, but whenever he thought of Linnil—which was most of the time—he would sink slowly into a morass of hopelessness. He tried to pull himself out, but the feelings clung ever tighter, sapping the energy he needed to fight them. Tiredness seeped through his bones.

The fortress itself did nothing to lift his depression. It was a forbidding place at the best of times. Now, in combination with the weather, it seemed to trap him in thick walls of loneliness and fear. He knew that something—perhaps some small vestige of inner peace—stopped him from cracking under the strain, but sometimes he felt perilously close to doing so. Sometimes he even wondered if Elsinoth himself had deserted him, but then he realised that the Mighty One was the source of that small spark of peace.

However, it was difficult to understand why Linnil had been captured. Surely Elsinoth could have prevented it? Even though Kess knew it was pointless, he continually berated himself for having tripped in Dargan's Throne Room. Occasionally he even blamed

27

his friends, though it was not their fault either. In the blackest moments he would again direct his frustration and anger at Elsinoth—how could he allow such a thing to happen when they had been fighting on his behalf?

At the moment he just felt drained. Nearly two weeks had passed since they had arrived at the fortress. Despite its well-defended battlements, he doubted whether he would ever again feel safe while Dargan was alive. How could he forget the ease with which the Dark Master had immobilised all the company in his Throne Room? Kess shivered as he recalled those malignant eyes sweeping over him, his muscles suddenly freezing in response.

This won't do! he thought. *I'm going to be no use to Linnil like this—defeated before we've even started searching for her!*

If only they knew where to search. ...

Standing in the courtyard, Merric watched Kess' lonely figure peering over the parapet. He knew what Kess was going through: he felt it too. He desperately wanted to look for Linnil, but it was pointless until they had at least a clue to where Dargan had taken her. The Tark had at first flown off in a northerly direction but had then circled higher into the cloudy sky until it was difficult to trace its movements, even with his sharp eyes.

Many scouts had been sent into the Southlands to search for signs of their whereabouts. Linnil ... he could see her now, the curly auburn tresses gently tantalising him, and the peaceful green eyes that held promises of friendship and love.

He quickly pulled himself together. The scouts would not return for some time, he knew. Meanwhile, it would be best if he could try to lift Kess' mood a little. It was so difficult when he felt the same pain himself. He had tried playing his lute or the beautiful wooden flute Tolledon had given him, but it was no use. Since Linnil had gone there was only sadness in his music.

Somehow the pain of losing her was made even greater by watching Vallel and Hesteron. The two were virtually inseparable. He rejoiced at their growing love for each other; it was bringing the two Crafters a greater understanding of each other's Craft. It was also healing Vallel's grief over the loss of her sister. However, it reminded Merric of the happiness he and Linnil might have experienced together if Dargan had not parted them so cruelly.

His thoughts were interrupted by shouts of greeting. Moments later a huge, lumbering bear of a man burst into the courtyard accompanied by Athennar, Hesteron and Vallel. Delighted, Merric rushed over to meet him. 'Gatera! Good meeting! Are you well? And how do our Rrokki friends fare?'

'Good meeting, friend Merric! The little rock men are well. It was good to spend time with them and learn some of their understanding of the land. However, I fear I'm wasting away. I've had to survive on a diet of berries and juice and the like!' The Land Crafter patted his enormous girth and grinned widely.

Merric smiled in response. Gatera's frame was as colossal as ever. 'I suspect you probably finished their year's supply of guest food!' he said.

'Well, perhaps I didn't fare too badly after all—but I could do with some food now,' boomed the Land Crafter. He lowered his voice as he spotted the figure brooding on the battlements. 'How is Kess? Still taking it badly?'

The minstrel nodded in response.

'In that case, we must make sure his mind is kept busy. Kess!' he roared.

Kess looked down in surprise, jerked out of his dark thoughts. Seeing the Land Crafter, he ran down the flight of stone steps that led to the courtyard. 'Gatera, it's good to see you! How's Rrum? Have the Rrokki found out where Dargan and Linnil might have gone?'

The Land Crafter grimaced at the hopeful expression on the young man's face. 'No—no news, I'm afraid. Still, I'll tell you all about what Rrum and his friends have been up to while we have dinner—if I can persuade someone around here to make me some food!'

Athennar smiled and slapped him on the back. 'Some things never change,' he said. 'Let's go and see what we can find.'

An hour later, the friends were gathered around a hearty lunch. Tolledon and Meltizoc sat with them. Gatera's plate had been piled high with food—two grilled marducks oozing with mouth-watering juice, accompanied by spiced ragweed and dalroots. Now little was left, and he burped and gave a satisfied smile. Then he raised a goblet of pulberry wine. 'Good health, my friends! It is a long time since I have enjoyed such good food in such pleasant company.'

'Perhaps you could tell us some more of what has happened in the Southlands since we left,' suggested Athennar.

'There's not much to tell,' replied the massive Land Crafter, easing back on the wooden bench and leaning against the old stone wall. 'However, I do bring some good news. It appears that for some reason Dargan's hasty exit from his stronghold has weakened his power in the Land of Dreams. Whether

he consciously controlled what has happened there
we do not know, but I suspect not—it would have
taken too much of his time. All we know is that the
Mentars have discovered that they might at last be
able to overcome the nightmares that Dargan twisted
out of their dreams—the same nightmares we faced
on the way to Dargan's stronghold. The Land of
Dreams may once again become a place of
refreshment for travellers.'

Meltizoc stroked his white moustache thoughtfully.
'It may be that a link was formed between those
dream-forces and his own will. Such a bond may be
weakened—or even snapped—with increasing distance.'

'Do you mean like when Dargan left the Throne
Room and we were able to move again?' asked Valor,
who had been sitting next to Kess, unusually quiet.

'Not exactly. In that case, Dargan was directing his
will into one specific task—keeping you immobile. No,
the link with the Land of Dreams—and the Vale of
Miscreance—would have been much weaker.'

'Both places may become safe now that Dargan has
been ousted from his bastion!' Vallel added hopefully.

Hesteron squeezed her hand. 'Perhaps we'll be able
to go back there when this is all over,' he said.

'But we still don't know what has happened to
Dargan!' blurted Kess. 'What's to prevent him from
going back to his stronghold and rebuilding it?
Shouldn't some men have been posted down there to
guard it?'

'It would take him some time to repair all the
damage done by Zendos' sound tube,' Athennar
remarked. 'You may be right, however—perhaps
Hinno or I should have sent a contingent of men or
elves down there to guard it as soon as we arrived
here.'

'There's no need,' boomed Gatera. The others looked at him in surprise. 'I haven't finished telling you what happened when I stayed with the Rrokki. Rrum and his people were most concerned that they should play a part in restoring some beauty to the desolate areas of the Southlands. They also kept muttering something about defending the land.'

Kess smiled wryly at the memory of the Rronadd—the meeting of the Rrokki—that he and Linnil had attended. 'They didn't seem to know how they were going to do that,' he commented.

'But the Rrokki did stop those Zorg reinforcements from reaching the fortress,' Hesteron reminded him.

'Well, they have now decided that there is something else they can do,' continued Gatera. 'Just before I left they were calling the community together. They had made up their minds to visit Dargan's stronghold and see what was happening there. They were pretty determined—any Zorgs that were still there wouldn't last long.'

Kess shivered as he remembered the devastation caused by the rock people in the Zorgs' underground hideout. The Rrokki were not gentle with their enemies.

'They also intended to set free any prisoners they found still alive, and to destroy all Dargan's books and belongings. Then they were going to ensure that no one could ever use the stronghold for evil purposes again.' Gatera heaved a sigh and glanced quickly at Athennar. Then he continued, 'Rrum will then travel up here to join us, I believe. For some reason he wants to see your motley faces again. He'll be able to answer any other questions you have then. Now, is there any food left?'

The others around the table laughed at the good-natured Land Crafter, but Kess remained silent. It

was all very well destroying Dargan's lair after the
Dark Master had left, but how would that help them
to find his sister? If only the scouts Tolledon had sent
out could find her! Failing that, perhaps Rrum and
his people might find some clue to suggest where
Dargan might have taken her. It was a feeble hope,
but the only one he had at the moment.

Athennar's mind followed a similar path. Perhaps
the Rrokki would find Melinya among the desolation
of Dargan's stronghold ... unless Zendos had
somehow recovered and escaped with her. But would
Elsinoth allow such a thing? He hoped desperately
that he wouldn't, but somehow he felt he still had a lot
to learn about the ways of the Mighty One.

5
Destruction and Discovery

The grotesque faces guarding the entrance to Dargan's stronghold leered down at the group of Rrokki. Rrum ignored them, and ambled between the two grey pillars into the mouth of the tunnel, followed quickly by the others. Several of them held torches, and the yellow light flickered off the slime-covered walls. It was at least an improvement on the sickly green light he had seen when he had last walked along the passage. This time when they reached the junction the entrance tunnel did not disappear. The little rock man gave a slight grunt. Ignoring the two side corridors, he beckoned his band of Rrokki forward up the central passageway.

After a hard climb they passed through the stone door into the little corridor that led down to the dungeon cells. The lock still hung uselessly from the side wall. Rrum and his party carried on upwards. There would be time enough later to check whether there were any prisoners left in the dungeons. First he wanted to make sure that there were no Zorgs left in the place.

In the upper corridor he sent some of his people to check each room. The rest of the group followed him to the huge oaken doors that guarded Dargan's

DESTRUCTION AND DISCOVERY

Throne Room. One of these lay cracked on the ground, knocked from its hinges by a huge block of masonry. The Rrokki worked their way cautiously forward into the scene of devastation inside the great hall. The air was still heavy with dust, and huge chunks of stone lay haphazardly among broken tables and benches. A large, gaping hole had appeared in the ceiling, letting in the cold grey light that filtered down through the dust and wreckage.

Carefully and methodically, the rock people began their search, sorting through the tangled mass of shattered furniture, pieces of masonry and smashed flagstones. At the far end of the hall, the black onyx dais had been demolished by a large lump of fallen ceiling. The rough wooden throne was broken and twisted, and the grim face-mask with its leering eye sockets had been spilt in two by a deep crack. Rrum grimaced and sighed: there was no sign of Zendos anywhere. Either the sorcerer had survived the room's disintegration or his body had been taken elsewhere by the Zorgs. He suspected it was the former as the Zorgs were unlikely to care much about Zendos while their own lives were in danger.

A small female Rrokki coughed behind him. Rrum wheeled around.

'We have foundd no Zorggs.'

'Goodd. Search the restt of the forttifications andd reportt backk to me.'

'Agreedd.' The rock woman left to continue the search.

Rrum picked his way forward over the rubble to Dargan's antechamber. The door was ajar and he scrambled through to the room beyond. Various leather-bound ancient tomes lined the walls. Dusty maps lay draped across tables and an assortment of pieces of parchment, scrolls and skeletal birds' heads adorned a huge desk over at one side. Moving to the shelves of books, Rrum picked one of the volumes at random.

The cover of the book was plain, but inside were strange words. They looked as if they should have been familiar, but for some reason he couldn't quite recognise them. Rrum had read few books but he was sure there was something evil about this one. Turning over the page, he was confronted by an illustration so gruesome that it made even his stocky frame judder in revulsion. He flung down the book and had a brief look at the pieces of parchment on the table. Dargan had scribbled rough notes on them, but again the rock man couldn't decipher what they said. Pondering for a moment, he decided that although some of the material might be helpful to his friends, he couldn't afford to risk anyone making use of the dark secrets within the books. Neither could he risk them falling into Dargan's hands again. No, he would order the whole lot to be burned.

Wandering over to the staircase, he climbed upwards. Emerging onto the battlements, he looked down on the rock people scuttling around below.

'Foundd anythingg?' he called in his grinding voice.

'Only boddies.'

'Goodd!'

He looked briefly out over the scarred, pitted plains and wondered if this land could ever be beautiful, with running streams and the cries of birds. Wearily, he turned and made his way back down the steps.

Back in the corridor outside the Throne Room, Rrum had a brief discussion with the other Rrokki. It seemed that the only bodies found had been out in the open; most of them with the same fixed, petrified look of madness in their eyes. The rock man wondered what had terrified them so much. Several of the bodies had been Zorgs, but others were strange, often deformed, creatures.

He sent a few Rrokki off to burn the contents of Dargan's chamber. Some of the others were told to complete the work of destruction on the stronghold: he wanted to be sure it could not easily become a hiding place for evil again. The remaining rock people accompanied him on a search of the prison cells.

Rrum led the way to the top of the spiral staircase, and they descended cautiously to where Athennar and the others had been imprisoned. All the cell doors stood open. Rapidly investigating each one, they soon discovered that all the occupants had left and, except for one or two corpses, the cells were empty. He motioned his people over to the top of the next stairwell at the far end of the room. The steps were steeper here, making it difficult for their short legs, but eventually they reached the lower level. Even in the torchlight it had a grim and sombre appearance. The rock walls were rough and black, and the floor pitted and worn. Rrum groaned to see Elsinoth's beautiful rocks marred by such ugly use.

Most of the cell doors were again open. The Rrokki split up in order to check each cell, with Rrum going to the one cell with a closed door. To his surprise, it opened easily. In the flickering torchlight he could see the silhouette of a man cowering pitifully in the far corner of the cell. The figure whimpered as he approached, and pressed against the wall, as if trying to melt into it.

'Keep away!' the man shrieked. 'There is no one here!'

Rrum halted, pondering how best to proceed. As he watched, the man straightened and sidled carefully towards another corner, as if hiding from the Rrokki's eyes. Despite his pathetic appearance he seemed like someone who had probably once been proud and strong.

'I will not hurtt you,' grated Rrum.

The man halted. 'Hurt?' he cackled maniacally. 'Oh, they all hurt. They hurt in here.' He pointed to his head.

The rock man wondered what mental tortures Dargan had inflicted upon him. 'How longg have you been here?' he asked as gently as he could.

The man glowered and then lowered his head sulkily. 'Don't know. Don't know where or when. Long time—perhaps for ever. Don't know. I ache.' He cradled his head in his hands and rocked from side to side, groaning.

Rrum watched with concern. He wondered who the man was and how he had come to be one of Dargan's prisoners. An innocent wanderer who had ventured too near to the stronghold, perhaps? 'I can helpp,' he said, advancing a couple of steps.

The man stopped groaning and looked up, start- led. 'Who are you?' he snapped.

Rrum was taken aback by the sudden assertiveness.

It didn't last. The stranger's voice again took on the tone of mindless fear that he had first heard. 'There is no one here! Go away!'

A distant rumbling noise filtered down to the dungeon cell. The Rrokki were obviously obeying Rrum's requests to destroy the buildings. A judicious use of their jaws in grinding away some of the remaining supporting pillars, no doubt. It was time to move. Rolling over to the man, he gently gripped his arm.

The stranger screamed as if in dreadful agony and wrenched himself free. Taken by surprise, Rrum could only watch as the man darted for the door.

Then, recovering rapidly, he gave chase. Fortunately, three of his fellow Rrokki were waiting just outside the cell and caught the prisoner as he rushed by. The man wriggled furiously but could not free himself. After several piercing screams he abruptly fell silent and went limp.

'He is sttill alive,' confirmed one of the rock people.

'Goodd. We will leave now. Didd you findd anyone else alive?'

The Rrokki shook their heads. 'No one. The boddies we foundd in the oppen were probabbly prisoners.'

Rrum nodded and motioned them forward. He wanted to get out of this place. Every inch of it oozed with evil.

Standing out on the scarred plain, all the Rrokki took a last look at the huge rock that housed Dargan's stronghold. A column of dark smoke billowed from the top, tinged with occasional streaks of yellow and green. Rrum grunted and turned his attention to the prisoner, who was beginning to show signs of recovery. The glare of insanity in the man's opening eyes seemed to dim as he noticed the smoking bastion.

'Death to Dargan!' he muttered darkly. 'And to Zendos!'

'Whatt do you know of them?' demanded Rrum.

'Don't know.' The haunted look had returned. 'Dargan has gone. Don't know where. But Zendos ...'

'Yes?' prompted Rrum.

'Take me home!' shrieked the man suddenly.

'Where is home?'

'Don't know. Somewhere. Mountains? Leave me alone.'

Rrum began to feel exasperated. At one moment, the man seemed almost lucid, and the next as if he had stepped over the narrow ledge that separates sanity from madness. He wasn't sure what to do with him. They would go back to Rronadd now, but then what would happen? He couldn't see the man settling happily there, and they wouldn't be able to send him home if they couldn't find out where he lived. He decided to try just once more. The circle of Rrokki around the stranger was beginning to get restless; it was time to be moving away from this desolate scene.

'Who are you?' he asked. 'Where do you come from?'

The man shrugged. 'Don't know. Tired. Confused. I have lost it.   Dargan tricked me—me, Carnak! Its Keeper! Tired. Go away.'

Rrum listened with interest and sudden under-standing. So that was the answer to his questions. This gibbering figure was Carnak—the one who had stolen the Sceptre and taken it to Dargan! This was the man who had betrayed his trust and killed Valor's father. He looked again at the pitiful figure. Shaking his head wearily, he motioned his people to coax the prisoner towards Rronadd.

6

The Ravings of a Madman

Rrum spent some time alone with Carnak after their
arrival at Rronadd. The Keeper had passed through
several violent changes of mood on the journey,
sometimes lapsing into near lifelessness before again
breaking into periods of intense agitation or frightened confusion. Although much of what Carnak now
said seemed to be just the wild ravings of a madman,
Rrum was gradually able to piece together something
of what had happened at the Dark Master's lair.
Either Dargan or Zendos—possibly both—had tortured the prisoner, probing and enslaving his mind.
Quite how they had done this was impossible to tell,
but hatred for both of them burned deep in the
Keeper, often threatening to engulf him completely
in its poison.

Rrum also learned the reason for the assortment of
bodies his men had found in the open. Apparently
Zendos—who must have escaped from the collapsing
Throne Room—had appeared unexpectedly in the
dungeons. He had opened all the cells and herded
the prisoners upstairs and into the courtyard. There
they were pushed to the ground before two Tarks. In
his moments of greatest lucidity, Carnak described
how Zendos had brought the prisoners as offerings to

the Tarks. There had also been a female prisoner, he
claimed. Zendos had bargained with the creatures to
fly him and the woman somewhere. At this point the
Keeper started rambling again and Rrum was unable
to find out any more.

Exhausted, the Rrokki trundled over to his parents'
shelter to tell them all he had been able to find out.
Rrokk and Rrudda sat quietly on the stone bench,
occasionally asking short questions or nodding their
approval of his actions. When he had finished, Rrum
fell silent and waited for his parents to speak.

'You didd well.'

'Whatt aboutt Carnakk?' Rrum asked.

Rrokk pondered for a moment. He looked
enquiringly at Rrudda, who nodded as if in reply to
some unspoken comment. 'You mustt take him to the
forttress. To Athennar,' she said. 'He will know whatt
shouldd be done.'

Rrum nodded his agreement. He had been wanting
to go and rejoin his new friends—he would rather be
doing something positive than sitting quietly at
Rronadd. 'Itt is goodd,' he said.

The small group arrived at the fortress a few days
later. Two other rock men had joined Rrum for the
journey, to help him with Carnak and then to report
back to Rronadd with any news from the northern
army. Rrum was to remain at the fortress with his
friends.

The Keeper had been strangely silent for most of
the journey, striding almost purposefully along,
although his eyes were still glazed. Once or twice he
became excitable, and once he collapsed, sobbing for
no apparent reason. The Rrokki waited patiently for
him to stop before continuing.

Eventually they neared the sombre bulk of the

Fortress of Fear. Carnak's eyes grew wide when he first noticed the huge structure. 'No, no! Tarks .... must get away!'

'The Tarkks have ggone.'

'No. Not here. I have lost it. Where has it gone?' The Keeper sank into an untidy heap on the ground, muttering to himself. Rrum shrugged and motioned the other two Rrokki to pick him up. To their surprise, Carnak gave no resistance, but kept mumbling as they carried him unceremoniously towards the nearest gate.

They had already been sighted by sentries on the battlements, and the great gate creaked open.

Inside the fortress, several of Rrum's friends were talking in the courtyard. Valor was enraged when he saw Carnak and, shouting wildly, started to run towards him. Athennar and Hesteron moved quickly to intercept the Mountain Guard, and managed to restrain him.

However, Carnak had already slumped to the rough stone floor of the courtyard, gibbering wildly once more. When Valor realised the state of the Keeper's mind, the hatred and lust for vengeance rapidly drained away, leaving him feeling cheated and empty. The direction of his life in recent weeks had been governed by his promise to avenge his father's death, but it appeared that Carnak had already paid a heavy price for his treachery.

Athennar barked some orders, and Carnak was helped to his feet and led away. Valor stood miserably, his shoulders hunched in defeat.

'Come!' coaxed the Hallion man. 'Once Rrum is rested, we will hear his news. If you would rather go and ...'

'No!' A spark rekindled in Valor's eyes. 'Spare me any pity! I've been a fool! All this time I've allowed my

desire for revenge to drive me, consume me. Now ...'
He sighed and shook his head. 'Now I know that my
father would never have wanted that. I just hope I can
find something else to fill the gap that is left.'

'Let love replace the hatred.' Meltizoc's voice,
surprisingly gentle, came from behind the young man.
'And let Elsinoth be your inspiration. His way needs no
hatred or fear to drive us forward. Just the power of
love.'

Athennar nodded in silent agreement. 'Come, let us
go inside.'

A little later the company was gathered around a large
table, listening to Rrum. Tolledon was busy elsewhere,
but all the others were present.

Athennar pursed his lips as he pondered the little
Rrokki's news. 'So Zendos is still alive! And Melinya—
she must have been the female prisoner that Carnak
saw.' He gazed down the table at the squat figure of the
rock man. 'I should have gone back to the Throne
Room to check,' he continued.

'It wasn't safe,' interrupted Merric. 'And as far as we
knew Zendos was buried somewhere underneath the
rubble.'

'It's my fault,' groaned Kess. The others looked at
him. So far, he had been quiet throughout their
discussion. 'Athennar, you know you would have gone
back but for me. Instead you sacrificed the chance to
find Melinya because you had to get me away from that
place.'

'It's not your fault that Dargan caught Linnil!'
exclaimed Valor, troubled by his friend's deepening
sorrow.

'No one is to blame,' interjected Meltizoc. 'What is
done is done. It is pointless to live in the past, regretting
what might have been. We must look to the future!'

'You are right, as usual, my friend,' Athennar sighed. 'I apologise. As my father said some time ago, we have not lost yet. Perhaps we can find out more from Carnak.'

'Itt is difficultt. His mindd wandders.'

'I think Carnak began to lose control of his mind the day Dargan entered his life,' Meltizoc commented. 'I'm sure that the constant pressure of Dargan's will—for such it must have been to make him betray his sacred trust—took its toll. Then losing the Sceptre to the Dark Master must have been the final blow, though no doubt Dargan and Zendos encouraged the process of deterioration. I know how you feel about him, Valor, but I believe he never meant to betray his trust; he really loved the Sceptre.'

'Perhaps,' Valor conceded grudgingly. 'I know he used to be proud of his position as Keeper. But he had no reason to kill my father—they had been friends.'

Meltizoc nodded in understanding as the memory of Rustan's death flooded back to Valor. 'It would perhaps be better if you were not present when we question him,' he said.

'No, I want to hear what he has to say.'

'Very well,' said Athennar. 'We will see if we can learn any more. Guard! Bring in Carnak!'

'While we are waiting, Rrum, do you have any more news from your people? Have any of them seen anything that might give us a clue to Dargan's whereabouts?'

'I fear nott. He has disapppeared.'

'Don't you have any idea where he might have taken Linnil?' asked Kess.

'The Southlandds are very bigg—even if he is sttill there.'

At that moment the guard returned with his prisoner. Athennar motioned him to seat Carnak next to

Rrum at the end of the table. The Keeper was looking even paler than usual, and stared wide-eyed at the assembled company.

'Where am I? You don't trick me, Dargan!' he said, staring up the table at Athennar. 'Where is it? I know you have it!'

He rose to his feet, jabbing the air with his finger. 'You have it. It is mine. You tricked me. Give it to me!' He thumped the table and then sat down again, sobbing.

'You are safe here. We are no friends of Dargan's,' said Meltizoc gently. 'But we need your help to find him.'

'Where is it? Have you got it? I shouldn't have taken it, I know I shouldn't. He made me.'

Meltizoc raised an eyebrow. This was going to be difficult. 'Carnak!' he called sternly. 'You must try to concentrate. We cannot get your beloved Sceptre back unless you help us. Do you know where Dargan is?'

The Keeper looked up slowly. He seemed to be struggling with hidden emotions. Suddenly his eyes caught sight of the Mountain Guard. Any remaining colour in his face drained away. 'Valor!' he croaked. 'But I thought you were dead. Or was that your father? I forget. It was all so long ago.'

'You murdered my father!' shouted Valor at the pale, pathetic figure. 'You killed him—do you understand? Killed him!'

Athennar held him back. 'Peace, my friend. There is nothing to be gained here from anger.'

Carnak gazed stupidly at the young man. He began to whine. 'I'm sorry. So sorry. I didn't want to. But he would have taken it away. I couldn't let him do that.' Then he slumped down again, his head between his hands.

'Carnak, we need your help. *Do you know where Dargan is?*' persisted Meltizoc.

The Keeper shook his head wearily. 'I don't know. I can't remember anything.'

'Well then, do you know where Zendos is?'

'Zendos? The scum. He wanted it as well. He told me. I remember. But he would never get it from Dargan. Where is it? Have you got it?'

'Concentrate!' Meltizoc said sharply. 'Where is Zendos? Where were the Tarks taking him?'

'And who was with him?' interrupted Athennar, leaning forward.

'A girl. Don't know who. And Tarks.' The Keeper shuddered with revulsion. 'I heard him. I escaped and hid. The Tarks didn't see me. I heard him.'

'What did he say?'

'I got away when they weren't looking. Hid behind a barrel. Wasn't going to let them suck my mind again. Ghastly things. I hate Tarks. I hate Zendos. I hate Dargan. I want it back. Where is it?'

'Carnak, what did Zendos say? Think, man!'

'He was going away. Leaving. Taking a girl with him. He had to bargain with those Tarks. I hate them. I wasn't going to let them feed off me. I hid.'

Athennar looked in exasperation at Meltizoc. 'It's no use—we'll never get any sense out of him.'

'We must try, Athennar. He is our only key, however poor.' Turning back to Carnak, Meltizoc used a softer tone. 'Did Zendos say where he was going?'

'I heard him. I listened. I was hiding behind a barrel. Away from those Tarks. He wanted to go north. They wouldn't take him until they had fed. Horrible. Disgusting. They tried it on me once. He won't like it there, though.'

'Why not?'

'You know why. The white eyes—lots and lots. Hope he dies. Where is it? Have you got it?' The Keeper slipped back into gibbering to himself and started cackling maniacally. He ignored all further questions.

Meltizoc beckoned the guard to take Carnak away. 'Well, we know Zendos went north—but where? And where is this place with all the white eyes?'

'I know of no such place,' Hesteron murmured, while Merric and Vallel nodded their agreement.

'I have never heard of any race of people with white eyes, either,' remarked Meltizoc.

'I know Carnak better than any of you,' Valor said quietly. 'I am used to his accent. He didn't say anything about white eyes. He said 'white ice'.'

7
A New Quest

'The Ice Kingdom!' exclaimed Athennar. 'It has to be.'
    Meltizoc nodded his agreement.
    'But where's that?' asked Kess. 'I've never heard of it.'
    'That's not surprising,' replied Hesteron. 'It's in the north, three days' travel from Winderswood. It's an inhospitable region up in the mountains.'
    'But the people who live there are reputed to be peace-loving, ruled by the wisdom of the Ice Kings,' remarked Merric.
    'Nevertheless, I suspect that is where my wretched cousin went,' replied Athennar. 'As boys we often used to talk about the place. It always held a fascination for him. I have no doubt that he thinks he has sufficient power to deal with any resistance from the Ice People. He's probably looking for a people to enslave—in a pathetic imitation of Dargan's powers. Yet he's not ready to fight his former master, which is why I suspect he has moved a good distance away. Northwards is also the one direction he would not expect us to search should we discover that he hadn't died at Dargan's stronghold.'
    'Who are these Ice Kings and their people?' asked Valor.

Tolledon slipped quietly into the room. 'Perhaps I can answer that,' he said. He drew a seat up to the table. 'Much about them still remains a mystery, however. I have met them twice, when visiting their kingdom.'

'Don't they ever leave it?' asked Vallel.

'Very rarely. In days long gone, some Ice Kings unexpectedly turned up at a meeting of the peace-loving peoples of the Realm. They wanted to be part of the decisions made at that time, for there were then several Dark Masters who were growing in strength. The Ice Kings realised that the only way to hold back evil was for all those who opposed it to stand together. So they joined the meeting, despite the fact that they cannot easily live in a land that is so different from their own. They apparently had to wear layers of cooling clothing to protect them from the heat. Such courage in itself gave heart to the other races gathered there.'

'So what are they like—and how do they manage to live in such a hostile place?' asked Gatera.

'Hostile to us perhaps, but not to them,' Tolledon answered. 'As I said, they feel uncomfortable away from their home. Although their form is human in appearance, it is also totally unlike that of any other race in the Realm. It is as if they have been carved out of the ice itself. They also show little emotion— although they obviously long for peace, as we do.'

'Where did they come from originally?' asked Vallel.

Tolledon shrugged and looked at Meltizoc.

The wise man hesitated for a moment before replying. 'We can't be sure. We know that the Tissirim—to give them their proper name—are one of the ancient races of the Realm. Where they came from originally, or why Elsinoth breathed life into them, we may never know. Although they are naturally adapted to their icy world, they have few visitors, as not many men or elves would wish to stay there long. There is little available in the way of food—apart from a few snow berries; hardly enough to sustain anyone. Zendos must indeed be desperate to hide in such a forbidding land.'

'But how do the Tissirim eat? They must have some source of readily available food!' Merric exclaimed.

'Another mystery, I'm afraid,' replied Meltizoc. 'I too have spent a little time among them and I suspect that they draw what sustenance they need out of the ice.'

'So what do we do now?' Kess asked wearily. 'Can we really trust Carnak's word?'

'I have little doubt that he was telling the truth,' replied Meltizoc. 'At the moment it's all we have to go on. Finding Zendos appears to be our main hope as there seems little likelihood that the scouts we have sent southwards will find Dargan. I expect he has some hidden retreat we don't know about. However, it's likely that Zendos *will* know where it is.'

'In that case, some of us must leave immediately for the Ice Kingdom,' said Athennar, his dark looks chiselled into granite hardness. 'I will lead the expedition. If Zendos is in the Ice Kingdom, he will have Melinya with him or nearby. Don't worry,' he said in answer to his father's questioning look, 'I know my responsibilities—the Sceptre will remain our first priority. But I have searched too long for Melinya to give in lightly. Zendos has been within my grasp once—he won't escape a second time.'

His father nodded in understanding.

'I'll go with you,' said Kess firmly.

'And me too,' added Valor quickly. 'There's little left for me here now Carnak has been found.'

Athennar looked at Kess dubiously. 'Wouldn't you prefer to wait here for news of Linnil?'

'As Tolledon said, there's unlikely to be any, and I will only wear out the battlements with my pacing, and worry Merric even more if I stay.' He allowed himself a slight smile.

'You are right—it is best that you go,' agreed Merric. It was just what Kess needed to keep him occupied. Although the journey would be hazardous, the Quiet One would be in good hands with Athennar. 'But I will stay here,' he continued, 'lest there be further news of Linnil.'

Kess smiled gratefully at the troubadour.

'We will come with you also, Athennar,' said Hesteron, who had been discussing the matter with Vallel, and now sat with his arm around her.

'I was hoping so,' Athennar smiled. 'It may be that Vallel's craftship and understanding of water may help us when we reach the Ice Kingdom. Five should be a good number—unless you or Rrum want to join us, Gatera?'

'We will travel a little way with you,' rumbled the giant Land Crafter, 'but we'll leave you when we near Kravos. I must see my family again. I have missed them. Rrum will come with me so that I can return his hospitality. Then we'll return here to support Merric—I have a feeling we may yet be needed. While I can't say that I'm sorry not to be going to the Ice Kingdom, the idea of such a place intrigues me. Perhaps it is one place where at least two of our crafts—' here he paused and looked across at Vallel '—touch one another. I shall look forward to hearing more about this land made of water.'

'Good,' said Tolledon. 'You will need to stop along the way at Hallion, Athennar; we have special garments there for use in cold climates.'

Athennar nodded. Kess heaved a sigh of relief. He
would be glad to be away from this gloomy fortress.

The friends gathered next morning to bid farewell to
one another. A sparklingly clear sky greeted them as
if offering new hope. Their horses were led into the
courtyard by some elves.

Kess embraced Merric before mounting Blazer,
who was snorting and tossing his mane with
excitement. 'Thanks for all your help. I'm sorry you
have had to bear my burdens as well as your own
lately. I owe you a great deal.'

'You owe me nothing,' replied the troubadour.
'What is a friend if not someone who is there when
needed? You need never feel you are in my debt. All I
ask of you—as a friend—is to take care and come back
safely, I hope with news of Linnil.'

Kess nodded, a lump rising in his throat.

Meltizoc and Tolledon stood nearby, talking quietly
to Athennar as he swung onto the back of his proud
white horse, Windrider. Then, waving a farewell to
the troops of elves and men gathered on the battlements, the small group moved off slowly. One of
the great gates in the northern wall was swung open,
and the wide vista of the Northlands greeted the
company. They passed through the gate and on to
the plains beyond. Merric watched thoughtfully until
the group had dwindled even from his keen sight.

8

The Underground Prison

Linnil remembered little of the journey underground. Dimly she recalled Dargan unbolting a huge door at the end of the passage leading from the trapdoor. She wondered vaguely why the bolts were on that side of the door. Passing through, Dargan locked the door behind him.

Then there was a confusion of long, dark passages past strange edifices. Some, she was sure, were real, but others felt like the fevered imaginations of her weary mind. Later, Dargan had guided her along a walkway across the centre of a large mass of water. At the end, a great stone throne reared up threateningly, casting cold shadows in the weak torchlight. Gushing out of the rock behind it was a waterfall, the water tumbling down two channels on either side of the throne as it made its way to the lake. Linnil was taken across a stone bridge and down a narrow passage to a cheerless, dark room, where Dargan lit a stumpy candle on a table. As he bent over the candle, a long black shadow hovered menacingly on the wall.

'I think you will be safe in here, my pretty one,' he said quietly, using the soft, reassuring tones she hated so much.

Linnil felt him release the last of the mental bonds

that held her. Suddenly she felt unguarded and insecure. Dargan's powers, however binding, had also protected her from the full realisation of her predicament. Now she realised she was alone and defenceless in a strange and hostile place. Dargan had already relieved her of her weapons.

'Make yourself comfortable, my sweet. This is going to be your new home.' Cackling, he left the chamber, locking the door behind him.

Linnil groaned as feeling began to return to her body. She realised that she ached all over, probably from the buffeting of the wind and the long, stupefying journey on the back of the Tark. She shuddered in distaste as she thought of the loathesome creature. Perhaps it was as well that she had not been fully conscious for most of the journey.

She looked around her cell—for that is how she already regarded it. The furniture was all of a strange grey wood. Under the table in the middle of the room were two old wooden chairs. Against one wall was a small bed, again of the same uniform grey. A couple of thick, coarse blankets covered it, with a third folded as a pillow. Against the opposite wall of the windowless room was a bookcase. Like sentinels on either side of it were two grotesque stone statuettes that leered at her. The only other piece of furniture was an old wooden chest. Curious, she opened it: it was empty except for a spare blanket for the bed.

Wandering to the bookcase, she started to pull out a red-bound volume, but nearly dropped it in dismay. The cover had seemed to move as she touched it. Hastily she pushed it back and gingerly tried another volume further along the shelf; one with a rough animal skin cover. Opening it, she was greeted by a dazzling display of black and gold lettering. It seemed to shimmer and hurt her eyes. Pushing the book back,

she stumbled over to the bed and lay on top of the
rough blankets, gazing up at the ceiling overhead.
Light from the candle reflected from thin spiderets'
webs laced across the ceiling.

She wondered where Kess was now. With a jolt,
another face floated into her memory—Merric's. She
felt a pang of guilt for not having thought of him
sooner. Now his features and his kind ways came
flooding back into her mind. They had only just
realised how much they cared for each another, and
then they had been abruptly parted. She hoped that
he and Kess were safe. Saying a quiet prayer to
Elsinoth, she asked for protection for them both.

The sound of a key turning in the lock disturbed her
thoughts. Dargan reappeared, followed by a thickset
Zorg who bore a bowl of steaming green soup and a
chunk of bread. 'Some food for you, my little one. This
is Dun'grat. He will bring you your meals. I should
warn you that it is futile to try to escape. Should you get
out of this cell, it would take you a long time to find the
door that leads to the castle, and if you did, you still
could not pass through it. I have the only key.'

'What are you going to do with me?' demanded
Linnil, some of her defiance returning.

The Dark Master looked down patronisingly at her.
'Patience, patience, my sweet. All in good time. For
now, enjoy your meal—and be thankful you are still
alive. You may even learn to like this place.'

'Never! Please let me go—I'm of no value to you.'

'Oh, but how wrong you are, my dear. How wrong.'
Snapping his fingers curtly to dismiss the Zorg,
Dargan also withdrew from the chamber. Linnil was
left alone with her thoughts.

Dargan slipped quietly along the passageway to his
own room. Bolting the door behind him, he moved to

an ornately carved chair and slumped into it. He reached for the Sceptre, which was propped against a wall. Picking it up, he gazed for several minutes all along its length. Already he knew every inch of it, but it still gripped and fascinated him. He could almost feel the power hidden in the wood, throbbing, ready to be released. The beauty of the staff sickened him, as did the aura of health and vigour that seeped from it, yet he hungered for its power more than anything else.

But how could he unlock its secrets? He turned the problem over and over in his mind but came no nearer to a solution. He was sure there must be a way to tap the energy of the Sceptre; he would not be beaten by a mere strip of carved sapling.

He held it at arm's length. The lamplight threw delicate shadows onto the carvings that adorned its length. He must concentrate and not be distracted by such things. Focusing on one small section, he summoned his reserves of power. His eyes bulged as he tried to focus all his energy into the staff. One eye was still nearly useless, damaged when Gatera had smashed the jade Eye in his former Throne Room. Dargan ignored the pain, however, even though his head throbbed with the effort.

For an instant it seemed as if the staff went cold, but he knew he might have imagined it. He felt light-headed and nearly passed out. Rather sheepishly he realised he had been holding his breath. What would it take to gain control over this wretched staff?

As he relaxed, weird and unfamiliar images flickered through his mind and then were gone. He sat dazed, in a state of shock. What had happened? Had he actually touched some part of the Sceptre's power—or had the images come from the mental strain he had been exerting? That seemed unlikely, for he had trained and built up his mental strengths and agilities. Had he been too eager, too forceful?

Rising, he strode across to the shelves of books that lined two walls of the room. He reached purposefully for a book with a luminous yellow cover and leafed through it until he reached the page he wanted. Bright green serpentine script wriggled backwards and forwards across the page. Muttering to himself, he held his gaze steady. Slowly the dancing motion stopped, and his practised eyes unravelled the symbols. It seemed that he was correct. The images could not have come from his own over-exertions but were a product of the staff's own forces.

A puzzled frown creased his brow. The answer was almost at his fingertips—but what was it? How had he touched upon the Sceptre's secrets? It was not the first time he had tried channelling his will into the staff, yet he had never before been assailed by the strange visions. Perhaps the answer lay inside the Sceptre itself, rather than in the various methods he had been using to direct his powers into it.

He returned to the chair and sat down. Although his head still ached from his earlier efforts, he again forced himself to ignore the pain. Taking control of every muscle in his body, Dargan stilled himself until everything around him receded as he cleared from his mind all the clutter of thoughts. He concentrated only upon his battle with the Sceptre, mentally examining every detail of his latest attempt to penetrate its mysteries. Several times it eluded him, but finally he had it.

Dargan laughed aloud as his mind relaxed. The answer had been so obvious all the time. He had been too eager to test his powers while overlooking one of the simple truths of the infernal staff. It was not a matter of trying to overcome it by mental force. Rather, it was a case of submitting his own will to the Sceptre's powers. So obvious, yet so subtle! His smile faded as he contemplated the task ahead of him. He had spent years building up his powers, delving into dark mysteries, ever hardening his will. He had made himself invulnerable to the emotions and weaknesses experienced by other men; a solid rock barrier had long ago been built against feelings of love, pity, kindness—all had been entombed.

Now he faced a new challenge. He would have to open himself to the Sceptre's power, quite deliberately. For a while, he would have to choose to become weak and vulnerable; only by doing so would he be able to gain ultimate power. The experiment would have its own dangers—he was not sure how he would be able to tap the Sceptre's energies once they were available. His state of defencelessness might even cripple his powers. It would also take time to get to that stage: days, weeks, possibly months. Still, he had no alternative but to try.

He smiled again as his confidence returned. With a little practice, he would soon be able to experiment again—and this time he would be successful. The long years of toil and hardship had paid off; it would not be all that long now before the Realm would quiver within his grasp. His hand picked a large walnut from a bowl at his side. Closing his fist, he crushed it in a gesture of triumph. He opened his hand and a brown dust filtered through his fingers to the floor below.

Dargan threw back his head and laughed. Cold and long, the sound reverberated around the grim stone walls.

9
The Journey Begins

After two days of hard travelling, the seven friends reached the sheltered vale of Hallion. The soothing tranquillity of the place soon began to ease their tensions. Athennar disappeared to organise their clothing and supplies, having directed the others to a cabin where they could rest.

Easing his great bulk onto the nearest bunk, Gatera promptly fell asleep. Valor also threw himself onto a bed and closed his eyes. Hesteron and Vallel sat together in a corner talking quietly, their soft voices occasionally joining together in a light elven melody. Rrum settled down by the door, a contented look on his granite features.

Unnoticed, Kess slipped out of the cabin. He felt restless, the only one of the group who had been unable to relax. He wandered over to one of the tracks that rambled carelessly between the trees on the slopes of the mountains that enclosed Hallion. The sun filtered down through the intricate lacework of leaves. Summer was approaching. Shadows of the trees cast dappled patterns across the ground. There was a cool freshness in the air beneath their branches. As he climbed, memories of his own Valley home flooded back. It had been what—two months—since he left? It seemed like years!

Presently he reached a small clearing and, sitting on an old log in the sunshine, picked up a piece of broken branch lying at his feet. Searching through his jerkin, he found a sharp knife. The Quiet Ones had a natural love of wood, and he had often spent many a happy hour in the Valley carving and fashioning his own designs.

The piece of wood he now held was light, with a smooth texture. He started whittling it away; the action helped to soothe him. Slowly the sculpture began to take shape. He smiled as it brought back recollections of happier times with Linnil, and he decided to keep the carving as a symbol of hope that his sister would be found. She would be pleased with it, he thought. Turning it in his hand, he put the finishing touches to it. It was formed in the shape of the heart's-tear flower that Linnil so liked. He smiled again and put it in his pocket. Later he would find a leather thong to attach to it, in the hope that she would one day wear it around her neck.

His mood lighter than it had been for some time, he decided to return to the cabin. Perhaps he would be able to sleep without the recurrent nightmares that had troubled him for so long. He hadn't mentioned them to anyone—they were just another sign of his distress about Linnil's disappearance.

Rising to his feet, he started back down the hillside.

Athennar sat back against the rough timber of the cabin and surveyed the assembled company. It was good to see them so relaxed. They would need this rest with such a difficult and cold journey ahead of them. He was glad it was nearly summer—it would have been far worse had they been going into the mountains in winter.

Remembering something, he rose and went inside

the cabin. When he re-emerged he was carrying a large bundle of clothes. He threw a set each to Kess, Valor, Hesteron and Vallel. 'It's a relief that you and Rrum aren't joining us, Gatera,' he quipped. 'We'd have had great difficulty finding garments to fit you.'

The huge Land Crafter grinned. 'I knew there was another reason why we shouldn't go with you,' he rumbled.

The clothes consisted of doublet and long trousers, tied at ankle and wrist and made of a thick, white, fluffy material. A long white leather cape and hood went with each, as well as a pair of white leather gloves and boots.

'These are all made from the skins of the northern ice bears,' explained Athennar. 'They seem to offer great protection against the cold.'

'How would Zendos have survived the cold without special clothing?' asked Valor.

'No doubt by some cunning means,' replied Athennar. 'He has spent many years learning to shield himself.'

Kess looked at him. It was unusual to hear such bitterness in the Animal Crafter's voice. 'Athennar,' he began hesitantly, 'you have never really spoken much of Melinya. What is she like?'

It was Athennar's turn to be surprised. Turning thoughtful, his deep-set eyes gazed out across the peaceful valley. 'She is the fairest of all the people of the Realm,' he said wistfully, 'with a character to match her beauty. She comes from the same elvish stock as both the Water and the Air Crafters, but her features are even more serene, her hair an even purer gold. I believe you met Vesson when you visited Tarrelford. Melinya's mother, as Vallel could tell you, was Vesson's sister.'

Kess looked at the Water Crafter, who had lowered

her eyes as she remembered some distant but sad event. Hesteron put a comforting arm around her.

'When Vesson, Venya and the other River Crafters established their community at Tarrelford, Melinya's mother stayed behind at Hallion with the one to whom she was betrothed. They loved the Valley and unlike many of the elves could see the value of all the crafts.

'Melinya was born and raised in Hallion; I knew her since we were children. Her parents were killed by bandits on the way back from one of their rare visits to Tarrelford—that may be one reason why the Water Crafters didn't wish to journey here. My uncle—Zendos' father—took Melinya into his household and reared her as his own. We often played together, and as we grew older, fell in love. Zendos became insanely jealous, trying all manner of tricks to coax Melinya into his arms. The more she resisted, the more both his love and hatred of her grew, and the more twisted his mind became.

'When his father warned him off, Zendos killed him. Then he fled from Hallion and later met Dargan. After years spent learning dark secrets, he used some of his master's teaching to lure Melinya from Hallion a year ago. She has not been seen since.'

He fell quiet, a dark mood making his face even more sombre than ever. Feeling a soft touch on his shoulder, he looked up to find Vallel smiling down at him.

'Don't fear; we will find her,' she whispered. He gripped her hand in a gesture of thanks.

Kess realised how much Athennar must have been suffering during the past year. Weighed down by his own grief at Linnil's disappearance, he hadn't realised that Athennar had been struggling with similar emotions for much longer.

'Where's Sash?' asked Hesteron suddenly. The black leopard had joined them for the journey from the fortress to Hallion, but hadn't been seen since. All the friends had become fond of the gentle cat, though only Athennar could communicate with her.

'I sent her home for the time being,' said Athennar, his mood lifting. 'She would be too noticeable in the area around the Ice Kingdom. I expect she will join us again at a later stage. Don't worry, you haven't seen the last of her.

'Now we must rest,' he continued. 'We have a long, hard journey ahead of us.'

Two days later, the company arrived at the eastern slopes of the Mountains of Kravos. Gatera and Rrum said their farewells.

'May Elsinoth be with you,' said Athennar, grasping the giant's hand firmly.

Gatera grinned. 'And with you!' he boomed. 'Take care of yourselves, and may the land be firm beneath your feet.' He shook hands with the others.

'Look after him,' Kess said to Rrum. 'We will hope to see you on our return. I hope it won't be long.'

'Nott too longg,' agreed the little Rrokki, bowing.

The five friends mounted their horses and started off northwards. Gatera put a reassuring hand on Rrum's shoulder. 'They are good people,' he said.

'Yes, goodd.'

The two then turned westwards to find Gatera's family.

Two more days passed uneventfully for the diminished company as they journeyed northwards. They made good time on horseback, the countryside being mostly a flat and grassy plain. Nevertheless, Kess chafed at any slight delay. He was only too aware that every day they spent travelling was another day in which Dargan could be mistreating Linnil. 'Can't we go any faster?' he begged.

Athennar smiled patiently. 'We must spare the horses. There is little point in pushing them so hard that they collapse. I share your concern, but we are making good progress. Within another three or four days we should be within reach of the Ice Kingdom.'

'If we can find it,' muttered Valor darkly. He was weary of the endless travelling and had been feeling strangely unsettled since seeing Carnak at the fortress.

Hesteron's elvish sight noticed a strange shimmer in the sky ahead of them. 'There seems to be some sort of haze over there,' he called to the others.

'It must be a mist; I can sense water in the air,' added Vallel.

Hesteron took a deep breath and then nodded in agreement.

'That will be the Whistling Waters,' Athennar informed them. 'We pass nearby, but we won't go too close. Curious things are said to happen within the mists there.'

'What sort of things?' asked Kess.

'I'm not sure, but many legends grow up around such places and there is often a central core of truth in them, so it is best to be wary. Some of the tales tell of a strange woman, known by the somewhat whimsical title of "The Mistress of the Mysteries of the Mist".'

Vallel giggled at the name.

'Humph!' snorted Valor, making her giggle even more.

Kess smiled at the Mountain Guard, who glared back at first but then broke into a reluctant grin.

They camped that night in the shelter of a rock a mile or so away from the thickest mist. They all felt the dampness, which was accompanied by an uncomfortable, clammy chill.

Athennar decided against lighting a fire, so they had a cold meal of bread and cheese before settling down for the night. Hesteron had volunteered to take the first watch, a precaution partly against any roving Zorgs or bandits, and partly against any threat that might come from the mist.

Kess jerked awake suddenly. He must have fallen asleep, although he had only been on watch for a few minutes. The grey light of dawn was filtering through the mist, fingers of which were spreading throughout the campsite. He could only dimly make out the sleeping forms of his companions. He turned to see if there was any danger lurking nearby. Off to one side he thought he could see something moving. Sleepily, he rubbed his eyes and looked again. The shape of a woman flitted through the mist. It looked like Linnil!

'Linnil?' he called softly, urgently. Pulling his cloak tighter, he padded off quietly after the retreating figure.

10

The Mists of Death

The shifting form of the woman glided slowly onwards, keeping a constant distance ahead of Kess. He called out Linnil's name again, and thought he saw her turn briefly, as if she had half-heard something but then had shrugged it off. He started running then. At first he thought he was catching her, but somehow she managed to stay just out of reach. Gradually he was aware of distant whistling sounds. They somehow brought him back to his senses.

He looked all around. The mist was a thick shroud of grey, veiling everything. Shaking his head, he tried to clear his thoughts. Why had he followed the shape when he had been warned about such dangers? Had it just been his sleepiness, his longing to find his sister, or had he been drawn on by some spell? He didn't know—but he did know he was lost, not even sure of the direction of the campsite.

He shouted for help, but could hear no replies. *The camp must be at least a mile away*, he thought gloomily. Then the mysterious figure came back into view. She seemed to be beckoning him. What should he do? Kess decided to try and retrace his steps by going in the opposite direction from the woman. He knew now that it wasn't Linnil, and it was unlikely that she had his best interests at heart.

The ground underfoot was wet, and his footsteps made eery splashing sounds in the damp air. The mist seemed strangely thick; almost as if he could part it with his fingers. The water was soon sloshing around his ankles, and he stopped in despair, again calling for help. He seemed to be heading into the water rather than escaping it. The weird whistling started again—mournful, unearthly tones that tugged at him.

Changing direction, he started off once more. The haunting shapes of long dead trees reared out of the swamp, threatening him, mocking him. The thick, clammy mist seemed to be wrapping itself around his heart. He felt a sudden cold panic but fought to control it.

Pushing on through the greyness, he noticed that the whistling was growing louder. Desperately he tried to turn away from it, but it surrounded him, sounding even more ghostly with each step he took.

The water was now well above his ankles. Looking down he could just make out grey-green swirls circling around his legs, tendrils of mists climbing up and clinging to him. He stopped and cried out to Elsinoth for help. Even as he did so, he realised the cry was being deadened by the thick grey veil all around him.

Hesteron and Athennar had woken immediately at the sound of Kess' first call. They both sprang to their feet, alarmed at the mist. Athennar shouted out Kess' name, but there was no answer, and the call sounded hollow. Vallel and Valor then appeared.

'What's happened?' asked Valor anxiously.

'I don't know,' admitted Athennar. 'I heard Kess

call Linnil's name, but now he seems to have disappeared into this wretched mist.'

'We must follow him,' said Valor.

Athennar thought for a moment and then nodded grimly. 'We will go forward, about ten paces apart, making sure we are at least able to hear each other's voices all the time. It sounded as if he was going in the direction of the Whistling Waters, so we must go that way. Take great care, though, we don't know what we might face.' He sighed. 'It's going to be difficult to find him in this mist. I'll take the left flank. Valor, you come next, then Vallel, then Hesteron over to the right. Every twenty paces forward, give a call. Perhaps if Kess has fallen he will hear us and reply.'

'How will we find our way back here?' asked Hesteron.

'Windrider knows my call well. If I whistle, he will respond with a whinny. That's the best I can offer, I'm afraid. Perhaps one of us should stay behind, however, just in case.'

The others all shook their heads. 'We should go together,' insisted Vallel. 'The more of us who are searching, the better the chance we have of finding Kess.'

Athennar moved off to the left, while Vallel and Hesteron walked in the opposite direction until they were suitably spaced out.

'Ready?' called Athennar.

Valor shouted to the other two and then confirmed that they were ready to proceed. The four friends strode carefully forwards, periodically calling Kess' name and checking each other's position. It was an eery feeling moving forward into the mist, knowing their companions were nearby, yet unable to see them or hear them apart from the occasional shout. Valor felt alone for the first time since leaving Mount Tilt and meeting Kess and Linnil. It was disconcerting, and he was relieved each time he heard the others call out.

After some time the ground started to become marshy. Far from being reassuring, the slurping of their feet through the water added to the sense of unreality. A haunting, whistling tune began to float around their ears despite the denseness of the mist. It whispered subtly to them, drawing them onwards. Vague contorted shapes appeared out of the gloom. They seemed like armies of mist soldiers coming towards them, spears at the ready. Yet as they drew nearer the forms became insubstantial and dissolved. Tall ships appeared to sail proudly by, and the friends thought they could almost hear the sound of rigging slapping in an imaginary breeze.

Vallel leaned down and trailed her hand in the water as she walked. It was a curious sensation for her. Her years as a River Crafter had taught her much, but she was unprepared for this. The water was soulless, stagnant, seemingly purposeless, holding none of the vibrancy of a river, the playfulness of a stream, or the power of the sea. She sighed sadly and withdrew her hand.

Hesteron meanwhile tossed his head, irritated by the cloying feeling of the mist. All his life there had been some movement in the air, though at times almost undetectable. Ever since learning his craft, he had cultivated a small breeze which gently teased his hair as he walked. For the first time it had left him, weighed down by the clinging dampness.

In the distance he thought he heard a muffled shout. 'This way!' he called to Vallel. She passed on the message, and all four shouted as they made their way forward, groping through the greyness.

As she walked, Vallel nearly bumped into a charred

tree stump sticking out of the water. It had registered in her mind, but she had expected it to disappear like the other illusions they had seen. As she passed the stump, she caught sight of something out of the corner of her eye and an involuntary scream left her throat.

There was a calling of concerned voices and a splashing as the other three rushed to join her where she stood, transfixed. They followed her gaze. Through the mist, they could just make out details of the old tree stump. It wasn't a stump at all. It was a body, somehow rooted there, all of its features having been turned to the texture of burned wood. No wood carver, however, could have captured the look of terror in the face that peered out at them.

'By the Realm!' breathed Athennar.

Hesteron meanwhile comforted Vallel, who was slowly recovering from the shock. 'Who—or what—could have done such a thing?' she asked. 'Could it have been Dargan? The illusions around here seem to fit his way of working.'

'I think not,' replied Athennar thoughtfully. 'His influence does not extend this far north. No, it must be the work of the Mist Mistress, I fear.'

'Wherever we go there is someone intent on doing evil,' muttered Hesteron.

'Yes, evil abounds, but good also,' said Athennar. 'However, if more folk took a stand against evil, perhaps people like Dargan wouldn't grow so strong.'

Hesteron nodded as he recalled Kess talking about the reluctance of the Valley folk to get involved with matters outside their home.

'Take heart,' continued Athennar. 'We must be that force for good!'

'Do you—d'you think Kess has been turned into a tree stump?' Valor swallowed as he realised the horrifying implications of the corpse before him.

'I doubt the process is that rapid,' said Athennar. 'And Kess has strengths in him which I think few of us have seen yet. However, we won't find him by standing here. Spread apart again, and we will continue our search a while longer.'

They moved slowly forward again. More grisly wooden bodies appeared out of the mists. The whistling had turned to a terrible mournful wailing which shrieked of despair. They tried to close their ears to it as they trudged on wearily through the water.

As they struggled onwards the mist seemed to change. It was losing its greyness and was becoming a sombre brown colour. Athennar called the others to him for a meeting.

'I'm not sure whether there is any point in going further,' he said. 'We could hunt for days in this mist and go right past Kess without even knowing. Let's give one more call together, then try to return to the camp.'

He counted to three and then they all shouted at once.

'KESSSSS!' The sound hung for a moment and then evaporated. No answering call came; no eager splashing through the water.

They were about to turn around when the mists parted slightly. Just a little way ahead they could see some mysterious shapes. Athennar beckoned the others and they quietly followed him as he went to investigate.

When they reached the objects, it was with a sense of anticlimax. Four stout wooden poles stuck up out of the water. Athennar was about to suggest they turn back when Hesteron shouted. 'This pole has my name carved on it!'

The others gathered round to see. Sure enough, in crudely carved letters was the name 'Hesteron'.

'This one says "Valor",' said the Mountain Guard, who was looking at the next pole.

On inspection, each stake was found to have been inscribed with one of their names. As the friends looked on in confusion, the mist began to swirl again. Brown tendrils detached themselves from the main body of the mist and started wrapping themselves around their arms and legs. Even as the friends tried to resist, they found themselves drawn back roughly against the poles. The ropes of mist held them as securely as any real ropes could have done; each captive bound tightly to his own pole.

Out of the gloom came a mocking laugh that floated around their heads, seeming to circle them. A voice followed it; a chill, heartless voice.

'More volunteers for sacrifice! Welcome to the Mists of Death!' The tones turned into a fiendish cackle that echoed around them as they struggled hopelessly against their bonds.

11

Thoughts of Escape

Merric paced the battlements of the Fortress of Fear. He half wished he had travelled northwards with his friends, but he held onto the strange instinct that he must stay at the fortress. Perhaps the first news of Linnil would come from the south. If so, he wanted to be there when it came, ready to respond.

He smiled grimly to himself as he realised he was becoming as moody as Kess had been before leaving the fortress. He wondered how the company was faring in the north, and whether or not they had yet reached the Ice Kingdom. More than that, he again wondered where Linnil was, what Dargan might be doing to her and whether she was thinking of him. If only they could get some clue as to where she was being kept prisoner!

Merric's mood darkened further as he recalled his visit to Carnak the previous day. He had been to see the Keeper every day since the company had left, hoping to glean more information from the man's ravings. Yesterday had been different, though. Instead of the usual ramblings, Carnak had been totally silent, not even grunting in reply to Merric's questions. There had been a peculiarly detached look in his eyes that had sent a shiver down the minstrel's spine.

After several futile attempts to get some response from the Keeper, Merric had conceded defeat and left the room. Barely an hour later, Carnak had suddenly let out a terrible scream. Rushing in to see what had happened, the guard had been attacked by the madman. When the guard drew his sword in defence, the crazed Carnak threw himself on its point. A single sigh of relief had hissed from his lips before his life had slipped away.

Merric regretted the Keeper's passing, even though he had no great love for the man. It also increased his sense of frustration; another fragile hope of finding Linnil had disappeared.

Climbing wearily from the battlements, he went to his room and picked up his lute, although he knew that even music would give him little solace.

It was a beautiful instrument, crafted by his father's own hands. Delicately inlaid around its belly were circles of tiny flowers, interwoven with slender leaves. Cradling the lute lovingly, he began to pick out a gentle melody, his fingers rippling smoothly over the strings. The music was soft, haunting, questioning. All his aches, all his fears, were poured into the making of the melody. When it was formed, rounded, teased into shape, he began to add words. His voice floated around the room. It was a call to the one he loved; a call that he knew would be unanswered until time itself drew forth the reply:

> 'Features fair, lithesome grace,
> Float on by as on a breeze
> Briefly met yet swiftly rent
> Leaving tattered memories.
>
> Green of eyes, smile serene,
> Sinking deep into my heart

Slipping past and lost from view;
Distant dreams now we're apart.

Bright and clear, walking light,
Stillness in a soul of peace
Waiting now 'neath distant skies
Lonely notes, cold melodies.

True lady, know I think of you
With russet hair and emerald gaze
And when I find you we will be
As one until the end of days.'

He stopped and put the lute aside. Burying his head
in his hands, he gave way to his grief. *Where are you,
Linnil?*' he cried.

Linnil stood quietly behind the door of her cell, one
of the statuettes from the bookcase raised above her
head. The lock clicked and the door swung open. A
figure moved forward into the room, and the Valley
girl brought the statuette crashing down on its head.
The body of her Zorg guard crumpled to the floor,
giving a slight groan as he did so. Linnil dropped her
makeshift weapon and stepped quickly over him.

As she reached the doorway, she found it blocked
by a dark, menacing shape. Her mind constricted
under the strength of Dargan's mental powers as he
forced her back into the room.

'Well, well, my little sweet. I see there is still a little
fire left in you. Good!' He scowled at the Zorg who
was moaning lightly on the floor. Dargan prodded
him with his foot. 'Get up, you fool! That tough
leather head of yours should have protected what
little brain you have. Perhaps that will teach you to be
more careful in future.'

The Zorg struggled to his feet and glared at Linnil.

She thought for a moment that he was going to attack her, but another scowl from Dargan sent him shuffling out of the room, muttering.

'Forgive him—he has no manners,' said Dargan in his sickly sweet, sarcastic tones. 'He should have knocked before he came in. I thought it was time I visited you again. I'm afraid I've neglected you lately as I've been rather busy for the last week or two.'

Linnil groaned inwardly. Had she really been here that long? Dargan's mind control had obviously affected her as she had spent much of the time in sleep. Only today had her thoughts really turned to escape, despite Dargan's earlier warning.

'I told you that you could never escape,' gloated Dargan. 'It seems that you have to learn these things the hard way. No matter. I will leave you to ponder your foolishness. Unfortunately, because of your— er—reprisal against your guard, it will be a little while before anyone can be sent to replace him. I'm afraid if you need anything you will have to bide your time.'

Having spoken, he bowed mockingly and snapped the door shut behind him.

Linnil felt his mind-hold dissolve, and sank down onto the nearest chair. Now what could she do? Of all the times to choose to attack her guard, she'd chosen the one time when Dargan was there as well.

It was then that she realised she hadn't heard the key turn in the lock when Dargan left the room. In the confusion, he must have forgotten! Rushing to the door, she gingerly tried the handle, held her breath to listen, and then waited. She almost squealed with delight as the door opened, and she slipped quickly through the gap and into the gloom of the passageway. *Free at last!* Her hopes rose. Perhaps there was a chance of escape after all!

In the darkness of a nearby alcove, Dargan

chuckled to himself. So she had taken the bait. The
girl needed some mental exercise, and it would
provide an amusing diversion for him, as well as
being a reminder to her of the futility of trying to
escape. He needed a break from his experiments with
the Sceptre, even though he felt that he was at last
making good progress. It would not be long now
before he had mastered its power. For the moment he
would have some entertainment at his prisoner's
expense.

Linnil meanwhile had reached a place where the
passageway opened out into an enormous natural
chamber. She peered around cautiously before emerging from the tunnel. To her right was the roar of the
underground waterfall, charging headlong to the
ground, then rushing towards the back of the throne.
There the waters split and went either side, where
they were spanned by two bridges. She could just
remember having been brought across the one on this
side—so that must be the way out!

She ran lightly across the bridge. On either side of
the throne was a stand with a torch mounted in the
top. Reaching up, she took the nearest one as she
passed. At least she would have some light. Cautiously
but quickly she made her way along the walkway
across the middle of the underground lake. Even as
she hurried on, she noticed how old and worn the
path seemed, and wondered who could have built it
and why. Was it originally some subterranean kingdom unheard of by those above ground, and unused
for centuries until Dargan had happened upon it?
She would probably never know.

In places, the walkway was quite slippery, and she
had to slow down. Memories of the Scorbid that had
killed Vosphel came flooding back, and she cast
several nervous glances at the lake. She hoped there

was no similar monster in these waters; she was all too aware of her defencelessness. The waters swirled strangely, almost hypnotically, and were streaked with grey and black whirls. Looking away, she concentrated on her footing.

When at last she reached the other side of the dark pool, a single wide passage stretched away in front of her. The torch cast flickering shadows across the walls, making her feel she was being followed. She knew that if any of Dargan's Zorgs were nearby they would soon spot the light. The tunnel bent after a short distance, taking her out of view of the lake. However, she couldn't shake off her sense of unease—a shiver kept running up the nape of her neck, as if it was being stroked by a cold finger. Shutting out the thought, she began to hurry. It felt good to run after being cramped up in the little chamber for so long.

A little further along, the passage opened out into a circular room with a huge, grotesque statue in its centre. All round the edge of the chamber were identical passages leading off into the darkness. She had no idea which to choose, and walked slowly past each opening hoping that something might jolt her memory.

As she came back past the front of the statue, there was an awful groaning noise. Linnil looked up in horror to see the stony eyes of the figure grate open, revealing a flickering redness. A huge coiled tongue wound and unwound from the statue's mouth, dripping a hideous-smelling fluid onto the cavern floor. Screaming, she ran into the nearest corridor, desperate to escape whatever evil was embodied in the stone image.

She had been running for a few minutes when she heard a noise that sounded like falling rocks.

Skidding to a halt, she peered into the gloom beyond the torch's light. The floor of the tunnel was disintegrating—falling into a black void! Dargan's evil enchantments were at work even here.

As she watched, cracks appeared in the ground in front of her, and it too started to cave in. She had no alternative—she would have to return to the horrors of the circular chamber. Racing back down the tunnel, she gasped for breath, while behind her the sounds of crumbling rock followed her flight.

When she reached the room with the statue, she didn't even pause to look at it, but darted rapidly into the next passage. This time, once she had travelled a reasonable distance down the new tunnel, she slowed to a walk. She felt tired, and was beginning to question the wisdom of trying to escape at all. At least in her cell she had been supplied with food and had been allowed to live; well, at least for the moment.

No, she refused to admit defeat. She thought of Kess, of Merric, and resolved to find her way out of this place. Perhaps this was the right tunnel. Even as the thought crossed her mind, the corridor widened into another big cavern. Pools of water dotted the floor and the path disappeared in a maze of little tracks around these pools. Linnil aimed for the far side of the cavern, taking the paths that would keep her travelling in that direction.

For a while, all went well. Then, as she neared the opposite wall of the cavern, she found that several pools had merged to form a wider strip of water, barring her way. She would have to wade across.

Kneeling down beside the water, she tried to gauge its depth. As she did so, her knee knocked a little pebble into the pool. A great hissing and frothing surrounded the stone and Linnil leapt back in alarm. This wasn't water—it was some kind of horrible acid!

She suddenly realised that there was a constant hissing all along the edge of the pool; the acid was dissolving the rock away. Looking behind her, she noticed with horror that some of the pathways were beginning to disappear.

Leaping up, she rushed back along the nearest pathway. If she didn't hurry, she would be too late—trapped by an expanding network of acid!

It became a desperate race. Twice she had to turn round and retrace her steps because the track in front of her had suddenly crumbled away. She was already tired, but fear lent strength to her legs. By the time she neared the tunnel entrance, several pools had again joined together in a narrow stretch of acid, preventing her exit. With a superhuman effort, and with the agility she had inherited from her elven ancestors, she didn't hesitate, but sprang across in a tremendous leap. Her heart was pounding as she fell heavily on the other side, scrambled to her feet, and hobbled to the passage. The hissing had stopped, but behind her the cavern floor had become a massive pool of the deadly fluid.

Linnil collapsed on to the floor of the tunnel. She had to have a rest, even if all the monstrous evils in this place, all the acid underground, surrounded her. The feeling of hopelessness and frustration again boiled up inside her but she pushed it down, forcing herself to breathe deeply.

When she had recovered, she arose wearily and worked her way back along the passage. At least she had managed to hold on to the torch.

This time, when she arrived back at the circular room, she bit back her fear of the statue and slowly examined the other passages. Although all the tunnels had looked the same at first sight, on closer inspection one of them appeared slightly wider than the others. She decided to try it, still dreading what new horrors might await her.

As she proceeded, the passage started to grow gradually narrower. Eventually she could barely walk without scraping her shoulders on the walls on either side. The tunnel also kept taking sudden right angled turns, so she was no longer sure whether she was indeed still moving away from the central chamber. She went round one such turn and unexpectedly found herself in a small, square room.

None of its walls had an opening. She had walked all this way to find a dead end! The thought of yet again having to retrace her steps almost reduced her to tears. Just as she was about to step back into the passage, there was a sudden rumbling noise and a huge slab of rock descended, blocking off her only exit. She was trapped—imprisoned more certainly than ever before. She pounded on the slab with her fists, pushed and heaved at it, but to no effect. It wouldn't move at all.

Utterly defeated, she collapsed on the floor of the room, half-sobbing, half-choking from the dust that had been raised by the slab. Why hadn't she listened to Dargan? He had said there was no escape.

As if in confirmation, a cold, dry voice floated into the room. 'Don't say I didn't warn you.'

Linnil gave a gasp of disbelief as Dargan seemed to materialise through the stone. As he did so, it faded and the passageway reappeared. 'Just an illusion, my dear,' he said mockingly.

'But how …?' she said.

'The mind is a powerful thing. Sometimes you can so convince yourself of something that even beating upon thin air can hurt you.' The Dark Master's gloating voice was hateful to Linnil. He continued, sneering, 'You don't really think I would be foolish enough to leave you a means of escape, do you? You had to be taught that I am in total control. Perhaps now you will not entertain such foolish notions again,'

He snapped his fingers and two Zorg sentries appeared from the passage and grabbed Linnil's arms. 'These two—er—gentlemen will see that you find your way safely back to your room,' chuckled Dargan. 'There you can continue to enjoy both rest and my hospitality.'

The Zorgs bundled her roughly down the passage. Dargan watched them go with a crooked smile of satisfaction. The girl had spirit but had learned now to see the futility of her situation. She had learned that a little fear is the best prison guard of all. Yes, she would be a fine specimen for his tests.

The Dark Master walked back along the tunnel, grinning mirthlessly to himself.

12

Whisper

Still enshrouded in fog, Kess hung his head and said a silent prayer to Elsinoth. What was he going to do now? Whichever way he turned, he seemed to go deeper into the marsh. He wanted to brush the mist away, to stop it from clinging to him. He breathed slowly to calm himself.

Out of the corner of his eye he noticed a slight movement—the figure of the woman. She beckoned to him yet again. This time he decided he had little choice but to follow. Ready for any trickery, he kept his hand on the hilt of his sword.

The figure floated away in front of him, pausing if he lagged behind. Kess laboured forward, noticing with relief that the water didn't get any deeper. He wondered who the woman was. Could she be the 'Mistress of the Mysteries of the Mist'? If so, what cruel fate was in store for him?

He tried calling his friends again, but there was still no response. Perhaps they hadn't even noticed he was missing. Even if they had, they were unlikely to find him now.

He suddenly realised that the woman had disappeared. Directly ahead of him was a great tree, its dead, stark branches reaching vainly upwards, as if

WHISPER   85

seeking to break through the stranglehold of the mist.
As Kess looked up, he saw the woman sitting on one
of the branches, motioning him to join her. He waded
to the tree. To his surprise, he saw a tall door in its
trunk.

Opening the door, he stepped through, but found
himself on the other side of the tree. Looking back, he
could see no door in the trunk.

'It's an illusion,' called a faint, dream-like voice
above him.

Kess looked up again. He could see her more
clearly now, though her shape seemed to shift in the
mist that draped itself around her.

'Come up!' came her soft tones. 'There are steps in
the side of the trunk.'

Kess looked and saw rough chunks cut out of the
bole of the tree. He hesitated but then decided to
obey. Relieved to have his feet out of the water at last,
he scrambled up.

Reaching the branch, he found the top was
flattened and wide enough to walk on. He moved
carefully to join the woman, who welcomed him with a
smile.

'Good meeting,' she said formally. 'My name is
Whisper.'

'Good meeting,' Kess replied. 'I'm Kessek.'

'I know,' she said, and smiled at his surprise. She
had moist grey eyes, skin of ivory, and sleek jet black
hair that fell down and swung around her neck.

Kess had to admit to himself, rather reluctantly,
that she was beautiful. 'How do you know?' he asked.

She smiled again, but said nothing.

'Are you the Mistress of the Mist?' Kess asked.

This time she laughed. 'No, far from it. I am her
captive. Most people who fall into her snares perish to
satisfy her cruel whims. She has been here for

centuries. Yet even someone with her power can become lonely. She trapped me a long time ago, and keeps me to talk to. She treats me well, yet I am a prisoner. I cannot escape save ...' She looked pensive and changed the subject. 'This is my look-out tree,' she said, suddenly laughing again. Her laugh was light and airy, contrasting with the murkiness all around.

'But you can't see anything!' protested Kess.

'I know,' she laughed, 'but I come here and imagine things that I remember from the world outside. Tell me, does the sun still shine brightly? Does the wind still ripple its way through the grass and the wild flowers?'

Kess nodded, not knowing how to reply. 'Why did you bring me here?' he demanded suddenly.

'It is the only place where I could talk safely to you. Were we touching the Whistling Waters, the Mistress would know of all our conversations. It has been ... so long since I spoke to anyone *real*,' she added wistfully.

'Are you going to let me go free?' Kess asked, half-afraid of the answer.

'I was hoping you would be able to free me,' she said. Seeing his puzzled expression, she explained: 'I have learned much from the Mistress since I was first captured. A spell is on the water that prevents me from leaving it, save at such sanctuaries as this. But if someone were to carry me out ...'

'Would it work?' asked Kess, and then, suspiciously, 'Why should I believe you, anyway?'

'Without my help you will never leave here alive. My Mistress left me to deal with you because she now has others—um—other details to see to. As to whether our escape will work, who can say until it is tried? I'm afraid, though, it is the only hope for both of us.'

Kess peered down at the dingy colours of the water barely visible below. He must escape this dreaded mist and get back to his friends. As Whisper had said, he didn't really have any choice but to trust her. 'Very well,' he said, 'but no tricks.'

Whisper smiled. 'Once you are carrying me, we must not speak,' she said. 'I will point out the direction we need to go. Just carry me carefully and do not let me drop into the water. Now, if you are ready, the sooner we go the better—while my Mistress is still distracted.'

Kess moved back towards the trunk of the tree and climbed carefully down until he was once more standing in the murky waters. Whisper followed, and when she reached the bottom step, lowered herself cautiously into his waiting arms.

Kess balanced himself, breathing raggedly. He did not mind carrying Whisper, for she was surprisingly light, but her beauty left him almost breathless. He tried to look away from her face, but kept glancing out of the corner of his eyes to see her gentle, half-mocking smile.

She pointed the way ahead, and he waded slowly through the clammy marsh. His mind was full of her pale eyes, the glossy blackness of her hair, the feel of her arms around his neck. Berating himself for such foolishness, he tried to keep his mind on the journey ahead.

The walk through the marsh seemed to take for ever. Did Whisper truly know her way through the mist? Despite her lightness, Kess' arms became more and more tired and it grew increasingly difficult to keep her feet from dangling in the water. Just as he thought he would have to drop her, the ground began to rise slightly. As he took his last step out of the water and on to the dry land, Whisper gave a little gasp of pain. He lowered her carefully and looked at her. 'Are you safe now?' he asked worriedly.

She nodded. 'Whatever bond tied me to that place has now been broken.'

'But won't the Mist Mistress know, and come after you?'

'Oh, she'll know all right, but she won't be able to do anything about it. She's a prisoner there just as much as I was. For her, there is an even stronger bond; she is both a captive of the mist and waters, and at the same time, the one who keeps them there. In a way, the marsh-mist is her soul, her very life-force.'

Kess shuddered at the thought. 'Let's find our way out of here, and back to my companions,' he suggested. 'They may have woken and realised I am missing.'

The mist was thinning, but they could still see only a few yards ahead. However, grey wisps floated past them as if drawn back into the centre of the marsh. As they walked, it quickly dissipated, and they suddenly broke through into the light of morning.

Whisper shielded her eyes with a cry: 'Oh, It's so bright!'

Kess persuaded her to sit down and let her eyes gradually adjust to the light. He watched her closely as she then lay on the grass, her eyes shut and shaded by her hands. 'Who are you really?' he asked quietly.

Her eyelids fluttered but didn't open. 'I am Whisper,' she replied. 'My past is best forgotten.'

'Who, then, is the Mistress of the Mysteries of the Mist?' he persisted. 'Why should I believe you when you say you aren't the Mistress?'

'Because if I were, I would have dealt with you in the security of the mists, on my own terms,' she replied. 'As for who she is ... there have been many stories, but I think I know her well enough to know which is truest.'

'Well?' said Kess when she fell silent again.

She opened her eyes slowly and carefully and looked at him with an openly approving gaze. 'You look even more handsome in this clear light.'

Kess reddened, taken aback by her frankness.

'You don't know what it has been like to spend so long in the same grey fog,' she said, gazing around. 'I had forgotten what true colour is; how sharp and bright everything appears.'

She paused for a moment. 'You were asking me about the Mistress. She is a cold creature, without feeling. It is said—and I believe it—that centuries ago she was the wife of a past Guardian of the Realm, but was captured by a Dark Master. He wanted to make her his own, but she spurned his advances and remained faithful to her husband. In an act of revenge, the Dark Master imprisoned her in the waters of this place. She was bound by the mist, drained of all goodness and truth, drained even of the ravages of time—left to live for ever in a misty tomb. Yet just occasionally I have seen glimpses of her former self—somehow, rarely, her true self breaks through, and she speaks of her loneliness and longing to be freed of her prison for ever—freed by death. It is this loneliness which led her to hold me for company in her misery.'

'How terrible! What will she do now you have gone?' asked Kess.

Whisper shrugged. 'She will return to her solitary existence.'

'It is a sad tale; I wish we could help her.'

'I don't think anyone can help her—now or ever.'

'What will you do now you are free?'

'I am not completely free; I have yet to be fully released from her spell. I will speak more later, when we are further away from the mist.'

Kess nodded and helped her up. In the distance he thought he could see the rock under which the company had camped the previous night. 'We'll find my friends and discuss it there. Perhaps we can help you in some way.'

Whisper looked at him gratefully and took his hand, squeezing it in gratitude. Her touch was cold and clammy, a reminder of the recent mists.

'Come on,' said Kess, withdrawing his hand, 'the others will be wondering where I am.'

A little while later, they arrived at the campsite. Blazer gave a snort of greeting, but there was no welcoming shout from the company. Kess' heart dropped as he realised that all his friends had disappeared. 'They're not here,' he groaned. 'They must have gone to look for me in the mist.'

Whisper nodded in agreement.

Kess noticed an odd look in her eyes, and his own opened wide in sudden understanding. 'You *knew*!' he shouted accusingly. 'That's what you were talking about when you said the Mist Mistress would be distracted. You made me carry you out of the waters while my friends acted as a decoy.'

'And what other choice did I have?' Whisper demanded, her eyes pained.

'You—we—could have helped them, instead of saving ourselves.'

'How?' said Whisper scornfully. 'That is her domain. Have you any idea of her powers? She turns her victims into charcoaled tree stumps. My powers are not sufficient to stand against hers; otherwise I would have done so years ago.'

Kess went pale at the thought of his friends turned to wood. He suddenly felt helpless. He was sure Whisper was speaking the truth, however unpalatable it might seem. 'Is there nothing we can do?' he asked, his head bowed.

'Nothing,' she replied. 'No one has ever escaped the clutches of the Mistress.'

'But *we* did," he said. He fell to his knees in confusion and despair. 'Help them, Elsinoth!' he cried in anguish.

Whisper looked at him disdainfully. 'You don't really believe Elsinoth is interested in us, do you?' she asked bitterly. 'Even if he was, it would be too late anyway. By now your friends will be dead.'

13

The Mist Mistress

Athennar, Valor, Hesteron and Vallel fought against
the writhing bonds of mist that gripped them. Vallel
had been pinioned against her post while she was
brushing her wet hair from her eyes. As a result, one
arm was free, with just a few misty strands clinging to
it, but she could do nothing to release the bonds. The
rest of her body was tightly bound and she couldn't
loosen her sword or dagger. Even if she could cut
through the strands, she guessed they would probably merge together again. Each time she grasped
one of the filaments, it felt slippery and cold, constantly shifting yet somehow solid.

The chill voice drew nearer. 'Struggle is hopeless.
All is hopeless.'

'No!' cried Athennar in defiance. 'Release us! We
have done you no harm.'

'You have entered the domain of the mists. No one
leaves without my permission. I never have, nor ever
will, give that permission.' The voice was at once both
sepulchral and ethereal.

'We will not harm you. Let us go!' shouted Hesteron.

'Never! You must die the death I cannot.'

As they listened, they could just discern the vague

outline of a figure approaching them. At first they
thought it was an apparition, but as it drew closer, it
resolved itself into the shape of a woman. She was like
the bonds that held them: solid, yet at the same time
somehow insubstantial. Her hair was a light, almost
transparent grey, and floated down to her waist. She
wore pale brown-grey robes which matched the mist
around her and added to her ever-changing nature.

'Why should we die? Our deaths won't help you,'
protested Valor.

'It enables me to observe the end that eludes me.
And it is my wish, and none can gainsay my wish.' She
drew a grey dagger from her robe. 'When death
comes—as it will—you will welcome its embrace,' she
whispered softly. Moving over to Valor, she touched
the point of the weapon against his left hand. A mist
flowed from the dagger and seemed to seep into his
skin. The Mountain Guard gave a cry of pain as his
hand went cold and heavy, the muscles tightening
and loosening in spasms.

'The dagger of death,' intoned the Mistress, as she
waved it in front of his face.

Valor shrank away, and she sneered at his fear. 'It
has not yet entered your body,' she said mockingly.
'You have had just a taste of what is to come. As I
touch each limb, it will become slowly strangled,
drained of life; but that is yet the start. Only
when I have observed each one suffering in turn
will I plunge my little blade into your hearts, one
by one. You will then die quickly, but painfully;
your bodies absorbed into the poles that bear your
names.'

'That's *horrible*,' shuddered Vallel.

'Oh, yes,' replied the Mistress. For a moment, a
troubled look crossed her face, then she continued, as
if in explanation: 'I have suffered long. I need to see

others suffer and die—that perhaps at some time I might also learn how to die.'

An involuntary shudder ran down Vallel's back as the Mistress moved in front of her and gazed at her through colourless eyes. She stepped closer to the Water Crafter, stroking her dagger absent-mindedly.

She was about to speak again when she stopped abruptly. 'No!' she screamed. 'She cannot defy me!' Rushing off, she was soon out of sight.

'What in the Realm caused that, I wonder?' asked Hesteron, bewildered.

'I don't know, but it at least gives us a little time,' commented Athennar. 'Quickly—does anyone have any ideas?' He strained to look at the others.

'Vallel, can you reach your sword and cut yourself free?'

'No, and weapons are unlikely to work against these bonds, I fear.'

Hesteron went red in the face as he struggled to burst out of the misty cords. 'It's no use!' he gasped.

'I think Vallel is right—we won't break our way out. But I have another idea,' said Athennar. 'Hesteron, your Craft teaches you some control over the air currents, doesn't it?'

'A little,' replied the Air Crafter, slowly. 'But I'm not sure ...'

'It may be,' interrupted Athennar thoughtfully, 'that if you concentrated, you could stir the air currents—indeed, perhaps even free us.'

'How? Only my head is free.'

Athennar paused for a moment. 'If you can somehow conjure up the small breeze that usually follows you, it could cause the mist to disperse, and these bonds, strong as they are, might melt away. Try, Hesteron—you must try for all our sakes.'

'I could help!' cried Vallel excitedly. 'I think I

might be able to work upon the droplets of water in the mist. If I can make them fall as rain, that would also help the air to clear.'

'Good,' Athennar urged, 'then start straight away—we don't know how soon it will be before she returns.'

Hesteron closed his eyes for a moment in thought. Then he pursed his lips and started blowing gently but firmly, moving his head in a circular motion as he did so. Little swirls of air wound their way clumsily into the thickness of the mist. 'It's doing little good,' he panted after a while.

'Keep trying!' encouraged Athennar. 'It's our only hope.'

'Toroth, aid me now!' whispered Hesteron, using the elven name for Elsinoth.

Vallel, meanwhile, felt the dampness of the air with her hand, touching the wetness, seeing in her mind the millions of droplets in the mist. She waved her hand in a peculiar gathering motion, willing the droplets to unite. Gradually—painfully slowly at first—a few drops of drizzle fell upon her. She tried to extend the movement of the drizzle towards Hesteron, to help him.

Hesteron continued battling to strengthen the small breeze that wafted the mist away from him. He was partly aware of Vallel's struggles, but could not let himself be distracted. As some of the water around him began to fall, so he found it easier to whip up the breeze.

Within a few minutes, the area around the four friends was clearing. A light rain had fallen, then eased off. Their bonds were beginning to disintegrate. They had almost forgotten the Mist Mistress. Soon, however, they were reminded as her cold tones came ringing from the remaining mist.

'What happens here?' her voice cried in rage and dismay.

'Quick!' urged Athennar in a hoarse whisper. 'Turn the rain and wind towards her!'

Hesteron had now freed his hands. He waved and blew the air towards the eery voice. Vallel did likewise, and a wide swathe of breeze and rain cut its way through the greyness. For a moment they glimpsed a figure clad in mist. Then, as the air around her cleared, the Mistress uttered a strangled cry.

Even as they watched, amazed, she began to dissolve. The Mistress of the Mist gave one last great cry; partly anguish, partly triumph and release: 'Death comes!' A shrieking whistle followed, fading into a sorrowful howl. Then a brief shower of rain fell where she stood. When it stopped, she was gone.

With the end of the Mist Mistress, the bonds around them faded, and sunlight began to filter through the vanishing mists.

The friends shook themselves free of the last remaining tendrils and took stock of their situation. Athennar gazed around; he could see for some distance now. There was no sign of Kess: just the water stretching away with the grisly wooden corpses at intervals, and an occasional tree. 'Let's get back to dry land,' he said to the others, and started wading through the cold waters towards the nearest grassy slope.

Valor groaned slightly to himself; his hand was cold and numb. However, he said nothing and followed the others, only too glad to be leaving the marsh at last.

'Look,' called Whisper. 'something is happening to the mist.'

Kess was jolted out of his gloom by the tone of her

voice. Standing up, he moved over beside her. Sure enough, the mist that had hung over the Whistling Waters was dispersing. 'The others must have escaped!' he shouted in delight.

'No, it's impossible,' declared Whisper.

Kess ignored her and started racing towards the marsh. He didn't even wait to hear if she was following.

Within a few minutes he could see four figures coming towards him. He yelled a greeting as he rushed to meet them.

'Kess! It's good to see you.' Vallel gave him a great hug as he reached them, and the others gathered round, patting him on the back.

'I thought you were all dead,' Kess said breathlessly.

'As we thought you might be,' Hesteron answered, his voice full of relief.

'But the Mistress of the Mist—Whisper said she would kill you.'

'Whisper?' asked Athennar.

Kess looked round, suddenly remembering. In the distance, a woman walked slowly towards them. 'Whisper has been a captive of the Mistress for years,' he explained. 'We broke out of the mist together, but I think she may need our help—she says she is not yet totally free.'

Valor noticed the restrained excitement in Kess' face as he watched the approaching figure. *There is more to this than meets the eye*, he thought.

'Whisper,' Kess said, 'these are my friends. I've just been telling them about you.'

Whisper looked warily at Kess, but he smiled.

'Don't worry—it was unfair of me to blame you for my friends' plight,' he reassured her.

'I suppose it was you two who made the Mist

Mistress angry, and gave us time to escape,' added Athennar. 'Our two Crafter friends here showed strengths I suspect even they did not know they possessed.'

Hesteron and Vallel smiled wearily. 'It just shows how our two Crafts can coexist,' Vallel said gently.

Then, remembering how the Mistress had touched Valor's hand with her mist dagger, she turned and looked at the young Mountain Guard, who had been standing unusually silent beside her. 'We had forgotten!' she exclaimed. 'How is your hand?'

Valor shrugged. 'I've lost the feeling in it,' he admitted.

Athennar peered at him. 'Forgive us for being so thoughtless,' he said. 'It was such a relief to be free that all else faded from mind. I'm afraid I know of no remedy for such an affliction. Will you be able to continue, or would you rather return to the fortress and see if my father has a cure?'

The Mountain Guard gave a wry smile. 'I'm coming with you. Fortunately, it's not my sword hand, though I won't be able to use my bow until it's better.'

Athennar knew the Mountain Guard was putting on a brave face for their sake, probably because he didn't want to miss any further adventure. 'Let's return to the camp and dry off. We can discuss such matters at greater length there.'

An hour later, the company rested at the campsite, having eaten a quick makeshift meal.

'And now,' Athennar said to Whisper, 'perhaps you can tell us what you were doing in the Whistling Waters.'

Whisper told them about her imprisonment by the Mistress of the Mist, and how she had persuaded Kess to rescue her.

'What did you mean when you told me you were

not completely free?' asked Kess, looking intently at her.

Whisper averted her eyes. After a pause, she started talking softly, as if to herself. 'Because I was so long in the mist under the powers of the Mistress, she somehow gradually and subtly changed my being. She told me of it some time ago, knowing it would make me think I could never escape. She knew that if I somehow did, eventually my body would start to break up and disperse, just as hers did in the end.'

Kess groaned in disbelief. 'Then why did you let me carry you out?'

'As I told you before, the Mistress was once the wife of a Guardian of the Realm ...'

Athennar interrupted her sharply. 'What do you mean?'

'Just as I say—she was captured by a Dark Master centuries ago, and has been bound in timeless agony ever since. She longed for death.'

'Did you ever hear her name?'

'Occasionally she would talk to herself and call herself Dirpha.'

A light of understanding gleamed in Athennar's eyes. 'Gwindirpha! It must be! She was the wife of the second Guardian—and disappeared mysteriously one night. No one ever found out what had happened to her. Her husband was said to have died shortly afterwards of a broken heart.'

'Anyway,' continued Whisper, 'when she was taken prisoner, she was looking after a key for her husband. It seems that the key belonged to a chest hidden away from most human knowledge. The chest—if it still exists—holds some items that were once of importance, though they may not be so now. There is apparently an ancient map of the Realm, a learned book of magic or some such thing, and several phials.

One of these contains a fluid that heals the body. I know, because the Mistress often wondered if it would make her whole, able to walk the world again.

'However, there was no way she could get to the chest. She wouldn't trust anyone else; they might steal its contents. The years before her capture had been ones of unrest; the chest had been well hidden, and just a rhyme left to hint at its whereabouts in case the Guardian should die. It was hoped that only someone who knew and cared for the Realm as he did would fully understand the rhyme. I—er—stole the rhyme and the key some time ago, hoping I would find an opportunity to make use of them.'

Pulling out a fragile piece of parchment, she started to read the words:

'A book of where and how and what and why
Of those who have the truth that lies behind each
    lie.
When secrets of the past again are opened wide;
The strands revealed from which all life is tied.
Where stones are things of beauty, made of wood,
Tho' hollow heart be covered, your chest is stained
    with blood.
When all that has lain quiet comes crashing,
tumbling down
Then in the centre, deep inside, the source of
    wisdom's found.
To find what is within, the seeker has to see
That that which is within must truly be the
    key.'

She slipped it carefully back inside her tunic. 'I think I understand the last part,' she said. 'It simply means that to find what is in the chest, the key, or clue, to its location is within the rhyme. I assume the first few

lines probably have something to do with the book—
but I have no idea about the rest.'

Athennar had a thoughtful expression on his face.
'Something sounds familiar. I'm sure that if you took
it to my father—the present Guardian—he would
probably know some of the answers.'

Whisper looked excitedly at Kess. 'I must find the
chest,' she said. 'And it may even be possible that the
map or book could help you to find your sister.'

Athennar looked dubious. 'That is unlikely.
Besides, Kess is coming with us.'

Kess himself sat quietly, thinking over what he had
heard. His emotions were being pulled in several
directions. He wanted to be with his friends, but he
also felt indebted to Whisper. His friends could
manage without him—he had no illusions about
that—but could she? And if there was any chance at
all that the contents of this chest might help him to
find Linnil, could he afford to ignore it? Also,
whenever he looked at Whisper, he felt a strange
tugging at his heart that his mind wanted desperately
to deny.

Finally he made up his mind. 'I will go back to the
fortress with Whisper,' he said. 'If there is any chance,
however slim, that it might help Linnil, I have to go.
Besides, they may have had news of her by now.'

Valor looked at him in surprise. 'You can't believe
this woman!' he said. 'You've only just met her. Surely
Linnil will be better served if you came with us?'

Athennar nodded his agreement, but Kess was
adamant. 'No, as I said, I have decided. I'm sorry to
let you down, but I must do what I feel is best.'

Athennar smiled at him. 'I cannot argue with that,'
he said. He rose to his feet. 'The rest of us must carry
on with our journey, however. We have already lost
too much time today.'

The company gathered their belongings together and mounted their horses. Whisper leapt up in front of Kess, on Blazer. The faithful horse could easily take her light weight as well.

Kess felt very aware of Whisper's presence in his arms. A lump came to his throat as he said goodbye to his friends.

'Strength in weakness, peace in trouble,' said Valor, gripping Kess' hand with his own good one as he passed by on Sundust. Kess smiled gratefully at him. Hesteron also shook Kess' hand, and Vallel leaned over to kiss him on the cheek.

'Farewell,' said Athennar, gripping Kess' shoulder. 'May Elsinoth go with you.' He reined Windrider to the north, and Valor and the two Crafters followed.

Kess held Blazer back and watched them as they disappeared into the distance.

'Don't worry—they'll be safe,' said Whisper.

'I hope so,' replied Kess, sighing. He also hoped he had made the right decision. Nudging the horse into a trot, he started the long ride back to the fortress with a troubled frown creasing his face.

14

The Fire Crafter

Two days later, Athennar led his friends into the shelter of a long valley as the day began to wane. The hillsides glowed orange in the dying rays of the sun.

'We should be able to find somewhere nearby where we can rest for the night,' he said. Windrider tossed his head as if in agreement.

'What's that light?' asked Hesteron, pointing to a deeper glow some distance ahead. 'It looks as if a small patch of the hillside is on fire, yet I can't detect any traces of smoke in the air.'

'There's only one way to find out,' replied Athennar, coaxing Windrider into a gentle trot.

As they drew nearer, they could see that the glow came from the central cave of a group of three, clustered together in the side of the hill.

Motioning the others to dismount, Athennar looped Windrider's reins loosely over the branch of a tree. It would be wisest to approach on foot from here. The four friends spread out and cautiously made their way towards the cave. They would have to cross a wide grassy slope to reach it, but all four could move swiftly and lightly when the need arose.

As they ran softly across the slope, sudden explosions of bright blue flame erupted from the ground before them, and they halted, startled. The flames died down, and Valor gasped as he realised that the grass hadn't even been scorched by the heat. He took an experimental step forward, but another streak of flame shot from the ground.

'Stay where you are.' said a harsh voice from the cave.

The friends shielded their eyes from the intensifying orange glow. They could just make out a small, hunched shape standing in the cavern entrance.

'Who are you, and what do you want?' the voice continued coldly.

'We are travellers; we mean you no harm,' said Athennar. 'We are seeking shelter for the night before continuing our journey.'

'And where are you from?' asked the voice sharply.

'From Hallion, where manners are somewhat better than here, and where all peace-loving creatures are made welcome,' answered Athennar.

'Hah!' snorted the voice. 'Perhaps you are right. You may proceed, but I warn you—don't try any tricks.'

The friends moved carefully forward, wary of any further outbreaks of the blue flames. They reached the entrance to the cave to find the figure had already retreated inside.

'Well, come in,' snapped the voice.

As their eyes adjusted, they saw that a circle of alternate blue and orange fires lined the walls of the cavern. In the centre was a large area, spread with a thick, ancient rug. Cross-legged on the rug sat a small figure with a hunched form and sharp features.

Hesteron immediately drew his sword. 'A thunder goblin,' he snarled.

'Put away your blade,' counselled Athennar as the fires suddenly roared upwards in response. 'Our host is a gnome, not a thunder goblin.'

'It is fortunate for you that you are so observant. Now sit.' the gnome said, gesturing to the rug in command rather than invitation.

The travellers settled themselves, Hesteron reluctantly re-sheathing his sword. The flames sank lower again.

'Good meeting,' said Athennar politely. 'I am Athennar, son of Tolledon. I bring with me Hesteron from Winderswood, Vallel of Tarrelford, and Valor, a Mountain Guard of Candra.'

The gnome nodded curtly at the Animal Crafter. 'I have heard of you. I knew your father, long ago. He is a good man. I might seem brusque to you, but these are strange times, and not all peoples walk the land with peace in their minds. My name is Fashag. All my family are peace gnomes, but I broke away to become a Fire Crafter.'

Athennar nodded in understanding.

'Fire Crafter?' asked Valor. 'I thought there were only Water, Air and Land Crafters—oh, and Animal Crafters,' he added hastily, looking at Athennar.

Athennar smiled. 'I am not the only one who chose to follow a lonely path. Fire Crafting is by nature a solitary existence. I have heard my father speak of you, Fashag. We do not wish to disturb your thoughts for long. As I said earlier, all we seek is a resting place. In the morning we will be gone.'

The gnome nodded. 'The caves to either side of this are unoccupied. They are cold, but I will light fires that will provide warmth.'

The companions had already noticed that despite the number of fires burning in the central cave, the heat was pleasant rather than overpowering.

'Why isn't this cave blazing hot?' asked Valor.

'I do not discuss my skills,' barked Fashag. But, mellowing slightly, he added, 'Suffice it to say I have learned to control the amount and quality of both light and heat given out by each fire. Now go, collect your provisions. You might wish to shelter your horses in one of the caves and have the other to yourselves.'

Athennar cocked an eyebrow at the mention of the horses. Obviously they had been under observation from afar without realising it.

By the time they returned with the horses, each cave glowed with gentle firelight. After tending their animals, they left them in the cave on the right. The horses seemed contented, quite unconcerned by the firelight. The company moved to the other cave. Pallets had been laid on the floor for them, and a small table laden with fruit stood in the centre of the room.

'Eat and rest well,' called Fashag from the entrance. Waving them a curt goodbye, he retreated to his own cave.

'He's a strange one,' remarked Hesteron.

'It must be difficult for him, if he is unused to company,' said Vallel.

Athennar nodded in agreement.

Valor meanwhile was investigating the fires. He called to the others. 'The fires burn and give off heat, yet there doesn't seem to be any fuel,' he said. 'It's as if they spring from bare rock.' Experimentally, he prodded the fire with a stick. The flames leapt around the wood, but when he withdrew it there were no signs of scorching or damage.

'A mystery indeed,' commented Athennar. 'I think all we are likely to learn, however, is that Fashag is very skilful at his craft.'

'He might be a useful, if somewhat surly, companion in the Ice Kingdom,' suggested Hesteron.

Athennar looked thoughtful. 'I believe you are right,' he said finally. 'His talents could well come in useful—if indeed he would be able to use them in such a hostile place. I will broach the subject with him tomorrow. In the meantime, let us feast and rest!.'

The following morning they rose early. Fashag appeared again and invited them to eat with him in his cave. He left without waiting for their reply.

When they joined him, bowls of crushed nuts in warm goats' milk awaited them. The food was tasty and refreshing. Having finished the meal, Athennar explained the purpose of their journey to Fashag. The gnome listened quietly, occasionally asking curt questions.

'Your talents would be of great help to us in such an inhospitable climate,' concluded Athennar.

Fashag gazed at him in silence, then slowly shook his head. 'I am not accustomed to company,' he said. 'It would be too much of a strain—both for me and for you. I have no love for the Dark Masters, but neither have I any wish to engage in conflict.'

'But we need you,' exclaimed Valor.

'I have given my answer,' the gnome said gruffly. 'Now I think it is time for you to go!' He stomped out of the cave before any of them could speak further.

As they left the cave, they could see him sitting on the grassy slopes below. In the daylight his skin was a pale yellowish colour and his sharp hooked nose gave him a fierce look. Hesteron was about to go down to talk to him, but Athennar restrained him. 'He has made his decision,' he said. 'We have no right to force him to go on a quest in which he is not involved.'

Down on the slope, Fashag was muttering to himself, a habit accumulated over the long and lonely years. 'Intruders! People come here and stir up trouble. Why don't they leave me alone? My fires are all I need. People are trouble. The sooner they go, the better.'

However, when he heard the travellers bringing their horses from the cave, he went over to bid them farewell. 'I cannot go with you, but I hope you succeed. May the earth fires warm you!'

The friends thanked him for the food and shelter, and mounted. Within minutes they were leaving the valley on the final stage of their journey northwards.

By early evening the company had reached the lower slopes of the ring of mountains encompassing the Ice Kingdom. The travellers continued upwards, going as high as they could on horseback. Just before sunset, they stopped on a flattish strip of rough ground under the shelter of some trees.

'We will camp here,' said Athennar, to the relief of the others. 'Tomorrow we must continue on foot. We may, however, need some guidance getting over these mountains. I have a friend who may be able to help us.'

The others looked at each other in surprise. The Hallion man hadn't mentioned the likelihood of anyone else joining them.

Athennar gave a loud, clear whistle, then walked off until he was a few yards away from his friends. There was a sudden, harsh call, and a white shape dived out of the gathering gloom of the skies. Athennar held out his arm, and a bird swooped down and landed on it. Speaking in strange, shrill tones to the bird, Athennar returned to his three friends. The bird flapped nervously as he spoke to them.

'This is Kal, a white hawk. She has been travelling in the skies above us for some time; she often accompanies me on my trips in the north. She and Sash have become good friends, but she is unused to humans other than myself. However, she will tolerate your presence for the time being, though she is unlikely to come near you.'

He had only just finished speaking when Kal rose lazily from his arm and flew to Valor, landing on his shoulder and nibbling gently at his ear. The Mountain Guard's training prevented him from jumping in surprise, and he smiled and slowly but gently stroked the hawk's head. Athennar looked on in astonishment. 'I have never known her do that,' he gasped. 'She has obviously taken to you, Valor.'

'Oh, I've spent some years with hawks, training them for hunting. Perhaps I send out the right signals,' he laughed.

Kal nibbled him once more and then flew back to Athennar.

'Perhaps you and I should talk more together about Animal Crafting,' Athennar said.

Valor coloured and smiled awkwardly. 'I would like that,' he replied.

'Good! Well, for now, let us settle beneath the trees and eat. Tomorrow we have a long climb ahead of us.'

15
The Tissirim

Zendos was pleased with his selection of the Ice Kingdom as a place where he could build up his powers. The ice mirrored his soul—cold and hard— and there were ready subjects over which to exert his influence. Oh, most of them might be unwilling now, but he would tame them in time. With his powers, the Tissirim could become an almost invincible army. All they needed was the protection against hostile environments that he, eventually, would be able to give them. Then there would be no stopping him. A legion of ice warriors, virtually invulnerable to pain or wounds. Oh, yes, they would welcome him as their leader in time.

He had landed not long ago at the base of the mountains in the Northlands. As he had untied the dazed Melinya from the back of her Tark, she had suddenly pushed him away, and started racing towards a stretch of woodland. Although taken by surprise, Zendos soon recovered and chased after her. Still suffering the after-effects of the potion he had used to drug her, she stumbled and fell, and he caught up with her. Roughly pulling her to her feet, he slapped her hard across the face, and then bound her hands.

Zendos already knew that although he would be able to use his arts to shield himself from the cold, the woman was another matter. It would be far too great a drain upon his powers to attempt to shield her as well. He was tempted to take her with him anyway; it might teach her a lesson for constantly snubbing him. But some vestige of humanity had caused him to relent, and he took her to a secret location nearby where she was safely imprisoned, and where no one would find her. In due course, as his powers grew stronger and he found an easier way to protect her, he would fetch her. From that time she would always be beside him—whether she wanted to be or not.

Despite his pleas, the Tarks chose to wing their way southwards again, leaving him to make the rest of the journey to the Ice Kingdom on foot. It was a weary journey.

When he eventually reached its city walls, he found with dismay that there was no obvious entrance. After walking halfway round the city, he eventually ran out of patience. Drawing out the sound tube he had used in Dargan's Throne Room, he put it to his lips, pointing it at the wall. From the depths of his throat came a strange hum, which was channelled down the tube, gathering strength. Part of the wall disappeared with a loud crack, leaving a jagged hole. Zendos gleefully stepped through, finding himself in a narrow alleyway running along the inside of the wall.

Within minutes he met one of the Ice People. It looked just like a block of walking ice, cut in the crude shape of a human figure. The Tissir seemed relatively unsurprised at this stranger suddenly appearing from nowhere, but spoke in bell-like tones which Zendos could not understand. Of what use would these people be if he couldn't even communicate with them? Zendos hadn't anticipated such a problem.

Then the Tissir's tones changed. 'Pardon my clumsiness; it is long since we have had visitors, and I failed to remember to use a language that you can understand. How may I help you?'

Zendos breathed a quiet sigh of relief. 'I am a friend,' he said smoothly. 'I have come here to visit your people—I would like to learn more of your ways.'

'You are welcome in our kingdom. Perhaps I should guide you to a Tessar—one of our kings?'

Zendos nodded, agreeably surprised by the way his plans seemed to be working. 'That would be helpful.'

The Tissir turned and, without speaking further, moved off along one of the narrow streets, walking with surprisingly fluid movements. Obediently following, Zendos tried to memorise the route as he went. He noticed that none of the odd-shaped buildings seemed to have any entrances, and this intrigued him. He would have paused to look closer, but his guide showed no signs of slowing or waiting for him, so he continued to trot behind. They passed several other Tissirim, none of whom showed any signs of interest in the sorcerer, much to his annoyance.

After a while, they came to an open place within which stood a magnificent castle of ice, its white spires stretching into the sky. Even Zendos could not fail to appreciate its fine tracery of ice filigree, patterned like lace.

'This is the palace of the Tessari,' explained his guide in clear, tinkling tones. 'If you would wait, I will inform them of your arrival.' Motioning to a spur of ice—upon which Zendos assumed he was expected to sit and wait—the Tissir walked towards the palace walls. As the sorcerer watched, it seemed to melt into the wall and disappear. Zendos quickly ran to the spot to investigate, but the wall was solid. Bemused, he paced up and down irritably, impatiently awaiting developments.

Within minutes, the guide emerged, followed by another of its kind. Both seemed to crystallise out of the wall at the spot where the Ice Person had first disappeared. To Zendos, the only difference between the two figures was that the second one was slightly taller.

The first figure—the guide—walked straight past Zendos and back towards the street they had travelled along. The sorcerer watched it disappear, then waited as the second approached.

'Good meeting,' it chimed. 'I am one of the Tessari. Welcome to our kingdom.'

'Good meeting,' said Zendos, forcing himself to bow. 'I am called Zendos. I have come to visit your people for a time, if that is permitted.'

'It is permitted. You may find our city a little cold, I fear.'

'I am, er, protected well against your climate,' countered Zendos.

The Ice King made no enquiries, but nodded. 'You may stay for whatever length of time suits you. An empty ice house stands nearby which you may wish to use. An entrance will have to be made. Entry to our buildings may prove to be a problem while you are with us. As you see, all of them are sealed for privacy. Should you wish, I can provide an escort who will make openings for you when you need them.'

Zendos bit his tongue and forced himself to be polite in his reply. 'That would be very helpful.'

The Tessar called; a single, loud, clear note. Within moments, another Tissir appeared from a nearby building and walked slowly towards them. The new-comer conversed briefly with its king in their strange

language and nodded. Then the Tessar turned to
Zendos and said, 'You are free to explore the city. My
people will be glad to provide any assistance you
should need. I fear that I must ask you, however, not
to try to enter the Ice Palace. It is a place of special,
almost sacred, meaning to our people.'

'Of course,' agreed Zendos. However, he secretly
determined to investigate the palace at the earliest
opportunity.

The Tessar turned and moved off towards the
palace. Zendos' new guide beckoned him to follow as
it walked smoothly towards a nearby building.

Once there, the Tissir ran its finger over part of the
wall, chanting: 'Ice to water.'

In a slow but fluid motion, the section of the wall it
had touched melted, leaving a natural doorway. The
Tissir then bent down and touched the pool of water
that had appeared. 'Water to ice,' it said, as it drew its
hands upwards.

A thin sheet of white ice formed, slightly larger
than the hole. The Tissir then slid the ice door to one
side, revealing the hole once more. Zendos marvelled
at the creation of this sliding door. It seemed to cling
to the ice wall of the building even as it slid. Perhaps
he would be able to find a good use for some of the
Tissirim's creative abilities!

'We have been visited by such as you before,'
explained the Tissir.

They stepped inside the small building, and Zendos
gave a nod of satisfaction. This place would suit him
admirably as a base: it was close enough for him to
keep an eye on the palace, and yet he would also have
all the privacy he needed. So, the Tissirim believed
they had been visited by people like him before, did
they? They were going to get some surprises!

Over the next few days, Zendos explored the city

thoroughly. On some occasions he travelled with his guide. The Tissir opened entrances into any of the buildings in which he showed an interest and these were sealed up again as soon as they left. Most of the buildings, apart from the Assembly Hall, the Recreation Centre and the Palace, were merely dwelling places of the Tissirim. Zendos failed to discover how the Ice People entertained themselves; perhaps they had no need of such diversions. The Recreation Centre was used as a place of exercise and refreshment rather than entertainment.

At other times Zendos wandered around by himself, talking to the Tissirim he met and finding out as much as he could about their way of life. On one such occasion, he spoke with an Ice Person who seemed different from the others he had so far encountered—more friendly towards him .. and dissatisfied with life in the city.

'We are prisoners here,' the Tissir complained. 'Oh, to be free to explore the vastness of this land!'

'And if someone could help you to achieve that aim?' ventured Zendos.

'How?' asked the Tissir suspiciously.

'Oh, let us say by certain skills and arts—and by knowledge that could be used to enable the Tissirim to live in warmer climates without any ill effect.'

'If such a thing were possible then I, for one, would be very grateful,' replied the Tissir. Then its shoulders seemed to droop slightly. 'But I fear that such knowledge does not exist.'

Zendos could hardly believe his good fortune: here was the key for which he had been waiting! And if he could find similarly disgruntled Ice People to help him, his task would be much easier. It was also the first real expression of emotion he had found from any of the Tissirim.

Gradually, employing the wiles learned from his master Dargan over many years, he persuaded the unhappy Ice Person that he, Zendos, could develop a means of protection for the Tissirim, so that they might be able to venture more easily beyond the confines of their kingdom. He encouraged it to gather together any other malcontents.

Fourteen of the Tissirim were coaxed into service in this way. With a series of secret meetings, and using all his cunning, he convinced them that they alone would be the first to benefit from his powers: he would give them protection against warmer climates, enabling them to visit other places. Furthermore, he told them that it was in the interest of the whole Tissirim nation that he should be given complete freedom to carry out his experiments, even if all the remaining Tissirim would have to be imprisoned until he could demonstrate the freedom his powers would bring.

So persuasive was his silvery tongue that the fourteen Tissirim rebels agreed to a plan that would 'temporarily' imprison their fellow Ice People and their Kings. Zendos promised them that their countrymen would truly be grateful one day. Entranced by the sorcerer, they were only too willing to help, so after questioning them closely, Zendos soon devised a fiendishly simple way of gathering all the Ice People together in one place.

One day, when all his preparations were complete, Zendos blasted his way into the Ice Palace, using the sound tube. Within moments he was seized by the Tissirim within and marched outside. One of the Tessari emerged from the palace, almost tripping over his own feet in his haste.

Without any introductory words, the Ice King faced Zendos with the nearest to a show of anger the

sorcerer had witnessed. 'You have desecrated the
sanctuary of the Tessari. Never in our long history
has such sacrilege occurred.' Nodding to the six
Tissirim surrounding Zendos, he said, 'Guard
him well. This afternoon, a full assembly of the
Tissirim must be held to decide a suitable
punishment.'

Zendos grinned to himself as he was marched away.
Events were happening just as he had hoped. These
ancient traditions were useful sometimes.

That afternoon, the Tissirim gathered in the Assembly Hall, the largest building in the city. It was in fact
a single, enormous room, with a raised ice platform at
one end. Zendos was taken under guard through a
specially opened entrance, and hustled up onto the
platform. The sorcerer watched from his vantage
point as crowds of Ice People started arriving. It was
fascinating to watch them materialising through the
walls of the building. *If only my plan will work*, he
thought. Beside him were lined the ten Tessari, each
holding a long spear made out of a single piece of
clear ice. Apart from this, there was little to distinguish them from their fellow Tissirim.

The hall seemed to be full, yet still more Tissirim
filed in, and were somehow accommodated. Soon,
however, the arrivals ceased. The Tissirim, despite
their great numbers, stood as still as ice statues,
awaiting word from the platform.

One of the Tessari walked slowly over to a huge
white bell and struck it. The crystal tones reverberated around the room. 'People of the ice! We are
gathered together to mete out justice according to
our traditions. One has come among us who is not
one of us. At first we welcomed him, as befits the
customs of our peace-loving people. But he has

broken the trust we placed in him and has violated
the sanctuary of our lost ones.'

Zendos wasn't quite sure what the Tessar meant,
but at least the Ice King was speaking in a language
he could understand. He just hoped he would be able
to put his plan into action before anything drastic
happened to him. He had been slightly afraid that the
Tissirim might rush the platform in their rage.
However, the crowd remained quiet.

A second Ice King moved forward to stand next to
the first. 'As befits our ways, all of you must pronounce judgement. The contention of the Tessari is
that the stranger is guilty. He was given freedom to
roam our city and to enter all places except the Ice
Palace. He abused that privilege. There can be no
excuse.'

A third member of the Tessari now made his way to
stand beside the other two. 'The stranger must nevertheless be given the opportunity to explain his
actions. Justice demands that all explanations are
explored. This is the way of the Tissirim.'

An answering tinkling noise resounded from the
crowd in the hall, and then subsided. Zendos was
gently but firmly pushed towards the front of the
platform. He surveyed the waiting crowd, and for a
moment uncertainty almost conquered him: their
stillness and quietness unnerved him.

His hesitation didn't last long, however. Clearing
his throat, he began to speak. 'Honoured Tissirim! I
came as a guest among you, yet I have grieved you. I
regret the distress I have caused—it is mirrored
within my own heart. I can only explain my actions as
a moment of insanity; a madness came upon me and
caused me to break your trust. Once again, I
apologise.'

He tried to step back, but the Tessar accompanying

him held him firmly. 'We people of the ice do not fully understand your word "madness",' said one of the other Ice Kings. 'While among the Tissirim, you must abide by our ways. You have admitted your guilt—the judgement is clear. Punishment must be pronounced.'

'No!' shouted Zendos, wrenching his arm free. 'It's you who will be punished,' he cried. And he pulled two small pot flasks from his pockets. He flung one flask into a small space in front of the platform, and the other far into the crowd.

Both pots broke as they hit the ice floor, and a cloud of gas immediately issued from them and spread out across the surface of the ice, even working its way up onto the platform.

Confusion reigned for a few moments, with the Tissirim edging away from the gas. Within seconds, however, it had touched them all and immobilised them. Not one escaped, but all were riveted to the spot—they had become ice statues.

Choking from the fumes, Zendos raced across to the entrance and scuttled out into the open air. 'Now!' he called.

His rebel Tissirim, waiting outside, quickly sealed the entrance to the Assembly Hall before the gas could escape.

'Excellent,' the sorcerer beamed.

The Tissirim watched him with uncharacteristic doubt.

'Have no fear,' he reassured them in his most soothing tones. 'This will only benefit your nation and extend the boundaries of your kingdom. You will be hailed as the ones who helped your people to a new start.'

The rebel Tissirim shuffled away, their confusion forgotten. They had already come to rely on his voice, and to believe in it utterly. There was no doubt—it would be as Zendos had said.

The sorcerer grunted with satisfaction at his easy victory over the trusting Tissirim. He congratulated himself. The crowd of immobilised Tissirim would suffer no harm, he knew, but he would not release them from the hold of the gas until he could find some way to make them all do his will. As it was, the fairly simple control he held over the rebel Tissirim was only effective because it worked upon some vestige of discontent or greed for power within them. Zendos had to struggle to maintain such control. With a larger number, and with those opposed to his way of thinking, it would prove impossible.

However, he was confident that given time he would find a way to take full control of these people. Meanwhile, his rebel Tissirim had proved useful so far, but if they should turn troublesome, he could 'freeze' them as well. Soon the whole population of the Ice Kingdom would be under his control.

16

Into the Ice Kingdom

Valor sat on a rock and munched on an apple. There was a sharp bite in the air, and he drew the white cloak more closely around himself. His numb hand felt deathly cold. The company had set off early in the morning, and after three hours of travelling had reached the edge of the snow. Donning their protective clothes, they had left their other garments hidden behind a large rock. Then they had trudged on for another two hours before reaching their present position.

The rest was a welcome respite from the exertions of the climb. It had not been particularly difficult; just slow and tiring. Kal had glided above, occasionally swooping down to chatter to Athennar. The bird seemed to be able to guide them unerringly along the best routes.

Vallel had been intrigued by her first glimpse of snow. This was a new experience to her. Although she had of course heard of it before, none of the Water Crafters had either seen or expressed much interest in it. She found it fascinating, however—yet another mystery of her beloved water to unravel. Putting some to her mouth, she tasted it. The snow tingled on her tongue for a moment and then melted.

Experimenting further, she crushed some in her fist until it was tight and solid; different yet again from the soft powder all around.

Hesteron, meanwhile, was sensitive to the changes in the air as it became thinner and colder. Intrigued, he watched as his breath formed pale, wispy patterns. He found the air both crisp and refreshing. Of all the travellers, he was least affected by its changes, while being most aware of them.

Athennar spoke briefly to Kal in strange 'keeking' sounds. The bird flew off, and Athennar motioned the company to start walking again. 'When we reach the top of that ridge, we should be able to see the Ice Kingdom,' he told them, pointing to an area some distance ahead where a shoulder of the mountain thrust itself out.

Valor rubbed his numb hand and, with a struggle, donned his gloves. He had been glad of the rest, but it would be good to be on the move again. Briefly he wondered what dangers lay ahead, then put the thought from his mind.

It took them longer than expected to reach the ridge, the distances being deceptive in the snow. When they reached it, the view beyond took their breath away. In a natural dip in the mountains, a cold, frosty plain swept away, seemingly supported by the shoulders of three of the peaks. In the centre of the frozen wastes lay a city of white ice, glinting in the chilly glare of the sun.

It was like no city they had ever seen before, looking, even from this distance, as if it had been sculpted by nature rather than built by people. The city was entirely surrounded by a high ice wall. From their vantage point, however, they could see inside this. Of the buildings within, some were rounded domes, others irregular shapes, and yet others like wide, upward-pointing icicles.

'It's beautiful!' cried Vallel.

'Yes, but also dangerous, if Zendos is there,' muttered Athennar. Kal had returned some time ago, and was flying overhead, so he called the bird and then sent her off to scout around the walls. The bird dipped and glided into the distance.

'Won't they see us coming?' asked Valor.

'Unlikely,' replied Athennar. 'I can't see any figures moving down there. And Zendos should be too preoccupied to spend his time gazing up into the hills. There is no reason why he should be expecting us—as far as he knows, no one is even aware that he is alive.'

'At this distance, they would be unlikely to spot us in these white clothes, anyway,' commented Hesteron. 'And once we are down on the plain, their own walls will shield us from their eyes, unless they have lookouts posted.'

Kal soon returned and 'keeked' at Athennar.

'There are no openings at all in the wall,' Athennar reported.

'Then how do the Tissirim come and go?' asked Vallel.

'I suspect they rarely venture out of the city. I suppose they must do so occasionally, however. They must have some way of getting through or over the walls.'

'But how will we get in there?' persisted Valor impatiently. 'And how did your father and Meltizoc get in when they visited?'

Athennar thought for a moment. 'I remember them saying they passed through a gap in the walls— possibly cut especially for their visit, and sealed up again afterwards. Of course, it is always possible that there are gates down there that Kal was unable to distinguish from the wall itself. It is pointless to speculate further. We will be able to see for ourselves when we get down there.'

They made their way carefully down the rolling white slopes that led to the plain. At one point, Hesteron tripped, slipped and rolled for some distance before being halted by a mound of snow. Vallel and Athennar rushed down to help him while Valor retrieved his pack of provisions.

Minutes later, Valor also slipped. He automatically put out his hand to stop himself from falling. In the cold, he had forgotten its numbness, and it buckled underneath him. He rolled a few yards before managing to stop himself. He would have to take extra care from now on. What good would he be to the party with a useless hand?

It was then that he remembered what he had learned from their last expedition—strength can be a physical attribute, but it can also take many other forms. Grunting with determination, he clambered back to join the others.

It was late afternoon by the time they reached the city walls. Here they split up, with Athennar and Valor going in one direction and Hesteron and Vallel in the other, investigating the walls for any sign of access.

When they eventually met at the opposite side of the city, darkness was beginning to fall. None of them had managed to find a gateway, or indeed any break in the ice wall. Athennar pondered for a while, then led them to a point a little further along the wall, where Kal was perched. 'The largest building in the Ice Kingdom is apparently behind this section of wall,' he informed his friends. 'We have a choice of whether to try to get in now or stay outside until daybreak.'

'By staying outside, we only expose ourselves needlessly to the chill night winds,' counselled Hesteron, 'and we have to get inside at some point. We may as well do so under the cover of darkness. The reflections from the ice provide sufficient light for climbing.'

Athennar smiled gratefully at the Air Crafter. 'My own thoughts exactly. Now we have to work out how to get inside the city. These walls will be very difficult to scale.'

They all looked up at the walls which towered above them, almost three times their height.

Valor had an idea. 'If the ice isn't too hard, we could cut little steps into the side,' he suggested. 'It won't be easy, but it's worth a try.'

Athennar nodded his head in agreement. He pulled out his dagger and began carving at the wall. Within minutes he had produced a niche deep enough to give some kind of rather slippery foothold.

Hesteron had already started making a hole higher up. 'If you angle the cut downwards, it should make it easier to grip when scaling the walls,' he remarked.

For the next stages, he sat and then stood on Athennar's shoulders to cut holds higher up in the ice. After a while he jumped down, panting from his exertions. 'That's as far as I can reach,' he puffed. 'If only we could make one more step a few feet higher up, I think I might be able to climb to the top.'

'If you can sit on mine and on Athennar's shoulders, and Vallel could stand on your shoulders, she might be able to cut another step or two,' suggested Valor.

Hesteron looked doubtful, but Vallel seemed eager to attempt the feat, so he reluctantly gave way. 'Very well,' he said, 'but take care!'

Athennar and Valor braced themselves as Hesteron climbed onto their shoulders and then Vallel somehow scrambled up to stand rather precariously on Hesteron's shoulders. Fortunately, being of elvish stock, she was both light and also endowed with a good sense of balance. She hacked away at the ice until she had made a hole. To make the climb easier, she then reached up even higher and cut a final step a couple of feet below the top of the wall.

She then jumped down nimbly, rolling as she landed and scattering the snow in little flurries. Hesteron quickly followed, and Athennar and Valor moved away from the wall, rubbing their shoulders.

'When you've recovered, I'll try climbing,' said Hesteron, fetching a rope from his pack. Athennar and Vallel were both about to protest, but Hesteron held up his hand. 'Someone light needs to go up first, and it must be someone who will be able to take the strain of the next person who climbs up—it should be much easier climbing with the aid of the rope. Once I've reached the other side, I'll throw it back over. If Vallel follows next, I should be able to hold her as she climbs, then she can help me while Valor climbs. We can then all help to pull you over, Athennar.'

The Hallion man nodded, yielding to the sense in his argument. 'Very well. You might as well start reasonably high up. Climb back onto my shoulders—it will give you a good start.'

Hesteron threw the rope nimbly over the wall and climbed onto Athennar's shoulders. Reaching up, he jammed one leather-gloved hand into the highest hole he could reach. Then, gaining a foothold in one of the lower holes and heaving himself upwards, he began his perilous ascent. He found that his feet could grip fairly well in the angled steps, but he had difficulty getting a firm hold with his hands. However, he gradually inched his way higher.

As he neared the top, he reached for the lip of a hole, but one of his feet slipped out of its niche. He missed his hold and for a moment dangled from one hand. Quickly he found a foothold, easing the strain off his hand. This time he managed to grasp the edge of the next hole with his other hand and pull himself upwards again. With another step he was able to drag himself to the top of the wall.

The city below was impressive. The hawk had guided them well; within a few yards of where he sat was the largest structure of all. Like all the other buildings, its walls glowed gently in the gathering darkness. There was no one in sight.

He didn't pause for long to look at the view, however. His natural elven agility enabled him to jump lightly to the ground below, rolling as he landed. Speedily he picked up the rope, tied one end around his waist, and threw the other back over the wall. The rope was made of thin but very strong intertwined strands, long enough to reach the others.

It snaked down the other side of the wall. Vallel gripped it and began to climb, pulling herself up with the rope and using the steps mainly as footholds. Soon she was standing beside Hesteron, and helped him to hold the rope ready for Valor.

'You next,' Athennar said to the Mountain Guard. 'As you are not of elvish build, it would perhaps be better if you lower yourself down the other side of the rope, rather than try to jump from the top. I will hold onto the rope this side while you do so. Do you think you will be able to make the climb with your bad hand?'

Valor nodded, although he didn't feel as confident as he looked; he was worried about having to climb one-handed. He shrugged to himself and grabbed hold of the rope, heaving himself slowly upwards. The main difficulty came from trying to keep his weight evenly distributed. Although it was a strain, the strength borne of many hours of rigorous training helped him to ease his way towards the top.

Automatically, he reached up to grasp the lip with his numb hand, transferring some of his weight as he did so. His unfeeling fingers slipped, and he fell backwards. Clutching wildly at the rope, he missed and plummeted to the ground below.

Athennar grabbed at Valor as he fell, but couldn't catch him. However, he succeeded in breaking the fall a little. The Mountain Guard lay winded in an untidy heap in the snow.

'Valor?' Athennar knelt beside him.

Valor coughed and grimaced. He felt foolish lying in the snow, so struggled manfully to his feet.

'Perhaps you had better stay here,' Athennar suggested.

'No! I can make it,' said Valor defiantly. He grabbed hold of the rope and started climbing again before Athennar could argue with him.

Frustration and embarrassment lent strength to his climb, and he was soon at the top. He swung himself over awkwardly and, while Athennar steadied the rope, lowered himself carefully down the other side.

'What happened?' whispered Hesteron as Valor reached the ground. 'The rope went slack suddenly. We couldn't shout in case anyone heard us.'

'I fell,' replied Valor brusquely. Hesteron looked at Vallel and shrugged. Then Valor took hold of the rope with his good hand and helped the Crafters take the strain as Athennar climbed up the other side. Jumping down from the top of the wall, Athennar landed lightly despite his heavier frame.

The four friends looked at one another. They had entered the Ice Kingdom, but would they be able to find Zendos?

17
Echoes of Ice

They crouched in the narrow space between the city wall and the wide, white ice structure. A steady inner glow shimmered from deep within the icy shell of the building.

Athennar spoke quietly to Hesteron, and the Air Crafter sped off, running lightly and swiftly past the structure. After a little while he came back, emerging from the alley behind the waiting friends. 'I've been all the way round this thing,' he said, 'but I can't see an entrance of any kind.'

'Perhaps it's just a big monument,' suggested Valor.

'A *very* big one,' said Athennar drily. 'No, as we thought before, the Tissirim must have some way of passing through the walls that we have not yet discovered. However, if Zendos is here somewhere, there will probably be some buildings with an entrance—unless he, too, can pass through solid walls.'

'I wonder where everyone is,' said Vallel. 'The city is deserted.' She took one hand out of its glove and put it against the wall of the building. The coldness made her shiver, but it had a much friendlier feel than that of the soulless liquid of the Whistling Waters. There was something else as well, something beyond: a gentle vibration that seemed to speak of life. 'I feel sure that there is someone inside here,' she whispered.

'We will be able to find out once we can get inside,' replied Athennar. 'Meanwhile, we might as well search elsewhere for any signs of Zendos. If you and Hesteron make your way towards that tall icy spire over there—' he pointed to a white pinnacle some distance away, '—Valor and I will go in the other direction. If you find anything, one of you must come to find us. We will do likewise. If there are no clues there, search further. We will meet back here at dawn if all else fails.'

Vallel and Hesteron nodded and without further comment set off towards the spire. Athennar and Valor watched them for a moment, then started walking along a street that ran parallel to the city wall.

The street varied in width, some of the irregular icy structures spilling out onto it at intervals. The ground beneath their feet was covered in a hard crust of snow, and showed no signs of any other recent travellers. Some of the buildings they passed had pitted surfaces and odd icy projections, while others were as smooth as glass. Valor pressed his face against one of the smoother structures in an effort to see into the interior. But however much he rubbed the white ice, all he could see was a dim glow—and he couldn't make out whether this was coming from inside the building or from the wall itself; the structure may even have been solid.

When he put this suggestion to Athennar, the Hallion man shook his head. 'I think not,' he said. 'My father and Meltizoc mentioned these buildings to me. They are apparently hollow, though sparsely furnished inside. Some doorways must have been made for their benefit, though, as they never mentioned any difficulty in entering the buildings.'

As he spoke, they came to a small dome-shaped building. A jagged hole in the side gave access to the interior, but also gave the structure an ugly appearance; it seemed somehow unnatural.

'Zendos' work, I would guess,' Athennar whispered to Valor. 'Probably the result of that tube of his.'

The Mountain Guard grimaced as he remembered the battle in Dargan's Throne Room. He followed cautiously as Athennar drew his sword and crept silently towards the hole. Athennar crawled underneath the bottom edge of the hole until he was able to stand up on the other side. After he had signalled to Valor to draw his sword, they both peered around the edge and into the building. For a moment, they could see little, but as their eyes became accustomed to the light they realised that the building was unoccupied. Athennar sheathed his sword and climbed in, followed closely by Valor.

The walls of the building were about two feet thick, and the young Mountain Guard could see that the dim glow came from somewhere within their depths. The edges of the hole were rough and darkened, as if the light had withdrawn in pain. Inside the building, the single room had a smooth and polished white ice floor which, surprisingly, was not slippery.

A line of four different-sized spheres stretched across the far end of the room. In front of these were three solid, box-shaped chunks of white ice. Two long, thin, inverted pyramids of ice hung from the ceiling. Apart from these objects, whose geometry somehow seemed to provide a comforting reassurance, the room was empty.

Athennar moved over to the ice globes and tried pushing them. They would not move. Neither he nor Valor could think what their purpose might be, other than decoration. Having made a careful examination of everything, they moved back to the hole and climbed out. The cool night air hit them as they emerged onto the street, and they realised that it had been relatively 'warm' inside the building.

They walked on until their way was suddenly blocked by a small, squat structure. The street turned at right angles and shot off towards a rectangular building. They passed several more places rent with holes; none of these buildings was occupied.

'Perhaps Zendos has killed everyone, or turned them out of the city,' suggested Valor.

Athennar shrugged. 'I doubt it. He enjoys having power, and what use is power unless you have someone over which to wield it? Whatever has happened, it seems likely that the Tissirim are in trouble. They would not willingly desert their homes.'

'We must find Zendos,' muttered Valor. 'I only hope he is here.' He was becoming frustrated and restless, and felt a renewed sense of urgency as his thoughts turned to Linnil. She and Kess were his good friends; he missed them both at the moment. He knew only too well that even if they found Zendos, it would hardly be easy to discover Dargan's whereabouts from him.

When they reached the end of the street, they realised that a great number of other alleyways also led to the same rectangular building—as if it was the focal point of something important. It was tall, very long and thin. At the end where they stood was one of the now familiar jagged holes.

'This looks an intriguing place,' whispered Athennar. He had a quick look down some of the roads which radiated from the building. All were deserted. Valor, meanwhile, had started to climb through the hole. Athennar rushed after him, groaning inwardly at the young man's impetuosity.

Inside the building, an odd assortment of ice sculptures greeted them. Instead of the chunky geometric shapes they had observed in the smaller buildings, there were long sweeping slopes, steep spirals and curves. There were also several small spheres lying around, but these were movable, unlike the fixed spheres in the first building they had visited. Valor pushed one of them. It rolled easily across the ground, though in a jerky motion, as if its weight was unevenly distributed. Valor looked puzzled for a while. There was something vaguely familiar about the shapes. Then he gave an exclamation of understanding. 'Of course! It looks like some kind of recreational area.'

Athennar nodded. 'You may well be right, though it is difficult to be sure of anything in this city.' He moved over to a platform on one side of the room. Two triangles stood upright on it, a little distance apart. A thin, slender length of ice connected their two points. Hanging from this rod—suspended on icy threads—was an assortment of tear-shaped icicles. Athennar touched one of them gently. It emitted a beautiful, crystal clear note. He touched another, which gave a deeper note. He then ran his hand along the whole row, and a cascade of bright, tinkling noises filled the room.

'It seems that the Tissirim have some appreciation of music,' he said to Valor, who had been watching, entranced by the sound. 'What a pity Merric can't hear this.'

This first room was obviously just a small section of the whole building. At its far end the walls grew much thicker, leaving a narrow passageway through to the next room. The two men made their way across to the passage, Athennar silently cursing himself for having made so much noise in the recreation area. If Zendos was nearby, he would almost certainly have heard. The corridor soon opened out into another room, entirely different from the first; it was much darker, with only a feeble glow from the walls. It also gave the impression of vastness; they could see neither the far wall of the room, nor the ceiling above, and, as far as they could see, the room was completely empty.

As they gazed around, Athennar thought he could pick out pinpricks of light far above, like stars in a dark sky. Valor, meanwhile, was looking at the walls. He felt sure that the low glow kept fluctuating. It was eery and made him feel uncomfortable—the walls almost seemed alive!

'Athennar!' he called softly. The sound reverberated around the room in a growing crescendo of echoes: '—thennar,—Thennar,—THENNAR.'

'Quietly!' urged the Hallion man. This too echoed around disturbingly: '—etly,—Etly,—ETLY.'

As the echoes grew in volume, the words took on a shape, forming themselves into mocking likenesses of the two men. Several icy half-figures, looking in silhouette like Valor, danced mysteriously in the air and then floated to the ground. They were rapidly followed by taller shapes; ice-echoes of Athennar.

The Valor-shapes formed a circle and began to parade around the Mountain Guard, still chanting their strange call: 'Thennar! Thennar!'

Athennar drew his sword as his own ice-echoes gathered around him. He thrust his sword at the nearest shape, then yelled in pain as blood seeped from a wound in his own side—at exactly the same position where he had stabbed the ice-shape! Fortunately, it was not a deep wound, but it left him in a quandary.

'Don't attack them! You'll hurt yourself,' he

shouted to Valor. This time, the words echoed so loudly that they both had to cover their ears. Huge shadows leapt up from the new Athennar ice-echoes that had formed. The first circle of ice shapes closed in on Valor. Pushing one aside, he found himself falling backwards. He had actually experienced the sensation of being pushed—by his own hand! The young Mountain Guard nearly cried out in frustration, but even that release was denied him when he realised it would only produce more of the echoes.

The ice-echo men were now close enough to join hands around him. Although he knew they were reflections of his own form, no clear features were visible. He glanced over hopelessly to Athennar, but the Hallion man was having enough problems of his own. There were two concentric rings of ice-echoes around him—the first from his earlier whisper and the second from his shout of warning. Both rings were closing in on him, and he could see no way out.

Walking in a clockwise direction around Valor, the figures continued intoning, in loud yet muffled voices, 'Thennar! Thennar! Thennar!' The Mountain Guard put his hands to his ears. He tried not to look, but felt the vibrations passing through the floor, and dizziness came over him, forcing him to open his eyes, even as he fell.

The two rings of ice-echoes around Athennar were marching in different directions; the inner ring chanting 'Etly! Etly! Etly!', the outer ones calling even louder: 'YOURSELF! YOURSELF! YOURSELF!' The shapes began to speed up, their forms blurring and shifting, the words blending into a strange discord of tones.

Athennar sank to his knees. Valor was already prostrate on the ground, apparently senseless. Dimly,

Athennar for some reason remembered Kess. In his torment, and as a last act of defiance, he lifted his sword, shouting: 'Elsinoth, protect us!' Then he sank down, slumping to the cold floor.

18

The Wanderer

Gatera's wife Mardilla smiled at her husband as he loosened the belt around his hessian doublet. 'It was a good meal, husband,' she said, her voice resonating around the dell.

'Very good, wife,' Gatera grinned, patting his huge girth. Then he turned to his friend. 'Have you eaten enough, Rrum?'

The rock man had just finished chewing on a piece of his favourite rock. 'Thankk you, yes,' he replied.

'I wonder if the others have reached the Ice Kingdom yet,' mused Gatera. 'I hope they find Zendos. Perhaps we should have ...'

A polite cough from the edge of the dell interrupted him. A tall handsome stranger had appeared there. All three friends jumped in surprise.

'Excuse me,' said the man, 'I didn't mean to startle you. I wonder if you could spare a little food? I have travelled far, and am weary.'

'Why, of course!' boomed Gatera, suddenly remembering his manners. 'Good meeting. Please come and join us.'

'Good meeting. I am known as the Wanderer.'

'I am Gatera. This is my wife, Mardilla, and my good friend, Rrum of the Rrokki.'

The newcomer bowed slightly and smiled as the
Land Crafter rolled a large rock over for him to use
as a seat. Settling down gratefully, the man stretched
his long legs. He smiled again when Mardilla passed
him some food and water. The Land Crafters and the
little Rrokki then waited patiently as he ate and
drank. When he had finished, the Wanderer wiped
his mouth and thanked them.

'What brings you to these parts?' asked Gatera.

'As you will have guessed by now, I am a traveller. I
was passing and smelt your cooking, so thought I
might prevail upon your hospitality.'

'But of course. Have you travelled far?'

'My journeys take me over the breadth and length
of the Realm. Just recently I have been in the
north.'

'A group of our friends have been travelling northwards,' Gatera said. 'I don't suppose you saw them?
Four men and a woman? They were going towards
the Ice Kingdom.'

The stranger shook his head. 'I'm afraid not. It's
strange that you should mention the Ice Kingdom,
though. I saw a peculiar sight in the mountains near
there some weeks ago. Two great Tarks swooped
down from the sky, carrying a cloaked man and a
golden haired woman. Later, the Tarks flew off
southwards. By the time I reached the place where
the man and woman had dismounted, they had
disappeared—it's as if they were swallowed up by the
mountain.'

'Zenddos!' grated Rrum, his small eyes narrowing
even more.

The huge Land Crafter nodded grimly.

'Why would he land there, and not at the Ice
Kingdom?' his wife asked.

The giant shrugged. 'Perhaps they weren't actually

going to the Ice Kingdom itself—and perhaps Zendos had a hideout nearby. If that's the case, the others will never find him.' He turned suddenly to the Wanderer. 'Would you be able to draw a map so we could find this place?'

The Wanderer leaned forward. 'There would be no problem finding it—it's very distinctive. The mountain has a flat top. Near its base is a large cave beside a stream. I searched the cave, but it was empty, yet they disappeared somewhere near it. Here, this might help.' He pulled a series of maps from a pocket and handed one to Gatera.

'But …'

'It's all right,' the man said quickly. 'I know the place well enough to have no need of the map. I can easily draw another if I need it.'

Gatera fell into deep thought, but Mardilla spoke up. 'I think you will need to be on your travels again tomorrow, my love. If there's a chance that Zendos is hiding somewhere near there, you must find him.'

Gatera looked at her thankfully; she obviously trusted the stranger, even as he did. 'I must go and find out,' he confirmed.

'*We* mustt ggo,' Rrum corrected him.

Gatera laughed and slapped his friend, nearly sending the rock man rolling down the slope where they sat.

The stranger smiled. 'I'm glad to have been able to tell you some news to repay your kindness.'

Mardilla asked him, 'Won't you stay with us tonight?'

'No, I must be moving on. I feel refreshed now. May Elsinoth guide your feet.' A secret smile twinkled in his eyes.

'And yours,' they answered.

Taking his leave, the man was gone as quickly and as silently as he had arrived.

Early the next day, Rrum and Gatera set off northwards. Gatera strolled along, his big legs covering the ground rapidly. Sometimes Rrum trotted alongside and at other times he somersaulted or rolled. The two made good time, both of them happy to be roaming the countryside together. The sun warmed them comfortably as they walked. Gatera revelled in the feel and smell of the land; it spoke to him of strength and freedom. As he walked, he began to sing a marching song of the Land Crafters:

'I walk down dales and climb the hills
Where the rocks stand firm and the water falls
Where the baraks roar and the songbird trills
I am a free man; I build no walls.

Oh! The feel of the ground
Oh! The sight and the sounds
Oh! There's life all around
In the land.

I roam the country far and wide
O'er mountain top and lowly plain
And the land alone is my trusted guide
To see me safely home again.

Oh! The feel of the ground
Oh! The sight and the sounds
Oh! There's life all around
In the land.

And when my travelling day is done
And I lay my weary head to sleep
I'll set off once more with the rising sun
Across moors and vales and the mountains steep.

Oh! The feel of the ground
Oh! The sight and the sounds

Oh! There's life all around
In the land.'

The Land Crafter's joyful bass reverberated around the gentle hills. Rrum did a series of cartwheels and somersaults, sharing his pleasure.

Two days later, they had reached a valley some miles east and north of the Black Caves. Rrum was trotting tirelessly at Gatera's side when suddenly two gaunt men stepped out of a small grove of trees just ahead of them.

One of the two, a surly character with deep-set eyes and a sallow complexion, stood barring their way, his arms folded and a scowl on his face. His companion, seeing Gatera's size, opened his mouth in dismay, then with a look at the other man, closed it rapidly.

'Can we do anything for you, gentlemen?' Gatera rumbled as he came to a halt.

'Hand over anything valuable,' sneered the leader.

'We haven't anything valuable, and if we had, we certainly wouldn't hand it over to the likes of you!'

'Banddits,' grated Rrum.

'Oh, it talks, does it?' drawled the bandit leader. 'If you haven't any valuables, you won't mind leaving your provisions with us,' he continued, pointing to Gatera's backpack.

There was a dangerous glint in his eye, but Gatera ignored it. 'You've got a nerve, I'll say that,' he boomed, roaring with laughter. 'D'you seriously think that the two of you can intimidate us?' He stomped his foot, and the bandit's nervous companion leapt back a couple of feet. The Land Crafter laughed again.

'Oh, but there aren't just two of us,' the bandit leader said coldly, signalling with his hand. Four other rogues appeared from the bushes, armed with swords and clubs.

'I warn you,' said Gatera, his smile replaced by a hard, cold look, "that we are peace-loving people, but if you provoke us, we will fight to protect what is ours and our right to pass this way without hindrance.'

'You terrify me,' replied the bandit, waving his men forward.

The Land Crafter and the little rock man found themselves suddenly surrounded. Pulling his staff from his belt, Gatera swung it down on the nearest bandit's skull. The man crumpled silently. Continuing the motion, Gatera swung at the legs of the next bandit. As he collapsed, screaming in agony, the man fell on top of the staff, knocking it from Gatera's hands. Hitting his head on the ground, the man lay still. There was no time for Gatera to recover the staff, however—two more armed bandits closed in on him. One dived at his legs, and the Land Crafter also crashed to the ground.

Meanwhile, the other two attacked Rrum. One of them swung his sword at the Rrokki. It broke against Rrum's leathery skin. The second man grabbed hold of Rrum roughly. Picking up a rock, the first bandit brought it down on Rrum's head. 'Let's see how you like this!'

The Rrokki caught the rock in his mouth and started grinding it to pieces. 'Very goodd!' He rolled over, sending his captor flying.

The man groaned as he got up. His companion advanced uncertainly towards Rrum, but the little Rrokki started spitting out bits of rock at both men. Unnerved, they turned and fled howling into the woods.

One of the bandits attacking Gatera kicked him, and the giant yelled in pain. Then, dodging their clubs, he rolled over with surprising agility and leapt to his feet. As the bandits hesitated, he jumped forward and grabbed them. Before they could wriggle free, he cracked their heads together. This time it was the two bandits who slumped to the ground.

Grinning at Rrum, he said, 'They'll wake up with a nasty headache later! Shall we continue our journey?'

His friend mumbled an inaudible reply his mouth still full of rock. Gatera laughed and clapped him on the back. 'Sorry, I shouldn't ask you to talk while you're eating!'

Four days later, the Land Crafter and the rock man reached the foothills of a range of mountains. Gatera knew from the map that the Ice Kingdom must be somewhere nearby.

Rrum pointed upwards. 'Flatt topped mounttain.'

Gatera looked up and breathed a sigh of relief. He had thought it might take all day to find the right peak, but this certainly seemed to be the one that the Wanderer had described.

They looked for a stream or a cave as they walked along the lower mountain slopes. After a little while, they came to a small stream that emerged from a little higher up the mountain. There was no sign of a cave, however.

'That's strange,' muttered Gatera. 'This seems to be the only stream on this mountain, yet there's no cave. Perhaps we're on the wrong mountain after all.'

'No. Rightt one,' insisted Rrum. He tottered off up the slope beside the stream.

'Here!' he called.

Gatera scrambled up to join him. The entrance to the cave was hidden by a large bush. The Land Crafter congratulated his Rrokki friend and pulled a firestick and a torch from his backpack. Lighting the torch, he crept into the cave, followed closely by Rrum.

The cavern stretched back for several paces into the hillside, but without obvious tunnels or ledges. Disappointed, they returned to the fresh air outside.

'Whatt now?' Rrum asked.

'The Wanderer insisted that Zendos and the woman—presumably Melinya—disappeared somewhere very near here. There must be another cave somewhere, or perhaps a hideout set into the hillside. We'll have to search carefully.'

They scoured the area below the cave but could find no other clues to the sorcerer's disappearance. Gatera climbed past the place where the stream gushed out of the mountain. He had spotted a shrubby area higher up which he thought was worth investigating.

As he climbed, his tough but sensitive feet felt a change in the ground. Pausing, he realised it was probably just the channel cut out by the stream. He turned to go on, then gave a yell of delight. 'Rrum! Quick! I think I've found the answer!'

The rock man scampered up the hillside to join him as Gatera climbed down to where the stream gurgled out of the mountain. It issued from a large hole and, bending down, he peered inside. 'It looks as if it widens out further in,' he said to Rrum as he arrived.

'I will lookk.' The Rrokki took the torch and paddled into the stream, disappearing into the opening. After a few moments his muffled voice floated back. 'You are rightt.'

Gatera gave a sigh—half of triumph, and half of apprehension. He didn't like enclosed tunnels. He still had too many bad memories of the evil passages below Dargan's stronghold. Even so, taking a deep breath, he bent down and squeezed through the hole into the dark channel beyond.

19
The Castle of Ice

As Valor and Athennar collapsed, their ice-echoes fell on top of them and began to melt. Within moments, the icy water had vapourised. Not a drop was left on their skin or clothing.

Five new shapes detached themselves from the darkness at the far end of the room, having observed all the activity from a distance. The first to reach the two spoke in bell-like tones as he looked down at Athennar's body. 'The Hall of Cold Echoes is no place for strangers. For the Tissirim, this is a place for refreshment and renewal, but for such as you it would seem to bring confusion and chaos.' He gestured to the other four Ice People. 'Take these two to Zendos. He will know what to do with them.'

One of the Tissirim shook his head, as if trying to clear it. 'But they have done us no harm ...'

'Do as I say!' said the first. 'Zendos is our one hope to be freed of the confinements of this accursed kingdom. We must aid him all we can.'

The Ice People nodded and withdrew, carrying Valor and Athennar.

In another part of the city, Hesteron and Vallel made their way slowly towards the long spire that towered

above the other ice structures. Like Athennar and
Valor, they had come across buildings with holes torn
in their sides; they too had found no signs of life.
Now, as they trudged down the cold, deserted streets,
Vallel felt a sense of foreboding. It had been easy
enough to regard their journey so far as a challenge;
but now they were in the Ice Kingdom, and she knew
that they were dealing with a powerful and dangerous adversary: Zendos would not hesitate to kill
them if it so suited him. Like most elves, she did not
fear death for herself; it was merely a gateway into a
far greater kingdom, into the presence of Toroth
himself. But she hated the thought of being parted
from Hesteron so soon. Even worse, she feared his
death, leaving her behind. She couldn't bear another
such loss. Her sister Vosphel's death had left a gaping
hole—one that had been filled only by the Air
Crafter's love and care.

Hesteron was concerned with more mundane matters. He was beginning to feel cold. At first, he had
welcomed the crispness of the air and its invigorating
freshness. Now it just seemed bitter and harsh.
However, glancing at Vallel, a warmth crept through
him that helped to dispel the cold for a while.

After a long walk, they reached a street that led
straight to the spire. From this vantage point, they
could see that the pinnacle was the tallest of several
pointed structures that looked like fragile towers on
top of a tall, graceful castle of ice. The sheer elegance
of the building made the two Crafters pause in
admiration. It was like something out of a dream.

Vallel sighed, and Hesteron put his arm around
her shoulder and drew her to him. 'It's beautiful,' he
said simply.

She nodded, still lost for words.

'Come on,' he said, starting forward again. 'I have a

feeling that where there is beauty, Zendos will not be far away, trying to corrupt it.'

They moved slowly forward, treading cautiously now, and watchful for any signs of danger.

The Ice Castle stood alone in the centre of a huge circle of ice. It was as if the other buildings stood at a distance, in awe. The two Crafters paused before venturing any further. If there was anyone on guard, they would be easily spotted as they crossed the flat, open space.

Hesteron silently pointed to a large hole in the side wall of the castle. Vallel nodded in understanding, then watched as he raced swiftly towards it. When he was there, he signalled to her, and she ran to join him. There was no sign that they had been seen; no calls of challenge or sounds of running feet.

Peering into the hole and seeing no one there, they stepped warily inside. They found themselves in a small chamber, completely devoid of furniture or other objects. Another hole had been blasted in the far wall, and they cautiously crossed over to it.

The room beyond was much larger. Rows of rectangular ice blocks radiated from its centre. Hesteron stepped to the nearest one to look more closely. At first it appeared to be just a single big chunk of ice, then he noticed that on one end a face had been etched into the surface. 'This is strange,' he said to Vallel.

'Perhaps it's the Tissirim's art,' she suggested.

'I doubt it,' he replied. 'It seems to be more like some sort of memorial chamber.'

About thirty blocks altogether were arranged in a spiral, each one with a carved facial likeness. Hesteron was sure that there were differences between the faces, although they all looked similar.

At the centre of the spiral was one that seemed to

have been turned on its end. One face of this slab
comprised a full-length etching of what they assumed
must be an Ice Person. Drawn to it without understanding why, they both had the impression that this
was someone of regal bearing. A cold breeze swirled
around the slab, as if guarding it.

Hesteron paused, surprised by the wind. He concentrated and sensed its movements, the undercur-
rents and temperatures within it, then he shivered.
This was a breeze of mourning; a sad, cold, haunting
flow of air for a great life that had been cruelly
shortened. The Air Crafter sighed as he realised that
his first suspicions were correct. This was a room of
ice tombs: something akin to a burial ground for the
Tissirim.

Vallel joined him and huddled close—she too was
aware of the sadness, though she had felt it more
when running her hands over the silent tombs. 'Let's
move on,' she whispered.

Hesteron looked at her as if jolted out of a deep
sleep. 'Yes,' he replied softly, 'this sadness pulls too
deeply at my heart.'

They crept slowly away and towards an opening on
the other side of the chamber.

In the centre of the next room was a raised
platform with a single row of steps leading upwards.
Hesteron signalled to Vallel to explore the rest of the
room while he went up the steps.

Vallel browsed around the base of the platform,
which towered over her head. She could no longer
see Hesteron. Her eyes were beginning to ache from
the constant whiteness wherever she looked. There
was never any relief—apart from when she could
turn to look at Hesteron—only an unrelenting glare;
whether the cold glare outside as they had walked
down the streets, or the greater glow within the

buildings. Even the whiteness of her protective
clothing began to annoy her. Oh, for a splash of
colour; the green of meadows or the blues, greys and
browns of her beloved River Tarrel! She ran her
hands idly over one of the many pyramids that lined
the walls of the room, deriving some comfort from
the wetness. She preferred not to wear the thick
gloves unless absolutely necessary.

Dreamily, she wondered what purpose the
pyramids served. An idea floated into her mind and
she stroked the shape gently, summoning all her
knowledge of water, and adding to it those things she
had sensed about the white ice all around her. Gradually, the ice began to melt. Within a few minutes the
pyramid had disappeared, leaving a pool of water on
the ground. She smiled then, recognising that the
innate powers which she had wielded against the
Mistress of the Mist—borne out of years of understanding, and from those talents with which Toroth
had endowed her people—were stronger than she
had realised.

She turned to go, but a slight noise made her look
round. When she did, she gave an involuntary gasp.
The pyramid had re-formed, as if it had never
melted. Vallel stood in mute astonishment for a
moment, then was disturbed from her thoughts by a
cry from above. Forgetting the pyramid, she raced up
the steps.

Hesteron, meanwhile, had been investigating the
top of the platform. Six long blocks of ice—similar to
the ice tombs in the previous room—sat huddled
together in one corner. Before he moved over
towards them, he discovered that the floor at the
front of the platform was pitted with a dozen or more
square holes. The nearest two holes were empty, and
he could see that they sank to a depth of about seven

or eight feet—virtually the full height of the platform. The remainder of the holes, however, were
filled with a cold, white liquid. Although he knew
little about the white ice all around, he realised that
this water was probably an unfrozen version—though
quite why it didn't freeze puzzled him, as a frigid mist
arose from each of the holes. He stood over one,
trying to sense the air currents, but had to withdraw
as the air began to freeze his moustache and
eyebrows, and made his eyes ache with its chill.

Backing away, he rubbed his smarting eyes and
then stepped over to the six long ice blocks in the
corner. They were similar to the ice tombs, except
that they were semi-transparent rather than white.
Hesteron leaned over the nearest one to see if there
was an engraving on it, and then withdrew in horror.
In the depths of the ice block lay the clothed body of a
man! His face was fine-featured, and etched with
lines of kindness and wisdom. He looked very noble,
an impression heightened by the deep golden cloak
he wore.

In the other five blocks were similar figures—three
other men and two women. Although their features
were remarkably preserved, the Air Crafter sensed
that they had been entombed for many years, possibly
even centuries. He wondered what they were doing
here. The Tissirim were said to be lovers of peace.
Were these, then, ancient friends whom they revered,
or enemies whom they had frozen to remind them of
the evils of the world? Somehow the faces showed no
signs of evil, or of fear, but were all fair and gentle, or
proud and strong.

Pondering upon the mystery, Hesteron moved
over to examine two tall, upright slabs of white ice
that stood nearby. Carved upon the faces of both
slabs were strange rows of inscriptions that meant

nothing to the Air Crafter. He was about to turn and go back towards the steps when a scraping sound made him stop. Stepping carefully, he edged his way round to view the other side of the slabs. As he did so, a hand shot out and grabbed his arm. Hesteron looked up, straight into cold eyes that he recognised all too well. 'Zendos!' he breathed.

'Good meeting,' the sorcerer said sarcastically, gripping the Air Crafter's arm effortlessly.

'Let me go!' shouted Hesteron.

The sorcerer laughed; a laugh that was colder than the ice all around. 'You have slipped through my grasp before,' he said. 'You will not do so again. By the time I have finished with you, you will wish that you had died under the claws of the Fangers.'

Hesteron desperately tried to pull away, but the sorcerer was too strong.

'Perhaps you would care to tell me why you came here? I presume it was not by coincidence. In which case—who betrayed me?' continued Zendos. 'I expect your friends are with you. Perhaps you would also care to tell me how many of them are swarming around the city?'

'Never!' hissed Hesteron.

The sorcerer glared at him for a moment, then laughed again. 'No matter. You will tell me—in time. Ah, I see that your caring companion is here as well.'

Hesteron turned round to see Vallel running up the steps. 'Go back!' the Air Crafter shouted. 'Escape while you can!'

'But …' she hesitated.

'Go back, I say! You can't help me. Find the others!'

Torn between his command and her concern for him, Vallel hesitated for a moment but then ran off down the steps.

'Thank you for letting me know that there are

others,' remarked Zendos. 'Have no fear—they will all be found and dealt with. Your puny efforts are hopeless. Now, while I await your friends, I think we had better keep you "on ice", so to speak.'

He jerked Hesteron into motion and dragged him across the platform, calling in shrill tones as he did so. Several Tissirim appeared from the far side of the room and glided towards the steps at that end of the platform.

Zendos bundled Hesteron towards the pits in the floor, and pushed him into the nearest hole of icy-cold water just as the Tissirim arrived. 'This should keep you quiet,' he chuckled.

As Hesteron's head sank beneath the surface, the Ice People thrust their hands into the water and it immediately turned to ice. Pulling upwards, they withdrew the newly-formed block of ice from its hole, with Hesteron encased within it. The Tissirim slid it purposefully across to the corner of the platform, beside the other six ice blocks.

'Good,' muttered Zendos. 'Now we will wait for his friends to make an appearance.'

20

Ice Fight

Her heart hammering, Vallel dashed out into the street and raced across the open space to the shelter of some nearby buildings. What could she do? She must find Athennar and Valor, but she had no idea where they would be. It might be too late for Hesteron if she waited until dawn, when they were all due to meet again. She groaned, then quickly slipped inside a building when she saw two Ice People emerging from the castle. Somehow the place had lost its beauty for her.

The Tissirim were coming nearer, and she pressed herself against the wall of her hiding place, hoping desperately that they wouldn't stop to search. As they reached the building, the Ice People halted. Vallel held her breath, afraid that any slight sound might reveal her presence. The Tissirim were talking in a bell-like language which she didn't understand. Just as her lungs were about to burst, they moved on.

She risked a quick glance out of the entrance hole. The Ice People were disappearing down the street. Sitting down for a moment, she tried to decide which direction to take. Desperately, she willed her mind to recall any particular ice building along Athennar's and Valor's route, but she could remember none.

153

Only the Ice Castle came to mind. But she had to make a choice—and rapidly.

Stepping outside, she made the best guess she could, and started towards a nearby street entrance. She was just about to turn the corner when she heard footsteps and ducked behind the nearest building. As she peered out, her hopes fell. Four Tissirim were carrying the immobile forms of Athennar and Valor towards the Ice Castle. Burying her head in her hands, she let out a sigh of frustration. What could she do now? The fate of all her friends rested with her. No one else could save them now. Yet what could she do? Zendos had seen her and was sure to set a guard on the castle. It all seemed so hopeless.

As she sat, she heard a sudden squawk and the sound of bell-like voices raised in protest. She peered round the corner again. The Tissirim were halfway across the open space, but were being bombarded by Kal. The brave white hawk kept swooping down, clawing at the Ice People and then retreating. Despite their protests, however, the Tissirim were not really bothered by the bird. They merely knocked her away like a rather troublesome fly. Eventually Kal flew off. Vallel wished she could have called her. Even a bird would have been better company than none.

Summoning all her elvish reserves, she braced herself. If the answer to her friends' plight lay in her hands, so be it. It would be best for her to move swiftly, before Zendos had time to set any traps. The Ice People had already disappeared into the icy edifice. She paused for a while, wondering if they would emerge again. After a few minutes' wait, she decided that she could delay no longer. Her resolve hardened, she ran lightly to the side of the building. Giving one look over her shoulder to make sure that no more Tissirim were approaching, she sneaked to the edge of the hole, took a quick look inside the anteroom, and then shrank back.

A single Ice Person stood on guard in a corner of the small room. How could she pass it? Then she realised that the Tissir had been unarmed. Although she baulked at the thought of attacking a defenceless creature, she had no choice: her friends' lives were in danger. She was no swordswoman, but she drew her slim elven blade anyway. No icy guard would keep her from rescuing Hesteron!

She peered cautiously into the hole once more. Then, climbing boldly through the entrance, she waved her sword defiantly at the Tissir. The guard's blank face showed no emotion, but it walked heavily across the room, barring her way. Then it stopped and spoke, and this time she could understand the words, even though they retained their delicate musical quality. She stifled her surprise at its ability to communicate with her; she could not afford to be off-guard even for a moment.

'You are expected,' the bell-like tones announced. 'Zendos awaits you.'

'Then he'll have to wait a little longer,' said Vallel defiantly.

'You will come,' intoned the Tissir, moving forward again.

'Never!' said Vallel, swiping at the advancing figure with her sword. To her astonishment, the sword sliced deep into the waist of the creature—yet where it had passed, the gash healed almost immediately. The River Crafter backed away, unsure of her next move. She had to silence this guard somehow, otherwise he would alert Zendos to her presence. There was no going back.

The Tissir was advancing again. Vallel felt a cold shiver run down her back as she looked at its beautiful

yet expressionless face. It reached out for her, and
she slashed out desperately, slicing off its arm. The
limb fell to the floor and, within seconds, melted.
Apparently unconcerned, the figure knelt and thrust
the remaining stump into the pool of water.

'Ice to water to ice,' it said softly. The water began
to freeze again, once more taking on the shape of the
arm. The Tissir rose, its arm complete. Vallel circled
away from it, her pulse racing. The creature seemed
invincible! Perhaps she could somehow take advan-
tage of its relative slowness. As it approached her
again, she dodged around behind it and pushed it
into the wall. There was a resounding crash and the
Tissir fell, stunned. An arm broke off and started to
melt.

Vallel leapt to stop the Ice Person once and for all
by cutting off its legs. Almost unable to look, she then
swung her sword at its head before it could start to
chant again. She felt violently ill as the head also
began to melt, followed rapidly by the rest of the
body. Within a short time, the Tissir had become no
more than a pool of water.

The River Crafter gasped and sat down for a
moment, exhausted. Tears flowed freely from her
eyes—partly from relief, and partly from having had
to destroy a fellow being. But once she had recovered
her breath, she steeled herself and moved towards
the hole that led into the room of the ice tombs. Then
she heard a sound behind her. To her dismay, the
Tissir was again re-forming.

'Ice to water to ice, two are one,' came the familiar
intonation. Vallel almost wept again—this time with
frustration. There seemed no way to overcome the
Ice Person. In desperation, she turned to Toroth and
mouthed a silent prayer, asking for his protection.

Once more the Ice Person drew itself up and

advanced towards Vallel. Once more she dodged around it, this time swiping at its head with her sword. Once more the Tissir's head fell from its body, and rolled over near the wall and started to melt. Vallel quickly knocked the body over and chopped at it with her sword. She had had a sudden flash of inspiration. As the pieces melted, she placed her hands against the wall of the chamber, sensing the ice, the crystals of water, the bonding. As her hands played over the wall, it too began to melt, even as the pyramid had done earlier. She gritted her teeth and continued. The water flowed from the wall and joined the pool formed by the melting Tissir. Within moments, the waters had mingled, and Vallel gave a sigh partly of hope and partly of exhaustion. Now she could only wait.

A struggle was going on within the waters as they again began to freeze and re-form. The whole pool was being drawn towards the wall. Was it just her imagination, or could she hear strangled, tinkling cries?

Within minutes, the waters had once more become white ice. However, this time there was no Tissir, just a large bulge where his body waters had frozen with those of the wall. Vallel gulped back the tears. Although she had no doubt about the need to win the battle, this somehow seemed a cruel way to end it.

But she could not afford to stop and think. Hesceron and the others were still in danger. She hurried now into the room of the ice tombs, running lightly from one tomb to another, using their bulk to conceal her movements should anyone enter suddenly. Like a white shadow, she flitted across the room towards the opposite wall until she was close to the opening that ed to the next chamber.

She strained to detect any sight or sound. Two Ice

People were moving backwards and forwards in front of the platform, carrying spheres of white ice. Waiting until they were some distance away with their backs turned, she then sprinted across to crouch in the shadow of the steps. The muffled sound of Zendos' voice came from a distance—possibly even from another room. Vallel shivered, but was relieved to see the Tissirim move ponderously away in the direction of the sound.

The River Crafter leapt lightly up the steps until she came near the top of the platform. She wasn't sure where Hesteron was, but this had been where she had last seen him. If he wasn't here, it would at least prove a useful vantage point for spying out the layout of the rest of the room. After looking warily over the edge of the platform, she ran up the remaining steps. No one! She was relieved but also disappointed. What now? It was likely that Zendos held her friends captive in another room, but how could she tackle the sorcerer and his Tissirim helpers alone?

Hesitating for only a second, she slipped into the shadows of a group of ice blocks while she decided on a plan of action. Then she flinched as she looked into the icy depths of the nearest block and saw the human body of a warrior. So these too were tombs! Shuddering, she sat down with her back to the cold tomb. She ached to be near Hesteron once more; to see his smile, feel his light touch on her arm. That single moment of working together against the Mist Mistress had been exhilarating—lending the Air Crafter her strength and feeling strengthened in return. She also missed Athennar and Valor—both had become trusted friends. There was no point in delaying; she must find them now! She must at least see if she could find the room where Zendos might be keeping them.

Vallel crept noiselessly between the tombs. As she leaned on one of them, it moved slightly. She jumped, then stifled a scream as she saw a familiar face staring at her from the depths of the ice. *Athennar* There was a pleading look in his eyes. Somehow she knew he was alive despite his cold prison. Moving quickly to the next block, she discovered Valor gazing wide-eyed into space. Trembling, she hurried to the third ice tomb, knowing before she did so whom she would find there. Her beloved Hesteron looked up at her from his icy prison. She could almost sense his voice in her mind, pleading urgently: 'Free me!'

She leaned over the tomb, tears falling freely from her face. Where they fell, they melted little channels in the ice. This reawakened the River Crafter's hope. If she had managed to melt the pyramid and a small section of ice wall, could she not do the same with this huge block? It would take a great effort, but she was sure she had sufficient strength, and her love for Hesteron would help her.

Eagerly now, she rubbed her hands almost lovingly across the top of the tomb. She then breathed on it and stroked it in circular motions, varying the speed as the ice began to melt. Rivulets of water trickled down the side of the tomb. Vallel's concentration lapsed briefly as she again looked at the Air Crafter inside: he looked so helpless.

Suddenly realising her hands had stopped, she frantically began the motions again. The ice was receding slowly and forming a small pool around the bottom of the block. Vallel knew that if she paused from her labours for long, the water would start to freeze again. She persevered, occasionally glancing beyond the ice to the ever-closer form of Hesteron.

Just a thin layer separated them now. Soon they would be reunited!

She stopped in mid-stroke as a shadow fell over the melting tomb. Looking up, she groaned and beat her fists in frustration against the ice.

Zendos towered over her, a malicious grin on his face. 'Are you enjoying yourself, my dear? So pleased you decided to come and join us.' He motioned to two of the four Tissirim who had appeared behind him. Walking forward, they grabbed her arms before she had a chance even to think of escape.

Zendos produced a length of leather cord from within his cloak. Taking her arms from the Ice People, he roughly pulled them behind her back and tied them with the cord. 'I think that will prevent any more of your pranks!'

He signalled to the Tissirim again. Two of them pushed Hesteron's tomb back towards one of the square pits for re-freezing. The other two Ice People escorted Vallel firmly over to another of the pits. She struggled, but they held her securely.

'I assume as you came alone, that there are no more of you,' gloated Zendos, 'though I will send out some of my friends here to check. As for you, since you seem so fond of the ice, you can study it at extra close quarters.'

He nodded to the Tissirim, and they pushed her over the lip of the pit. She seemed to hang for a moment, then plunged into the icy depths of the water. Even as she tried to move back upwards to the air, she felt the fluid freeze around her. To her surprise, she could breathe and think, although she knew she was frozen solid. Her whole 'tomb' was pulled slowly upwards, and she flinched inwardly as it crashed into a horizontal position—but she felt nothing. She didn't even feel cold.

Zendos looked down at her through the ice and it was almost as if he was in another world. She did her best to glare coldly at him. Watching disdainfully, he simply threw back his head in a spasm of laughter.

21

Beneath the Mountain

The tunnel wormed its way ever deeper into the
mountain. For a while, the gently flowing waters of
the stream lapped around their feet. Then they
reached a gaping crack in the rock from which the
stream issued. The tunnel itself led off to one side.
Underfoot the ground became dry, although the air
still seemed dank and cool.

'Does this go on for ever?' growled Gatera. 'My
back aches from all this bending.'

'Itt's no probblem,' retorted Rrum, his eyes glinting
with sympathetic amusement in the torchlight.

Rounding a bend, the glow bounced off a blank
rock wall ahead. 'A dead end,' breathed Gatera in
disbelief.

'Perhapps nott,' Rrum replied.

The two friends peered closely at the rock face.
'You may be right,' muttered Gatera. 'There's a crack
around the edges of this slab of rock.' He tested
different parts of the huge slab, pushing as hard as he
could. Suddenly, it sprang open, catapulting him into
a corridor beyond. Equally quickly, the rock door
quietly swung closed behind him. He was left in utter
darkness; Rrum still being in the tunnel holding the
torch.

'Rrum!' he whispered fiercely, pounding his fists against the wall. The darkness clutched at him. He longed to cry out, but didn't dare in case Zendos or one of his cronies was nearby. *But what if Rrum can't open the door?* he thought. *What if I'm stuck in this blackness for ever? What if ...*

A blaze of light burst into the corridor as the door opened a few feet away. Rrum's face peeked round it. 'Hello,' he said. 'All rightt?'

Gatera nodded sheepishly. 'Fine! Let's have a look at that door, though, before you let it close. Here, let's brace it—quick! I want to make sure we can get out again when we want to.'

Taking the torch from Rrum, he examined the slab. Cut into the face on his side was a small groove, acting as a handle. Directing Rrum to return to the tunnel, Gatera let the door close again. When it was shut, it was flush with the corridor wall, its outlines barely discernible from where he stood. When he pulled on the concealed 'handle', the door swung easily open. 'All right. You can come through now,' he said to Rrum.

The little Rrokki stepped through and glanced up and down the corridor as the door closed behind him. 'Which way?' he asked.

'First we mark this door so we can find it again,' rumbled Gatera, pulling a lump of limestone from his backpack. 'A mark on the walls or floor might alert anyone else who comes this way,' he muttered, partly to himself, as he chalked a short white line on the roof of the passage.

Rrum was still looking in both directions along the corridor. There was nothing to suggest which way they should go, so he started ambling slowly to the right.

Gatera followed him. 'Might as well go this way as

any other, I suppose,' he mumbled quietly to himself.
He was a little nervous about the light given off by the
torch—it would give any enemies an instant warning
signal of their approach. However, they had little
choice. He certainly didn't fancy the alternative of
groping his way along the passage in clinging
blackness.

Cautiously, they made their way forward. There
was no sign of any side tunnels and although the two
friends stopped occasionally, they could hear nothing
besides their own breathing.

During one such pause, Gatera muttered to Rrum,
'Perhaps this place is deserted after all.'

'Shhh!' hissed the Rrokki.

Obediently, the big man fell quiet, and listened. In
the distance he could just make out a soft rustling
noise and what seemed like muted conversation.

Creeping along ever more carefully, they moved
down the passage towards the source of the noises.
masking the light from the torch as well as they could
Their feet made virtually no sound, but a reedy voice
suddenly called out. 'Who's that? Is it you sneaking
along to surprise us, Ganniwaggik?'

Gatera gave a sigh of annoyance and moved forward boldly now that they had been discovered. A
little way ahead, the passageway opened into a great
circular hall with tunnels radiating from it. In the
centre of the hall were groups of tables with figures
clustered around them. The light from Gatera's
torch reflected off many of their faces. The Land
Crafter gasped in surprise. Who were all these
people, and why had they been lurking here in pitch
darkness?

'You're not Ganniwaggik,' came the piping voice
from one of the nearer figures. 'You don't sound or
smell at all like him! You don't even breathe or walk

like him. Who are you? What are you doing here?
You haven't come for us, have you?'

Several of the figures squealed and cowered in fear.
Rrum and Gatera gazed at them. They were all so old
and thin. Some looked so frail that the slightest
breeze might have knocked them over. Others had a
hint of wiry strength despite their thinness. The Land
Crafter suddenly realised that none of them was
looking directly at him, but had their heads cocked as
if listening. He waved his hand but received no
response. These people were all blind—no wonder
they needed no light! Or perhaps they had lost their
sight from having to live in constant darkness. There
were far too many questions he wanted to ask. He
cleared his throat. 'I am Gatera, a Land Crafter, and
this is my friend Rrum of the Rrokki. We mean you
no harm.'

The old people cowered as his voice rang out across
the open spaces of the hall.

Gatera flinched. He had spoken more loudly than
he had intended. Softening his voice, he tried once
again. 'Who are you? What is this place? What are you
doing here?'

The figures shuffled nervously. 'What is a Land
Crafter?' squeaked one of them. 'Has a new form of
life been born in the outer world?'

'What?' boomed Gatera, then, more softly, 'I don't
understand your question. Land Crafters are not
uncommon in the Realm.'

'Have you come here to torment us?' piped an
elderly woman.

'We are friends. We mean you no harm,' repeated
Gatera gently.

'Yes. Friendds,' Rrum's voice grinded out.

There were several more squeals.

'They have come for us!' wailed a voice.

'We are doomed!'

'How did they find us?'

'No! No!'

Gatera interrupted the cries. 'Calm yourselves! I repeat—we are your friends.'

'You are not our friends. Our friends bring us food. Our friends give us shelter. Our friends protect us from the dangers of the outside world.'

The Land Crafter shook his head in despair. What in the Realm were they gibbering about? He looked at Rrum questioningly, but the rock man just shrugged.

Gradually the sounds of complaint and fear died away. One thin, pale old man—the one who had been first to speak when they had arrived—cautioned his friends. 'Remember the one who was not of us? She was no enemy, except to herself. These ones may be similar.'

Turning towards the two companions, he asked, 'Do you really mean us no harm? If so, please answer our questions. Where are you from? Why are you here?'

'I come from the Mountains of Kravos. My friend here is from the Southlands.'

'Then you must be rare survivors indeed; like she who was brought here recently.'

'Someone brought here?' asked Gatera quickly. 'We are looking for a friend who has gone missing. Can you describe her?' He then flushed as he realised that the old beings would have been unable to see their mysterious visitor.

'We did not meet her. But she had a beautiful voice, even in her fear. Our friends locked her away for her own safety. They said she was found outside, quite delirious. Indeed, we could hear her cries of anguish floating down the passageway.'

The Land Crafter wondered who these 'friends' were who had taken the woman captive—and who the woman could be. An insistent tugging at his sleeve caught his attention.

'Melinya?' Rrum asked quietly when he looked down, as if having heard his unspoken question.

'Most likely. Or possibly even Linnil. Or perhaps a complete stranger.' Turning back to the old ones he said, 'Why do you say we are rare survivors? The Realm hums with life—elves, men and Rrokki; even the cursed Zorgs and Tarks!'

'Spare us your pity—we know the truth. Our friends told us that all races perished in a massive war some forty years ago. Evil beings caused many of the mountains to collapse and rivers to flood. Fortunately we were safe here.'

'Forty years? Is that how long you've been here?'

'Forty-five, to be precise. Our friends call us the Ancients. They continue to have young, but we merely age and die. It will not be long before the thirty of us who remain live out our last days. Only a few more years perhaps.'

'Who are these "friends"? Why have they fed you with lies about the Realm and kept you prisoners here?'

The sightless eyes roved restlessly around, as if seeking something that was only visible to the old man. 'It is you who lie …'

'Yes, you lie,' came a chorus of shrill voices.

'Our friends look after us. They would not deceive us.'

'They look after you? In return for what?' asked Gatera.

'Oh, we help them. We make clothes and furniture. Sometimes we make more tunnels for them; dig out some rocks for them.'

'Hard black ones. Special rocks. Our friends use them to make heat.'

Gatera snorted in disgust. This conversation was becoming more far-fetched each moment. He decided to try a different approach. 'Can you lead us to this stranger who was brought in recently?'

'No. Our friends wouldn't like it. Besides, she is kept in a place near their quarters. We are not allowed there. We have not been there for many years.'

'You mean you just stay here? Haven't you ever tried to escape?'

'Escape? Why? From what? To where? The outside world is in ruin and chaos.'

'Then where do you think we came from? Or this stranger you told us about?'

The old man thought over the question for a while, then replied, 'It does not matter. This is our home. Here we are not pursued. Here we are at peace. Here we have a purpose—to serve our friends.'

'As slaves,' grunted Gatera.

Rrum nodded in agreement. 'How didd you first come here?' he asked.

'It was long ago. I almost forget. We were all outcasts of one kind or another. Some of us had been thrown out of our villages for no fault of our own, others had committed some crime and yet others were wanderers by choice. We joined together so we might be strong. For a while we were successful, living off the best in the land, raiding villages for our needs...'

'Bandits!' breathed Gatera.

'Yes. I suppose we were, though we never harmed anyone. However, our fortunes changed, and we were no longer safe. Everywhere we were hated, often just because people feared our strength. We became weary and longed for somewhere that we could call our home. One day when we were near this mountain we saw a figure emerging from a hole in the hillside. We hid, and when it was gone we explored and found these tunnels. But we were captured and imprisoned here, and treated harshly for three or four years.' The man gazed sightlessly across the chamber before continuing.

'After some time we made friends with our captors and continued to help them. Then, a little while later when we were about to venture into the world again, one of their number arrived with a message. Terrible fighting and disasters had occurred in the world outside. All races had suffered and died, and deadly plagues had broken out among the animal life. It was no longer safe outside. In here we at least had some protection from infection. Even so, we were affected because none of our women could bear children. This was the final proof, and we have been here ever since.'

'You've been tricked!' exploded Gatera. 'There has been no plague in the Realm. The world outside is green and beautiful.'

Several of the Ancients had drawn closer, but now leapt away in alarm. 'Lies!' shrieked several voices in unison. Their spokesman clapped his thin, white hands together, and the other Ancients fell silent. 'Why have we had no children, then?' he demanded of Gatera.

'I don't know,' admitted the Land Crafter. 'Perhaps something was put in your food, or perhaps it is something in the air down here. It could even be some kind of sorcery. What I *do* know is that someone has been fooling you for years. We are the proof of that. If everyone died, how is it we are alive? It can't make sense, even to you.'

Absent-mindedly, the old man ran his fingers over the crude table in front of him. 'You may be right. But what does it matter?'

'What does it matter? How can you say that? You could be free. You could wander in the air again, enjoy valleys and streams ...'

'Even if all is as you say, outside we would be lost—scattered, with no purpose. Who knows, there might still be those who seek to hunt us down! We know that little of our lives is left. We don't want to be "free". Here we know what we do, we are good at our work and we have each other. We also have our friends.'

'Friends who lie and cheat. You choose death when you could choose life. And just where are these friends? I'd dearly like to meet them. There's a few words I'd like to say to them.'

'Then this is your opportunity,' said a thin voice from the tunnel behind them. There was a scurrying of many feet, and the light from brightly burning torches burst into the caverns, casting grotesque shadows across the walls of the chamber.

Gatera and Rrum wheeled around, to be confronted by about twenty menacing forms. The Land Crafter groaned as Rrum muttered the words which confirmed his fears.

'Thundder gobblins!'

22

Trapped in the Ice Tomb

Athennar lay in his ice tomb, seeking desperately but vainly for some glimmer of hope. The plunge into the icy pit had taken place as he was recovering consciousness, and he had felt a terrible panic when he suddenly found he could not move. At first he feared he was paralysed, then his dulled senses became aware of the ice all around him, and of Zendos' face leering down in triumph. A cold rage swept over him then, but there was nothing he could do. He had to watch, wide-eyed, as Zendos gloated.

At last the sorcerer disappeared, and Athennar was left alone with his thoughts. Knowing that Valor would almost certainly be similarly entombed nearby, he wondered how the young Mountain Guard was faring. He was likely to be even more frustrated than Athennar by the restrictions on his movements. Athennar groaned inwardly—he had never felt quite so helpless before.

After a while, he noticed a shadow moving across the tomb. Vallel's face came into view, peering down into the ice. Desperately he tried to move, to call for help, but it was useless. She watched him sadly for a moment and then moved on. He wondered where she had gone, and where Hesteron was. Surely they

didn't think that he and Valor were dead? Why didn't
they try to break the ice? He wished he could scream,
or pound at the ice, or cry, but none of these was
possible. He knew that insanity was a hair's breadth
away.

Slowly but gently, he calmed himself, and decided
to concentrate on more hopeful thoughts, of his
friends and family. Images flickered hazily into his
mind before settling. His mother had died giving
birth to him, so he had never known her. He could
visualise her, however, from the many stories his
father had told him, and from her likeness lovingly
carved by Tolledon himself. The detailed carving
depicted a beautiful young woman skipping through
a woodland glade. Athennar felt that even though he
hadn't known her, part of her lived on within him.

His thoughts passed to his father, Tolledon, and
the strain it must have caused him to have to bring up
a young son alone while overseeing and guarding the
affairs of the Realm. It couldn't have been easy, but
he had never heard his father complain. Just occasionally he thought he had glimpsed a lonely gaze in
his father's eyes when he spoke about his wife. But
somehow he had always found time to teach Athennar about the beauty of the Realm.

As Athennar thought of all that was good in the
Realm, another face came once more into his mind
(though it was rarely far away)—Melinya! Groaning
inwardly, he wondered where she might be, or what
Zendos might have done with her. He knew that if
she was alive she would probably be thinking of him,
too. Each empty day they had been apart seemed like
a lifetime and he yearned to be with her again, to hold
her in his arms. He knew, too, that one day—if he
should ever break free from this accursed tomb, and
if he could find her—they would be united together

for ever. One day he would have to take on the mantle of responsibility for the Realm. There was no other woman he could envisage by his side, supporting him in such a difficult task. However, even if events turned out well, that time was likely to be far away. Guardians were blessed with long lives and his father, mercifully, was likely to live for many years yet.

His thoughts turned to his other companions. Most of all, he wondered how Kess was faring. Both Kess and Valor had become like sons to him, and he hoped the Quiet One was safe. Athennar puzzled over Whisper—who she could be and whether Kess was in any danger from her—but no answers came. At least Kess had a maturity beyond his years, he thought: a quiet strength that transcended his upbringing in the sheltered Valley, and that was rooted in his faith in Elsinoth.

He too had known something of the special peace given to all those who followed Elsinoth. Lately, however, he seemed to have lost some of that peace. He knew he had been relying too much on his own strength and had failed to look to Elsinoth for guidance. Silently he vowed to himself to make amends. From the stillness of his icy prison, he sent a voiceless cry to Elsinoth for help.

Zendos sat in one of the Ice Castle's rooms, brooding over his plans while sucking on a cube of ice. It had given him great satisfaction to capture his wretched cousin with his friends the previous day. The Tissirim had assured him that there was no one else in the city, so for the moment he needn't fear any further trouble. He wondered again how they could possibly have known where he was. Had it just been Athennar's inspired guess?

Again he pondered how best to deal with Athennar and his friends now that they were safely entombed. Perhaps he should leave them like that for a while longer. That alone might teach them a lesson. He could then free Athennar's head while keeping his body frozen—just so that his cousin could answer his questions. No doubt having suffered the agony of being unable to move yet remaining conscious would make Athennar more co-operative. Once he had supplied the required information, Zendos would think of a suitable way of disposing of him, and his fellow intruders.

First, however, he must make sure that he would be warned of anyone coming to rescue them. They might be missed in a few days' time. Rising, he strode out of his palace room, calling the Tissirim rebels to follow him. Eight of them were in the palace with him; the others were performing different duties elsewhere in the city. Zendos decided that he would station Tissirim guards at suitable intervals around the city walls to ensure that he would be given warning of the approach of any more troublemakers. Leaving two Tissirim guards in the antechamber—it always paid to be careful—he left the palace with the six remaining Tissirim. He would deal with his cousin's group later.

Athennar lay looking upwards, his mind reawakened. He supposed he had somehow slept, although he would never before have thought sleep possible with his eyes open. He wished he could close them; they ached from the constant glare, reduced though it was by the thick ice around him. Vaguely he wondered how long he had been imprisoned; it might have been hours or days. Time had somehow lost its meaning. He tried to yawn and stretch, and then remembered that he couldn't. How he ached to be free again. At moments like these, he almost wished he had not been born son of the Guardian, but had just been left free to roam the Realm with Sash and Kal and his other friends. The feeling soon passed. Responsibility brought its own reward—that of seeing people freed from the bonds of cruelty, released from oppression. How he wished someone would release him. If only he could get his hands on Zendos …

As the thought passed through his mind, he realised that something was happening to the ice around him. A blue light seemed to surround it, coursing through it. Was this, then, the first taste of insanity, or were his eyes betraying him because they were strained by the glare? The blueness seemed to pulsate rhythmically, almost hypnotically. No, it wasn't insanity after all. It was Zendos—returned to torture him.

Gradually, he became aware that the ice was getting thinner. All at once he knew what was happening— the ice around his head was beginning to melt. All he could do was wait helplessly, hoping that somehow it wasn't a dream—that he would soon be breathing fresh air again. A shadow fell across his eyes as a figure blocked out the light. Athennar suddenly realised that the dream might become a nightmare, for he had no illusions that Zendos would show him any mercy.

23

The Two Zorgs

A shimmering haze lay on the land. Kess mopped his brow as he trotted along beside Blazer. To give the faithful horse some rest—and to keep himself fit—he had taken to dismounting and running alongside whenever he felt able. Whisper sat on Blazer, mostly thoughtful and quiet. She was unused to the heat of the summer sun, and had it not been for the urgency of their mission, she would probably have fallen asleep.

Despite the trickles of sweat that ran down his back, Kess was relieved not to be riding on the horse with this mysterious young woman. She had unsettled him, and he needed time to think and to assess the situation. He was still unsure of whether he had made the right decision in accompanying her, but having made that decision there was little point in brooding over it.

There are so many unknowns, he thought, glancing up at Whisper. He wished he knew more about her. For the first day or two, she had chatted quietly as they travelled; mainly about the thrill of being away from the mist that had entrapped her for so long. She revelled in the sights and sounds around her but gave away little of her own story, even of her time in the mist. As the days passed she had gradually become more aloof, draping herself in a mantle of silence, only occasionally shrugging it off to converse with Kess. At least they were not far from the fortress now. Perhaps Meltizoc or Tolledon would be able to learn more from her.

As if reading his thoughts, she looked down at him with a slight smile on her face. 'Are we nearing the fortress?' she asked softly.

'We should reach it some time this afternoon,' he replied. Then, choosing his words carefully, he asked: 'Who are you, Whisper? Where is your home?'

She ignored the questions, just as she had done previously when he'd asked. 'I can't wait to be inside and to have a good night's sleep for a change,' she said. A furrow creased her brow as she thought of the people she would meet at the fortress. 'I hope Tolledon will be able to shed some light on the rhyme,' she added wistfully.

Kess shrugged, a doubtful look crossing his sun-warmed features.

'You will help, won't you, Kess?' Whisper demanded suddenly in urgent tones. 'I'm sure that the contents of the chest—when we find it—will help you to find your sister.'

Kess looked even more dubious.

'Cheer up! At least it's a fair possibility—and you would never forgive yourself if you didn't at least attempt to help me find it. You wait—you'll be glad you decided to help me.'

Kess didn't reply. He hoped she was right.

Two bedraggled figures wandered wearily over a long, straggling hillside. One of them—a squat, scarred character with an empty eye socket—shuffled grumpily over towards a large rock and sprawled unceremoniously in the shade.

'Get up, you lazy lump of dung,' grumbled the taller figure.

'Come off it, Gur'brak. This sun is burning me to a frazzle. I've had enough. I need a rest.'

Gur'brak looked at his companion sourly. For a moment, he considered kicking him into action, but then thought better of it. Anyway, he was exhausted, too. They seemed to have been wandering around this land for months. After travelling all the way to the east coast, they had failed to steal a boat in which they could get back to the Southlands. The Zorg captain had been relieved in a way because the sea journey would have terrified him, and he was by no means sure that they would have survived the voyage—especially with a useless companion like Bar'drash.

Eventually, and very reluctantly, Gur'brak had decided that the only way to return to the safety of the Southlands was via the Fortress of Fear. The longer they stayed in the north, the more nervous he became. He didn't want to suffer the same fate as his dead colleagues. The main problem with his latest idea was the question of how they could sneak into the fortress once they reached it, and pass through without being noticed. Perhaps they could slip through the gates at night behind some unsuspecting travellers. It was a slim chance because there weren't many travellers in these parts, but it was the only idea he could think of at the moment.

He looked at Bar'drash. His stumpy companion had already fallen asleep and was snoring heavily. Gur'brak gave a sigh, then slumped down beside him. Within moments, he too was fast asleep.

Two hours later, Gur'brak awoke from his snooze. He scratched his deformed ears and picked a scab off his face, flicking it over the rock. He looked at his

snoring companion, who was not a pretty sight, and
grunted. Getting up, he prodded Bar'drash with his
foot. The sleeping Zorg just turned over and snored
even more loudly. This time, Gur'brak kicked him,
and bellowed in his ear. 'Get up, you pathetic apology
for a Zorg! You make enough noise to be heard in the
Southlands.' He kicked him again.

Bar'drash staggered to his feet, rubbing both his
good eye and the empty socket from force of habit. He
yawned and spat on the ground. 'Aw, couldn't I have a
bit longer? We've only been here a few minutes.'

'A few hours, more like,' grumbled Gur'brak. 'With
you giving an imitation of a snuffling hog all the time.
It's time we were on our way. We can't be all that far
from the fortress by now.'

'That's what you said two weeks ago, before we
ended up at the other coast. *And* last week, when we
got lost in those hills. Anyway, what are we going to do
when we do find it? We can't exactly walk up to the
doors and ask them to let us in.'

'Very funny. I've got a plan. At least, I will have by
the time we get to the fortress. There's no need to
worry your pretty little head about it.'

'Like your plan to find a boat at the coast, I suppose?
Huh!' Bar'drash had been made bold by weeks of
frustration spent wandering hopelessly around the
countryside, sometimes going hungry for days on end
and other times having to survive on berries or raw
rabbit. He was encouraged in his boldness by the fact
that Gur'brak wasn't quite as ill-tempered as he used
to be.

Gur'brak's tongue had lost only a little of its biting
edge, however. 'Have you got any better ideas, Tark's
breath? If there was a brain inside your head instead
of sludge, you might come up with some useful
suggestions instead of moaning all the time.'

Bar'drash's empty eye socket glared at Gur'brak, but he didn't reply. Scratching his stomach, he yawned again, and climbed up onto the rock to see if he could spot the fortress.

'Now where are you going?'

'Hey, Gur'brak,' he hissed, 'there's someone coming this way.'

'What are you talking about, you demented shorot?' Gur'brak climbed up to join his companion. Sure enough, in the distance was a horse and rider, and another figure walking alongside. They were coming straight towards the rocks.

Gur'brak pulled Bar'drash down before they were spotted, and then sat and thought for a moment. 'This might be our chance,' he said.

Bar'drash looked at him blankly. 'How d'you mean?'

'It looks like a man and a woman. We can easily deal with them. Then, if we put their clothes on, we might be able to sneak into the fortress in disguise. If it's dark, and there are other people going in, we might not be noticed.'

'Like a Tark wouldn't be noticed in a flock of crows. Anyway, their clothes would never fit us.'

'We can easily adjust them a bit by cutting off the edges with our knives, and making a slit here and there so they're not too tight.'

'Hold on,' said Bar'drash suspiciously. 'Who's going to wear the woman's clothing?' He screwed up his face in disgust.

'Who do you think?' sneered Gur'brak. ''As captain, I have first choice. I always thought you'd look pretty in a dress.' He gave a loud, mocking guffaw, then fell quiet as he realised that the travellers must be getting near. 'Let's slip down behind that rock over there,' he hissed.

Bar'drash grumbled but followed anyway, despite having serious doubts about this latest 'plan'.

Kess directed Blazer towards the group of rocks, thinking that it would be good to find some shade and have a short rest. As they approached the hill, his sharp hearing picked up the sound of coarse laughter suddenly cut short. He looked up at Whisper and saw that she, too, had heard the sound. Drawing his sword, he motioned her to steer the horse away from the rocks. So far, they had managed to avoid the few groups of roving bandits that lived in the north, but he wasn't prepared to take any chances.

He was surprised when Whisper leaped nimbly from Blazer's back to walk beside him. There was a sudden shout, and two Zorgs hurtled out of the rocks and came at a stumbling run towards them.

Kess groaned to himself. This was all they needed. Striding forward to fend off the attack and protect Whisper, he found that she was following him. 'Get back!' he hissed. 'You're unarmed.'

'Not completely,' she replied.

Kess had no time to answer, as the first Zorg was upon him. The grimy creature swung his sword, but Kess blocked the blow. He stabbed at the Zorg, but missed. Gur'brak, seeing his chance, swiped at Kess, his blunt sword making a long, dark scratch on the Quiet One's leather jerkin. Knocking the sword away, Kess swung once more at his opponent. This time he cut into Gur'brak's tough skin. The Zorg gave an angry bellow. Kess knew he would have to beware. The Zorg may be slow, but he was probably much stronger than Kess. Even as the thought crossed his mind, the enraged Gur'brak slipped past Kess' sword and wrestled him to the ground. His weight was enough to ensure that the Valley man was unable to move. Grinning now, the Zorg drew his dagger.

Meanwhile, Bar'drash had decided to tackle what he considered the easier victim—the slightly built young woman. He waved his sword in front of her and cackled. 'D'you want to give in now, dearie, or would you prefer a fight?' he leered.

Whisper smiled back at him, unnerving him, and waved her hand gently in the air in front of the Zorg.

Bar'drash watched stupidly as a narrow band of mist formed, drifted over to him and wrapped itself around his head. 'I can't see!' he screamed, tearing at the mist, and scratching his own face as his hands passed straight through it. He danced round in circles, yelling desperately for help.

Gur'brak, distracted by his companion's shrieks, looked up just in time to see Bar'drash come reeling towards him. 'Watch out!' he shouted, but he was too late, and was sent flying.

Kess was quickly on his feet, and he pressed the sharp point of his blade against the back of the Zorg captain's neck. 'Drop your knife and put your hands behind you!' he commanded.

Gur'brak had no choice but to obey, expecting any moment to feel the sharp stab that would end his life. To his surprise, it did not come.

Calling Blazer over, Kess slipped his long rope from its sling holder and secured Gur'brak's hands with one end. He searched the Zorg for weapons, then pulled him roughly to his feet.

Whisper joined him, leading Bar'drash, who was still trying vainly to tug at the misty blindfold. She had already relieved him of his sword and dagger. Kess tied Bar'drash's hands with the same rope, keeping a good length by which he could control the Zorgs from horseback. Then he nodded to Whisper to indicate that he had finished.

Gliding gracefully over to Bar'drash, she passed her hand through the mist around his head. It vanished.

Bar'drash staggered and rubbed his eye again. 'How did you do that?' he demanded.

'I was just about to ask the same question,' Kess added.

Whisper smiled mysteriously. 'It was just a little trick I picked up from the Mist Mistress.'

'A very useful one,' replied Kess. 'My thanks!'

'Consider it payment of a debt,' responded Whisper, and she smiled again.

The two Zorgs didn't understand the conversation at all.

'Why did you have to crash into me, you miserable scum-bag?' snarled Gur'brak. 'I was just about to finish him off.'

'I couldn't help it,' complained Bar'drash. ''I couldn't see a thing. It was 'orrible. Awful it was: like a clammy hand over my eye. 'Orrible!' He shuddered.

'Oh, shut up! I should have known better than to leave you with even the simplest of tasks. Bah! Beaten by an unarmed woman. You brainless spawn of a barak.'

Whisper had meanwhile remounted Blazer, followed by Kess. The Valley man felt safer on the horse, despite the distraction of Whisper. 'I suggest you two stop talking and start walking,' he said, jerking the rope. 'Otherwise we'll start riding and drag you along behind.'

'Where are you taking us?' asked Gur'brak.

'To the Fortress of Fear,' replied the Quiet One.

The Zorg captain groaned.

'At least you'll have your wish to get into the fortress,' Bar'drash said to him sarcastically.

Gur'brak kicked him and then started plod-
ing reluctantly in the direction Kess had indicated,
pulling his disgruntled companion along behind
him.

24
The Riddle of the Chest

Merric paced restlessly along the battlements. Time
was passing too slowly, and he was constantly frustrated by the lack of progress. He had spent many
hours helping Tolledon and Meltizoc, poring over
vague maps of the Southlands, and planning where
best to send scouts. It was all guesswork, though, as he
well knew. If only they could gain some clue to
Linnil's whereabouts. The main hope—indeed the
only hope, it seemed—lay with the small group who
had gone in search of Zendos. They should easily
have reached the Ice Kingdom by now. He wondered
what they were doing and wished he was with them.
He knew, however, that he had to stay at the
fortress in case any news of Linnil arrived. He
wanted to be ready to set off in search of her
immediately.

The minstrel stopped his pacing and gazed out
northwards across the plains below the fortress. Some
figures were approaching slowly, two of them on
horseback. Merric started as he recognised the horse
and one of the riders. *Kess!* Rushing from the battlements, he shouted for the gates to be opened.
Tolledon and Meltizoc, who had been engaged in
earnest discussion in the courtyard, heard the

troubadour's shout, and followed him as he raced towards the huge gates.

Merric's surprise grew as the strange party rambled towards the fortress. Kess seemed to have captured two Zorgs and a woman—single-handed! As he watched, the Valley man coaxed the Zorgs into a shambling run. When he reached the gates, he leaped from Blazer and embraced the minstrel.

'Merric! It's good to see you again.' Kess shook hands with Tolledon and Meltizoc, but then burst out urgently, 'Is there any news of Linnil?'

Meltizoc shook his head. 'I fear not. But who are your captives? And where are the others?'

Kess turned to look at Whisper, who was still astride Blazer and watching with bemusement. 'Oh, this is Whisper—she's a friend I met some days ago. These two Zorgs attacked us this morning, but we managed to overcome them.'

Meltizoc raised an eyebrow at these revelations.

'But where is my son, and your fellow travellers?' Tolledon asked sternly.

'They carried on towards the Ice Kingdom. They were all well when we parted. Whisper needs your help, so I came back with her.'

'Perhaps we had better discuss all this inside,' suggested Meltizoc. 'I expect you could also manage a good meal.'

Tolledon nodded his agreement, even as he ordered some guards to take away the Zorgs and feed them. Merric noticed Gur'brak's surly face light up with surprise. Perhaps he had expected to be tortured and killed, not fed!

'Now,' said Tolledon, when they had finished their meal, 'perhaps you could tell us a little more about yourself, Whisper.'

Kess had already related the tale of the company's encounter with the Mistress of the Mysteries of the Mist.

Whisper appeared hesitant. 'There's nothing much to tell,' she answered slowly. 'I can't remember much of my past—only dim snatches of it.'

Meltizoc looked at her doubtfully. 'You seem to have a very clear memory of your time in the mists,' he said. 'Why should you not remember the time before that?'

Flushing angrily, Kess was about to leap to her defence, but the wise man waved him back.

'I—I vaguely remember being on a journey and wandering into the mists when I was very tired,' said Whisper, her soft tones barely audible. 'But why I was alone there, I don't remember.'

'Very well,' responded Tolledon, although far from satisfied with her answer. 'Your account of Gwindirpha—if indeed it was her—seems to fit what little I know of her disappearance aeons ago. You explained earlier that you need our help to find a chest, and that you had a rhyme that I might be able to help you solve. Could we hear it, please?'

Whisper nodded nervously, and produced her tattered piece of parchment. She began to read it, her voice gathering courage as she did:

'A book of where and how and what and why
Of those who have the truth that lies behind each lie.
When secrets of the past again are opened wide;
The strands revealed from which all life is tied.
Where stones are things of beauty, made of wood,
Tho' hollow heart be covered, your chest is stained
     with blood.
When all that has lain quiet comes crashing,
tumbling down
Then in the centre, deep inside, the source of

wisdom's found.
To find what is within, the seeker has to see
That that which is within must truly be the key.'

Looking hopefully at Tolledon, she added, 'I think the last section means that the rhyme is the key to where the chest is. Your son thought that you might understand the remainder.'

She passed the parchment to the Guardian, who studied it carefully.

Meltizoc also peered over his shoulder at the words. The wise man gave a slight gasp of realisation. 'The book! I thought it had been destroyed!' He paused, realising that the others were bewildered by his strange outburst. 'The first four lines refer, I believe, to the long-lost Great Tome of Neldra. Neldra was a wise man and historian who, as well as writing the Learned Scrolls of Neldra—recounting the history of the Realm—also wrote the little known Great Tome. Apparently this book contained details that hinted at many mysteries, including that of the specific where-abouts of the various objects Elsinoth made as reminders of his powers. This could be the "where, how, what, why" of the rhyme; those who hold the objects would be the "who". As the rhyme also tells, the objects symbolise the very strands from which life is composed. If the Tome were indeed in the chest, it would truly be a valuable find. But I'm not sure I understand the rest of the riddle.'

'I may be able to suggest a solution to the other part,' Tolledon interposed. 'Beautiful stones are jewels; made of wood, they become the Jewelled Forest. The hollow heart must be a cave or something similar, covered—possibly with undergrowth—so it cannot be easily found. The blood-stained part is more difficult, but I seem to remember that in a certain part of the forest, the soil is made of a very deep red clay. Perhaps water seeping through this has found its way through into the cave. The "crashing, tumbling down" could mean that the cave was caused by a rock fall. However, some of these details may have changed since the rhyme was first written. Indeed, the chest may even have been found or destroyed.'

Seeing Kess' glum face, Meltizoc quickly added to Tolledon's words: 'Of course, there is a good chance that even after all this time it is safe—few folk live in the Jewelled Forest. Despite its lovely name, it is a cold, strange place.'

'We must go there,' decided Kess. 'It is the only hope for Whisper—and perhaps, too, for Linnil.'

'For Linnil?' repeated Merric, surprised.

'Whisper thinks that something in the book might help us to find her.'

Merric looked at the black-haired woman sharply but she just shrugged.

'Very well,' said Tolledon. 'I will send two of my best men with you.' Kess started to protest, but the Guardian interrupted him. 'Although the Northlands are safer at the moment, there are still groups of bandits—and occasional Zorgs, as you yourselves have discovered. They will think twice before attacking a group of four armed people. And there is more at stake here than just restoring Whisper— however important that might be.'

Kess nodded reluctantly. 'Can we start tomorrow?'

It was Tolledon's turn to nod. 'I will have four horses and the necessary provisions prepared. Meanwhile, I suggest that you both take some rest.'

Later, Kess lay in his room thinking over the recent meeting. It rankled with him that Meltizoc didn't seem to trust Whisper. Despite his own doubts, the Quiet One felt very protective of her.

A tap on the door of his room roused him.

'Come in!'

It was Merric. The troubadour looked tired and worried.

'What's the matter, Merric?' The troubadour had started pacing up and down the room, and his silence irritated Kess.

'I was wondering if I should accompany you. I am uneasy, my friend. Your friend Whisper is not all that she seems to be. I fear that she leads you into dangerous territory.'

'I'm going of my own free will,' replied Kess sharply, sitting up.

Merric gazed steadily at the young Valley man. 'I am just concerned for your safety.'

'I know,' said Kess, trying to take the edginess out of his voice. He shrugged, and ran his fingers through his tousled hair. 'But even Meltizoc said that it would be of help to find the Great Tome of Neldra. And it may just help in finding Linnil. I have no option but to try to find it.'

'Be on your guard. I fear that the young lady may not be telling you the whole truth.'

'Oh no?' snapped Kess, suddenly losing his patience completely. 'I seem to remember that you chose to conceal your true identity from us for some time. I have no need of your advice, nor of your company. Kindly leave!'

Merric paused, but then turned sadly and left the room.

In another room nearby, Whisper lay staring at the ceiling. It was good to be free at last. She contemplated the journey ahead and smiled. At least she had made sure she would be safe on her travels, even if the plan had involved raising Kess' hopes unfairly. Anyway, who was to say that his sister might not be found with the help of the chest's contents?

Even as the thought crossed her mind, she felt a slight pang of guilt. She had felt close to Kess on their journey together—even when they hadn't spoken much—closer than she had felt to anyone for a long time. She had almost told him everything but had stopped herself in time. No, if he knew, he would probably never trust her again. And now she needed his trust. Frightened that her strength might give out before the end of the journey, she had to know that there was someone who would do his best to make sure the chest was found before she faded completely. Although she hated to use Kess for her own ends—especially as she guessed he cared for her—she had little choice. She only hoped that if—when—they found the chest and the fluid, it would work as Gwindirpha had foretold, even after all these years.

The following morning, a small crowd assembled to bid the company farewell. Tolledon had selected two of his most trusted Hallion men to accompany Kess and Whisper. One was Marason, a tall, soft-spoken man who had been one of Hinno's three commanders in the battle to gain the fortress. The other was Callenor, another tall man, with a ready smile and quick reflexes. Both men were pleased to be sent on the mission; they liked Kess and also preferred to be outdoors rather than closeted in the stone confines of the fortress.

Kess thanked Tolledon and said his farewells to the Guardian and to Meltizoc. Looking up, he saw Merric standing on the battlements and felt a stab of annoyance. Turning from the minstrel's gaze, he kicked his horse into action.

Merric gazed down and sighed. These days he seemed to spend his time watching his friends leave on various expeditions. Wishing that he and Kess had parted on good terms, he sighed again and trudged down to join Tolledon and Meltizoc.

25
Rescue!

The figure drew closer, framed in blue light, as the ice began to thin. Athennar felt a wetness on his face and automatically shook his head. He could move it! He blinked the water from his eyelids so that he could look up at his tormentor. For a moment he stared in disbelief, then broke into a wide smile. 'Fashag!' he said. 'You'll never know how good it is to see you!'

The wizened face of the gnome peered down at him. 'Well, get up!' he said gruffly. 'I'll go and release the others.'

Athennar's smile grew wider. Slowly he stretched his aching limbs. A tingle ran through them, and they itched terribly. Carefully he tried moving one leg upwards, then the other. As the circulation returned, he gently levered himself upwards. Most of the ice that had surrounded him had vapourised. When he looked at Fashag, he could see why. The gnome rubbed his hands with an oily substance, then ran them over the ice block that held Vallel. Blue flames licked over the surface of the tomb, and the ice rapidly melted.

Athennar eased his aching back and stamped his feet. Then, remembering where he was, his hand went to his sword. It was still there, having frozen beside him. He gazed around but could see no signs of the Tissirim or of Zendos.

'If you're looking for those walking lumps of ice, forget it,' muttered Fashag. 'I passed six of them going towards the outer walls with a surly-looking character in a grey cloak. There were two on guard at the entrance to this place, but my fire proved more than a match for them. Come and help this young lady instead of just standing there!'

Still dazed, Athennar went to aid Vallel. Fashag had burned through the cord that held her wrists, and she was struggling to stand. The gnome meanwhile passed on to Valor in the next block.

'What ...?' said Vallel, looking bewildered. She hadn't seen her rescuer clearly.

'Fashag!' replied Athennar. 'He somehow found his way here—don't ask me how—and used his arts to free us.'

Very soon, Valor and Hesteron were also free. Valor's face was drawn and pale, but he was relieved to see his friends again. He suddenly gave a yelp of surprise. 'My hand! I can feel it! The ice must have countered the effects of the Mist Mistress' dagger. Either that, or the numbness has worn off naturally.' He smiled broadly.

As everyone began to recover, they all started asking questions at once, particularly of the gnome, but Fashag held up his hand. 'Let's say I came here out of curiosity. I thought some of this white ice might prove a challenge to my crafts. When I was part way up the mountains, a white hawk came soaring out of the sky and hovered above me. I thought it might attack, so I aimed one or two bursts of flame to scare it off, but it persisted, staying a little way ahead of me. Then I remembered that you're an Animal Crafter, Athennar. So I decided to follow it. The bird led me to the city walls and then to this place.'

As they all started to thank him, he again put up his hand. 'Don't waste time with thanks. The bird showed me where you were. Now let's escape while we can.'

'First we have to find and question Zendos,' said Athennar. 'That's why we came here, and so far we have failed.'

The gnome glared at the Animal Crafter for a moment, but then nodded. 'Very well,' he said tersely. 'It might give me a chance to practise more on those Ice People.'

Athennar allowed himself a slight smile. He wasn't fooled by Fashag's bravado, his brusque manner, or his excuses for coming. The gnome had a kinder heart than he cared to admit. As they descended from the platform, Fashag brushed past him and he noticed with surprise that the gnome's natural skin colour was deepened by a wafer-thin layer of glowing yellow flame. As Fashag walked ahead, small pools of water were left where he had trodden.

They passed through into the hall of ice tombs and then into the small chamber. Athennar motioned them to hide on either side of the entrance hole; footsteps were approaching. A tinkling call came. When there was no response from within, two Tissi-rim stepped through the hole. Before any of the others had time to act, red flames shot from Fashag's hands. The Ice People gave gurgling sighs, then vanished leaving a white steam that drifted in the air for a moment before disappearing.

'Did you have to do that?' asked Athennar.

Vallel spoke before Fashag could answer. 'It seems with the Tissirim that it is all or nothing,' she said. Had Fashag not dealt with them, they would have attacked us and continued to do so. If you slice them up with a sword, they only regenerate themselves and the same is true if you melt them.'

Hesteron raised an eyebrow. 'You obviously risked your life for us as well,' he said gratefully.

Athennar nodded his agreement and peered out of the hole. No one was in sight, so he signalled the others to follow him as he climbed out.

'Where do we go to now?' asked Valor.

'Back to the large building by the wall,' replied Athennar. 'I have a feeling that part of the mystery of the empty city lies within it, and Vallel thought that someone was inside it. Could you break through the ice walls, Fashag?'

'Of course,' the gnome said huffily, as if surprised that anyone could doubt him.

Hesteron pointed to a nearby street. 'I think that's the way that Vallel and I came,' he explained. 'If so, it's probably the most direct route back.'

The company ran across the open space and then moved cautiously down the street that led to the Assembly Hall.

A white shape suddenly fluttered down and landed on Athennar's shoulder. It was Kal. He stroked the white hawk affectionately. 'It's good to see you, old friend,' the Animal Crafter said.

They reached the Assembly Hall safely. Once there, Fashag muttered for a moment and rubbed his hands. The glow surrounding his skin deepened and spread over his light clothing. Without further ado, he walked to the wall and gently pushed himself against it. The ice sizzled and turned into a cloud of white steam. When it had cleared, a gnome-shaped hole had appeared in the wall. Another sizzling of steam, and Fashag re-emerged, having made the hole wider on his journey back. 'The place is packed,' he said.

Stooping, the four friends followed him into the hall. Inside, an amazing sight greeted their eyes. I

was just as Fashag had said—the hall was packed with
Tissirim, most of them in the main part of the room,
but a few scattered on a raised area at the front. All of
the Ice People were frozen in various strange pos-
tures, many looking as if they had been stopped in
mid-flight from some obscure danger.

'Zendos' work,' breathed Athennar. 'Can you do
anything for them, Fashag?'

The gnome's glow had subsided again. He gazed at
the nearest Ice Person. 'I don't think so. It's safer for
them if I don't go too near. But why would Zendos
immobilise all of these people?'

'Perhaps because they are peace-loving and would
never agree to his evil schemes,' Athennar ventured.
'However, he must have found a few whom he could
corrupt.'

'Quite right, as usual, dear cousin,' came an oily-
smooth voice from the entrance.

'Zendos!' Athennar said the name like a curse,
berating himself for not posting a guard.

The sorcerer climbed through the entrance, his
sound-tube poised near his lips, trained on the five,
alert for any sign of movement. He motioned them
towards a space near the platform. 'I must admit it
gave me a surprise to see you crawling into here,' he
said. 'Though I assume our little yellow friend here
somehow released you from your ice prisons. Have
no fear—you will soon return there.' Waving his
hand, he summoned six Tissirim guards through the
hole to stand behind him.

Fashag started to raise his hand to blast them with
fire, but Athennar grabbed his wrist. He felt a warm
glow tingling in the palm of his hand. 'Don't risk it,'
he hissed. 'If Zendos uses his weapon, it will kill you
and could also rebound anywhere.'

'Very wise, cousin,' sneered Zendos. 'Protecting

your friends again, as usual. Now put your hands behind you, all of you!'

The friends had no choice but to obey, and Zendos motioned three of his rebel Tissirim to tie their hands, using the long coil of rope still slung around Hesteron's shoulder.

'You really would use that weapon, wouldn't you?' Hesteron growled.

'Of course! You of all people should know that by now.'

'Even though it would probably destroy several of the Tissirim as well?'

'They are expendable—just as you are.'

Athennar caught the gist of Hesteron's questioning and joined in.

'And what do you hope to achieve here, Zendos? Hiding away in a bolt hole doesn't seem to be your style.'

'Quite right again, cousin,' gloated the sorcerer. 'In time, I will have a formidable ice army under my control.'

'But the Tissirim are basically peace-loving people,' protested Valor.

'They may be now, but they will soon be under my control. Then they will do as I bid them.'

A tinkling voice came from behind Vallel. 'But ... you said we would be ... set free,' a rebel Tissir said, obviously confused.

'Quiet!' barked Zendos. The Ice Person shook his head and then returned to his master in dumb obedience. 'As you can see, I have already had some success,' said the sorcerer, a twisted smirk on his lips.

'It must require concentration and energy to maintain such power,' remarked Athennar innocently.

'Of which I have plenty!' snapped Zendos.

Hesteron started coughing loudly, and Athennar called out a few shrill notes.

Zendos remained unmoved, another sneer coming to his face. 'Don't think you can so easily distract me,' he said.

Even as he was speaking, a white shape shot down from where it had been hovering high in the hall. Answering Athennar's call, Kal alighted on the sorcerer's head, embedding her talons in his skin.

Shrieking in pain, Zendos fell to the floor, dropping his sound-tube. The friends were still roped together, but Vallel managed to get close enough to kick it some distance away. Zendos struck the hawk away and shielded his head against further attacks. His face was contorted with rage. 'I will teach you all to meddle with me. This time you will all die.' He started for the tube.

A tinkling sound came from behind Zendos, and then: 'Ice to water.'

Zendos turned even as one of the Tissirim melted into a pool at his feet. 'What …?' he said.

'Water to ice,' intoned another Tissir. The pool of water started to freeze over, creeping up Zendos' legs, around his body and over his head. The friends heard a muffled scream and then he was bound, solid.

One of the remaining Ice People pushed him over and, before any of the company knew what was happening, Zendos' frozen form shattered into pieces.

'He will not return,' one of the Tissirim chimed solemnly. 'In the name of peace, it had to be done.'

'In the name of peace,' agreed the other four Ice People.

'But … your friend …' gasped Vallel, staring in disbelief.

'He sacrificed himself. We have done wrong. We sought freedom, but instead brought death among our people.'

'And to Zendos,' whispered Athennar, his face drained of colour. 'Now how will we ever find Melinya or Linnil?' And he bowed his head in grief.

26

Thunder Goblins

'It's Ganniwaggik!' came a cry from behind Gatera. The Ancients pressed forward, surrounding the two friends.

Gatera looked around in dismay. There were far too many thunder goblins to tackle. For a moment he thought of suggesting to Rrum that they make a bid to escape down one of the tunnels, but he realised it would be futile. The tunnels were unlikely to lead anywhere other than the Ancients' living quarters.

The big Land Crafter had no illusions about the 'friendliness' of the thunder goblins. Perhaps they somehow maintained a friendly relationship with the Ancients, but he felt sure that would finish if the old folk ceased to be of use. He looked at Rrum and shrugged.

'We are outtnumbered,' his little friend said.

The leading thunder goblin interrupted. 'I believe there was something you wanted to say to us?'

'They were telling us lies about you,' called out one of the Ancients.

'Oh, lies, is it? We know how to deal with liars, don't we?' A wave of nods came from the other thunder goblins.

'We are looking for a friend of ours,' said Gatera,

forcing himself to speak softly despite his frustration. 'Your friends here seem to think you may be keeping her somewhere.'

'Oh, looking for the girl, are you? Well why didn't you say so? You'd better come with us.' With a sly wink to his companions, Ganniwaggik motioned to the tunnel. Ten of the thunder goblins went ahead, and as soon as Gatera and Rrum followed, the other ten closed in behind.

Gatera turned briefly to call to the Ancients. 'Goodbye! Think on what I said!' Then they followed their guards into the tunnel. Somehow Gatera knew that the old folk would never change their minds and try to escape from these dark passages—they had become too dependent on the thunder goblins.

The two friends were taken past the concealed door and on along the corridor for some distance. Eventually they reached another large chamber which was similar to the one in which they had met the Ancients. Yet again, a number of passages led from it. The Land Crafter and the Rrokki were taken towards one of these.

There was a chill atmosphere in the tunnel. Furtive shadows chased each other along the rough-hewn walls. The passage was short, terminating in four doors, two on either side. Gatera and Rrum were thrust roughly into an end one, and the Land Crafter was relieved of his staff and double-headed axe.

'Your friend is next door,' mocked Ganniwaggik, 'But you won't be seeing her. You can stay here until we decide what to do with you, or until the sorcerer returns.' Giving a final sneer, he slammed the door shut behind him.

'Sorcerer, eh?' mused Gatera. 'That must be Zendos or Dargan. I don't think I particularly want to be around when he arrives.'

'No needd,' grated Rrum. 'I can eatt a hole in the ddoor.'

Gatera smiled as he remembered how the little Rrokki had chewed his way round a bolt in Dargan's stronghold. 'First we have to decide what we will do when we get free,' he counselled. 'We've somehow got to rescue whoever's next door and then get past about twenty thunder goblins in that large chamber. If they catch us, they'll soon overpower us.'

He fell quiet for some time while Rrum inspected the door. 'I've got an idea,' he said finally. 'It's a little risky, but it may just work....'

A little while later, the two friends eased their way quietly out of the cell and paused by the next door. Unbolting it, they slipped inside. On the floor lay a golden haired woman, her features serene and peaceful in sleep.

'She's beautiful,' whispered Gatera. Moving over beside her, he put his hand over her mouth to stifle any scream. The woman awoke abruptly, her eyes wide at this new fear.

'It's all right,' Gatera hissed. 'We are friends, here to help you.' He released his hand from her mouth.

'Who are you?' she asked, bewildered, in a soft voice. 'And how did you ...'

'There will be time enough for questions later,' interrupted Gatera. 'The most important thing now is that we get out of here. Can you walk?'

The woman nodded and rose to her feet. She was tall and graceful; her white robe, hemmed in gold, flowed lightly with her every move.

Gatera explained his plan quickly. 'Stay close by me,' he instructed.

'May Elsinoth be with us!' the woman whispered.

The Land Crafter looked at her in surprise, then

nodded. 'Aye, we need all the help we can get,' he said. Moving over to the door, he listened for a moment before waving his friends over. 'Our success depends on surprise,' he continued, 'so we must be as quiet as possible until we reach the goblins' main chamber.'

He opened the door, and Rrum and the woman followed him as silently as they could. The corridor was dimly lit by torchlight filtering down from the chamber ahead. As the three slipped cautiously nearer the source of the light, they began to pick up snatches of goblin conversation.

'... I think we should roast 'em alive.'

'Nah, they'd be too tough to eat.' Coarse laughter followed this comment.

'I say bash their heads in.'

'The sorcerer wouldn't be pleased ...'

'Well, he isn't here, is he?'

'What about the woman?'

'We leave her. If we harmed her, the sorcerer *definitely* wouldn't be pleased.'

Gatera sneaked to the passage mouth and peeked out. The thunder goblins were slouched around tables, eating and drinking. Four torches sat in brackets around the walls, their bright light reluctantly gleaming off the creatures' sickly faces..

Silently, Gatera waved the other two forward. He edged his way out of the tunnel along one side of the chamber, while his friends moved over to the other side. The goblins were so busy arguing and slurping their food that none of them noticed until he reached the first torch. Then one of them looked up and gave a whining shriek: 'The giant! He's escaping!'

Grabbing the torch, Gatera waved it around his head, distracting the creatures' attention from his companions. Then he sent it flying into the midst of the thunder goblins, causing instant panic. Rushing to the second torch, he wrenched it from the bracket and raced towards the main tunnel. As he ran, he saw his staff and axe propped against a wall and he scooped them up.

Rrum and the woman had meanwhile snatched the other two torches and were also running towards the tunnel. As they reached it, they threw both torches into the confused pack of goblins, the flames going out as they landed on the floor, leaving the cave in darkness. Holding the remaining lit torch in one hand, Gatera grabbed the woman's hand in his other and rushed down the tunnel, with Rrum somersaulting alongside. Fortunately their enemies took a little time to recover before chasing after them.

When the three reached the chalk mark above the concealed door, Gatera quickly doused the torch, using a sheet of soft leather from his backpack. 'Lie down as close to the wall as you can!' he hissed to the other two.

Within moments, there were cries from the approaching goblins.

'Where's the light gone?'

'Perhaps they've escaped to the outside.'

'I can't see!'

The voices came nearer as the creatures made their way carefully along the passage. They had almost reached the hidden door when the leading thunder goblins found themselves heaved back into the midst of their friends by a huge pair of unseen hands. Thinking they were being attacked, their friends struck out in all directions. Yells and screams from the injured only served to heighten their frenzy. If any came near Gatera, he swung his staff in what he thought was the right direction. Several times he was right on target, sending the creatures flying.

Some of the goblins decided they had had enough and started dashing back to the main chamber in search of spare torches. One poor unfortunate, dizzy and disorientated from the fight, started running towards the Ancients' chamber. There were cries of, 'Stop him! He's escaping!' and the rest of the creatures chased after him, leaving just one or two unconscious forms in the darkness of the passage.

Fumbling in his haste, Gatera found a firestick and relit his torch. He glanced quickly at his two friends, who were still lying against the wall. 'Time to go,' he urged. Desperately he searched for the handle cut into the slab of stone. Then he found it and yanked hard. The door swivelled open and he waved to the other two. 'Come on! This is no time for hanging around. The goblins will be back ...'

'Your friend!' said the woman. 'He isn't moving!'

'W-What?' stammered Gatera. 'Here! Hold this door and the torch!'

The woman glided gracefully across to comply.

Gatera ran to his friend and picked him up. There was no sign of life, and an ominous stain was spreading over Rrum's side. Some lucky—or unlucky—sword thrust must have pierced his tough skin during the fray. Gatera gritted his teeth and carried the Rrokki into the tunnel. 'Go ahead of me, please,' he said to the woman as the door closed behind them.

Soon they were paddling through the waters of the stream, and after a while, fresh daylight began to filter into the passage. The woman doused the torch as they emerged into the warm afternoon sunlight. 'How is your friend?' she asked gently.

'I don't know,' Gatera replied gruffly. 'But I'm not going any further until I find out. I'll have a closer look at him in the cave up there.'

Carrying the still form of Rrum, he scrambled up

the hill to the cave. Once inside, he laid the rock man carefully on the floor.

'I'll get some water to cleanse his wound,' the woman said.

Gatera nodded gratefully and knelt down beside his little friend. 'Come on, you can't desert me now,' he whispered, a large lump coming to his throat. He pressed his ear to Rrum's chest, but could hear nothing. Unfortunately, he didn't know enough about the Rrokki to know whether he *should* have been able to hear anything. Trickles of moisture worked their way from his eyes, and he rubbed them away fiercely.

There was a sudden cry from the hillside, and moments later the young woman rushed into the cave. 'The thunder goblins! I can hear them coming along the passage.'

Gatera grimaced. 'There's nothing we can do now. You see to Rrum. I will hold them off at the cave entrance.'

'But there are too many ...'

'Do as I say!' he barked. Then he looked at her sadly. 'I'm sorry. This is the best we can do. Perhaps we should have left you in there. I hope they won't harm you. Look after Rrum, and pray that Elsinoth will help us now.'

It was the woman's turn to nod as the Land Crafter had one last look at his little friend and then moved towards the cave entrance. Gatera knew that this would be one of the first places the goblins would search. Although it was partly obscured from below by the bush in front of the entrance, he had little doubt that they would know about it. He knew too that he couldn't hope to defeat them all, but he intended to fight to protect his companions until there was no breath left in his body. A new, controlled

anger had gripped him and hardened his resolve.
Through the branches of the bush, he could see a
little way down the hill.

The thunder goblins emerged from the stream
opening. After some arguing and shoving, several of
them made their way up towards the cave. As they
approached, they grew more uncertain, obviously
worried about whether they might find the escaped
trio there. One of them, a particularly nervy creature,
kept whining as he scrambled reluctantly up the
hillside.

'Shouldn't the others come with us?'

The leader of the group looked at him sharply.
'Shuddup! We don't need their help.'

'But what if they've got friends in there with them?'

'Shuddup!' repeated the leader, now beginning to
look distinctly uneasy himself. Then, deciding he
would show his companions that he wasn't really
afraid, he left them standing and marched on ahead
by himself, trying to maintain an air of boldness. As
he came round the bush, Gatera grabbed him and
knocked him unconscious with a blow to his head.

The other goblins waited for a few moments before
anxiously calling to their leader to ask if he had found
anything. When they received no reply, they climbed
a little higher and called again.

They soon received an answer. The dazed body of
their friend came hurtling over the bush, crashing
into them and sending them flying. The thunder
goblins ran shrieking down the hill.

Gatera smiled grimly to himself. If only they came
up a few at a time, he might be able to deal with them
after all!

However, it was not to be. The fleeing scouts joined
with the rest of the goblins, and this time they all
started to climb the hillside in a long line.

Gatera sighed, then picked up a nearby boulder and sauntered casually around the rock to await his enemies.

The thunder goblins marched slowly uphill, nervously eyeing the large rock in Gatera's hands. When they were within reach, the Land Crafter hoisted the boulder high above his head and flung it with all his strength at the approaching line. Three of the goblins crashed down. For a moment, the line hesitated, but then the thunder goblins closed ranks and started climbing again towards the Land Crafter, brandishing short axes and swords.

Once more Gatera smiled grimly to himself as the sun's warmth seeped into his muscles. It was a pleasant day on which to die.

27

Farewell to the Ice Kingdom

Vallel moved over to comfort Athennar, while Hesteron approached the Tissirim rebels. 'Thank you—you saved our lives.' He gestured towards the other Tissirim filling the hall. 'Do you know how we might save your people?'

They looked at each other, but shook their heads. Athennar, still pale, came to join the Air Crafter. 'Yes, thank you,' he echoed quietly. 'If Zendos was going to use your people, he must have had an antidote for whatever mixture he used here. If you lead us to his quarters, we may be able to find it.'

'But we must be punished. We have done wrong and are guilty. It is our tradition.'

'Tradition or not, the most important thing now is that your people are restored to normal.' Then the Animal Crafter turned to speak to Fashag. 'My friend, you have helped us much. From what my father told me of Tissirim traditions, they have no burial grounds. Those of their people who die in battle—and don't ask me how that can happen—are commemorated by having their likenesses etched into blocks of ice; the tombs we passed earlier.

'There is no suitable burial place for Zendos, and for his shattered body to remain here would be considered a taint on the ice. We cannot take him with us. Could you …?' He left the question unsaid, but the gnome nodded in understanding.

Athennar's jaw set firm, trying to push back the memories of earlier, once happy days with his cousin. He motioned the Tissirim to lead the group to Zendos' home. As they left, they heard a hiss of steam as Fashag commenced his grisly task.

A search of Zendos' dwelling place revealed one flask of brown liquid, a few scrolls, some provisions and very little else. Athennar couldn't read the scrolls, and decided it would be best to destroy them. The flask of liquid seemed to be the only possibility for reawakening the Tissirim. He removed the stopper and sniffed at it. It had a foul, pungent smell, and he quickly replaced the stopper. 'This must be it,' he said to the others. 'If this doesn't work, I'm not sure what we will do.'

They returned to the Assembly Hall, the five rebel Tissirim trailing obediently behind. Halfway there, they came across the other rebels who had been elsewhere in the city. The Ice People conversed excitedly, and then fell silent, the newcomers joining the procession.

Fashag was waiting for them, squatting on the floor outside the entrance hole to the hall. He nodded once in answer to Athennar's unspoken question.

The Hallion man grimaced, then turned to the Tissirim. 'I cannot know whether this fluid will revive your people. It is best that we try it on just one of them first. Is this agreed? It may not do any harm; it may cure, or it may cause irreparable damage. You have a right to speak if you feel the risk is not worth while.'

The rebels looked at each other uncertainly, then slowly nodded their heads. 'It is agreed,' one of them replied.

'Good. Perhaps you could fetch one of your colleagues.'

The Tissirim disappeared into the entrance hole and were soon back, carrying the rigid form of one of the Ice People. They placed the frozen 'statue' upright, and at Athennar's signal, moved a little distance away.

'I don't want to turn you into statues accidentally—this may be the liquid Zendos used to immobilise your friends,' the Animal Crafter explained. He asked Hesteron to stand next to the frozen Ice Person in case it should revive and collapse with shock. Carefully opening the flask, he held it gently beneath the Tissir's head. Nothing happened, and Athennar groaned in dismay.

'Look!' said Valor, pointing to the ground. A drop of the fluid had fallen from the stopper onto the ice. Where it had touched, a yellow sheet of gas spread over the ground, encompassing the area around the Tissir's feet and wreathing upwards around its body. The friends held their breath in anticipation.

The Tissir's head moved slowly, and then it took a faltering step, its hand moving slowly up to its head. Muffled tinkling tones filled the air, and then it spoke in the language they could understand. 'What happened?' Its voice was like the sound of a bell with a rusted clapper.

'It worked,' said Hesteron as he steadied the Tissir.

Athennar nodded to the rebel Ice People, who came over and escorted their friend to a nearby block of ice and sat him down. 'I will go inside and drop some of this on the floor. It is probably best if just one of us goes as the fumes may cause some discomfort.'

Athennar disappeared through the hole.

'He is a good man,' muttered Fashag. Then, realising he had spoken aloud, he hastened to cover his embarrassment. '... I suppose,' he added.

Hesteron grinned and slapped the gnome on the back. He was rewarded with a scowl.

Within an hour, all the Tissirim were fully recovered. Most went cheerfully back to their homes. The Tessari, however, gathered round the friends to thank them, shaking their hands and talking in high, clear voices. Fashag backed away against a wall—he didn't like all the fuss.

'We are truly grateful for all your help,' one of the Ice Kings said to Athennar. 'We have fond memories of your father and of Meltizoc. You must persuade them to visit us again. All of you, of course, are welcome here whenever you wish.'

Athennar smiled.

Vallel, meanwhile, was having a long discussion with one of the Tessari, explaining about the rebel Tissir she had frozen into the wall of the ante-chamber in the palace.

'Do not fear,' the Tessar tinkled. 'He will just be—should I say—"suspended". We will thaw him, then separate his body waters from the waters of the wall. His life-essence hasn't been harmed, so he should recover fully once he is refrozen. It will be a long process, but it is to be hoped that he will have learned from the experience.'

'What about the other Tissirim who helped Zendos?' interrupted Valor, who had been listening to the conversation.

The Ice King who had been talking to Athennar turned to the Mountain Guard. 'They have done wrong and will be punished.'

'Those who do evil must suffer the consequences,' agreed Athennar. 'But I would ask you to show mercy in this case. These Ice People rebelled and they *were* wrong, but much of what they did was under the

control of Zendos, and not of their own free will.
They did much to atone for that by saving our
lives—even at the cost of losing one of their own.'

After a pause, the Ice King replied: 'You may be
correct. What do you have to say?' he asked of the
rebels, who were standing in a small group to one
side.

'We have done wrong,' they replied. 'We were
promised freedom for all of the Tissirim. We had
forgotten we are already free. We risked the death of
our people.'

The Ice King turned back to Athennar. In a quiet
voice, he said, 'I think they have learned. We may give
them some light tasks to serve as punishment, but do
not fear. As you say, they have provided some
atonement already. Without their help there would
be no Tessari to pronounce judgement. They have
also given us cause for thought. Perhaps we have
been too long alone, and should be more involved
with the other peoples of the Realm.'

His voice turned more sombre, the bell-like tones
being strangely muted. 'The Tissirim are reputed to
show little emotion—yet we do feel, though perhaps
at different levels and in different ways from your
own races. We will mourn the passing of the five
whose bodies are no more. It is a rare thing for the
Tissirim numbers to be reduced.'

He saw Athennar glance at Fashag.

'Do not let your friend feel guilt,' he continued. 'He
put your lives before those he thought were seeking
to kill you. The Tissirim were in the wrong, as we
have said. He acted out of love for you.'

'The gnome seems cold, but his heart is warm,'
replied Athennar. Then, realising that he might have
offended the Tessar, he hastily added, 'I did not
mean to imply ...'

'Do not apologise,' interrupted the Ice King, giving the nearest sound to a chuckle that Athennar had heard. 'We understand your human ways of explaining emotion by degrees of coldness or warmth.' He grasped Athennar's arm. 'I am sorry that you had no chance to learn the information you needed from Zendos. Perhaps Elsinoth will reveal it in his own time.'

'You have heard of Elsinoth?' exclaimed Valor, unable to suppress the comment in time.

Another merry tinkle came from several of the Ice Kings. 'Of course!' one replied. 'We may be cut off from much that happens in the Realm, but we are not cut off from the Mighty One. He cares for all his people, wherever they are, and of whatever race. Perhaps, however—as my friend said—more contact with other peoples would widen our understanding of his ways.'

'And now,' the first Ice King said, 'the next few days will be very busy; repairing our homes and preparing for two days of mourning. Will you stay with us?'

Athennar wearily shook his head. 'I fear we must return in the morning with the news of Zendos, although it seems to end all our hopes.'

'While life remains, hope too is present, even though it may seem well concealed. Trust in Elsinoth.'

'You sound like my father,' said Athennar wryly.

'Thank you—he is a wise man,' countered the Tessar. 'Now we must find you all some rooms for the night.'

Early the next day, the friends were ready to leave the Ice Kingdom. Vallel, in particular, promised to return one day. The Tessari had been delighted to hear of her love for water, and had spoken at some length with her, both sides gaining in knowledge.

Hesteron and Valor were eager to be on their way once more, and Fashag was starting to fidget, muttering to himself.

The failure of their quest seemed to have aged Athennar. It was plain from his discussions with the Tessari that Zendos had given no clues as to Dargan's or Linnil's whereabouts. It was also clear that Melinya was not held within the Ice Kingdom. Although he knew his first responsibility was to his friends and the future of the Realm, he longed to be free to search for her. The one consolation was that Zendos would have no more opportunities to torment the one he loved. He just hoped Melinya could survive and had sufficient provisions to last until he could find her.

They reached the kingdom's outer wall. Fashag was about to melt his way through it, but one of the Tessari moved in front of him and ran his fingers over the wall, part of which melted instantly.

'I must find out how they do that some time,' the gnome muttered.

With a final farewell, the friends passed out of the city of ice and on to the snowy plains beyond. After a short distance, they looked back. The hole in the wall had disappeared as if it had never been there. Kal, who had perched briefly on Valor's shoulder, muttered a sharp 'Keek!' into the Mountain Guard's ear before rising up into the sky. The young man jumped, and then playfully shook his fist at the hawk. The others laughed as some of the tension of their time in the city drained away.

A light snow started falling as they crossed the plains of the Ice Kingdom. Reaching the ridge above the plains, they stopped briefly to bid farewell to Kal, who hovered over them before flying away to her home. Then, as they had just started making their way down the snowy slopes, a cold wind blew up.

Within moments, the way ahead was obscured. The wind whipped snow flurries into their faces, like thousands of tiny needles stinging their skin. The four friends pulled their cloaks more tightly around themselves. Fashag, while not liking the weather, seemed otherwise unaffected by it. His smouldering shield hissed constantly as it snuffed out the snow-arrows.

The company huddled together in a small hollow which gave a little protection from the worst of the wind. There was no point in travelling further until the storm had subsided; for all they knew they might even now be on the brink of a precipice.

The snow lashed around them for some time, cocooning them in a world of white misery and bringing with it a reminder of the hopelessness of their situation. They had failed in their task and now they were further away than ever from finding Dargan, Linnil or Melinya. Fashag tried to ease their misery by warming them, but the howling wind prevented any communication, and increased their sense of futility. Only Athennar, having recovered from his earlier dismay, and because of his love for Melinya and his rekindled trust in Elsinoth, still held out any hope. After all, the Mighty One had protected them in the Ice Kingdom, against all the odds. It seemed ungracious to admit defeat now.

At last, as quickly as it had begun, the storm passed. They brushed away the snow that had gathered around them and prepared to start off again. Then, noticing a movement to their right, Athennar hissed a warning. About fifty yards away, two gigantic ice bears were shaking the snow from their coats. They were truly magnificent creatures and moved with a grace that belied their size.

The company remained absolutely still, entranced

by the sight. Fashag, more conspicuous in his everyday clothes, hid behind Athennar and peeked out occasionally. Fortunately they were down-wind from the bears. Athennar wished he had time to try and communicate with them. Silently, he vowed to himself that one day he would return and try to befriend the creatures.

The bears' acute hearing picked up some small noise that was out of place. They both stopped and stood alert for a moment on their hind legs, sniffing the air. Then they turned nimbly and raced away across the snow.

The travellers breathed sighs of relief and admiration. They felt privileged to have seen such a sight, yet relieved that they had not been attacked by the bears. Forgetting their earlier despair for a while, they continued down the mountain.

28

A Test of Power

Dargan was pleased with his progress, though it had taken time; more time, in fact, than he had really expected. At last, however, he had been able to tap a small portion of the Sceptre's power. The effort left him feeling drained but also more triumphant each time.

At first he tried simple tasks, extensions of his own power. He strengthened the link between his one good eye and the jade Eye carried by his servants; as an experiment, he had sent Targul up into the sky with the object and found that the view in his mind was much clearer than it had ever been before.

Not content with such minor triumphs, the Dark Master delved deeper into the Sceptre, drawing some of its power into his own mind, caressing it, storing it. He knew that he understood only a fraction of the Sceptre's capabilities; he also knew he would have to proceed carefully to avoid losing control of his own powers. Slowly, he tried new experiments. Calling in a Zorg slave, he would bend the poor creature's mind to his own will. Whereas previously this had taken much effort and tended to be rather short-lived, he found that he could now have far more control, with much less strain upon his own reserves. What is more, the control seemed to last until a time of his own choosing. He could then switch it off as easily as he had started it.

New ideas came to Dargan's mind. The power of the Sceptre opened up a wide range of interesting possibilities. Above all else, however, he craved the eventual domination of the Realm. He would subdue its peoples and turn the land into a barren wilderness. Beautiful scenery irritated him: like an itch he was unable to scratch. Once, he had appreciated such beauty—now he saw it as a threat to his purposes. His one desire was to rid the world of such distractions; they were for weaklings. The world that he would create would be stark and cold. Oh, he might allow a few edible plants and vegetables to survive, in order to prevent his diet from becoming too boring—but nothing ornamental. He couldn't risk anything that might divert the attention of his new subjects from carrying out his will.

With renewed patience, he started stretching his control to other living things. At first he started with tiny seedlings and small insects. After much trial and error, he found that he could make the insects grow weaker. To his surprise, instead of shrivelling up, they began to fade. Over a number of days, they became increasingly transparent, until at last they disappeared completely.

Dargan gave a cry of elation. His enhanced powers were even greater than he had suspected. As he grew in strength, he would be able to alter the entire face of the Realm. Trees, shrubs, flowers, animals, birds—anything in fact that annoyed him—could be dispensed with!

He changed his attention from the insects to the seedlings. These proved more difficult to control and he had to experiment for days to learn how to manipulate his will to affect such things. The plants had no minds; they just lived and grew, existing without seeming to know they were doing so. However, with painstaking progress, and with careful use of the Sceptre's powers, he gradually unlocked their inner secrets. His will probed deep into each cell, exploring, sensing, modifying. Slowly, almost imperceptibly at first, the little plants also started to fade. Within days they had vanished.

Dargan cackled to himself. His face was drawn and lined from the hours of continuous work, and his eyes had once more turned a dull uniform grey. An onlooker may have thought that his madness was turning to mindlessness. However, he knew that the true situation was far different. As he drew increasingly upon the Sceptre's powers, his experiments would produce more and more dramatic results. A vision of empty landscapes flickered briefly through his mind. Yes, the plains around his old stronghold had been scarred and battered, but much of that was due to his minions ravaging the countryside, scaring the animals away, poisoning the land. This was different—it involved total mental control!

He knew then what his next task must be. Working his powers upon the feeble Zorgs was all very well, but the creatures had undeveloped brains and put up little resistance. Total control of a human would take much more strength and more subtlety. He was nearly ready. When the moment came, he would fetch the girl.

Linnil lay on her small grey bed, staring up at the ceiling. How long had she been here? Why didn't Kess and the others come for her? And what was Dargan doing? She had hardly seen him since he had played the cruel trick on her, letting her think she could escape. That had been the blackest day of her life. To experience such agony, knowing that her every move had been anticipated by Dargan's warped mind, knowing even that he had somehow created the illusions that had seemed so real at the time—it had all proved too much. For days she had lain on her bed, barely eating, refusing to speak to her Zorg jailer.

Gradually, from deep within, she had summoned strength. Whereas she had felt deserted, she now felt reassured that, whatever else befell her, Elsinoth still cared for her and watched over her. Quite where the feeling came from, she wasn't certain—maybe it had grown from the small core of peace that had always been with her. It was reassuring, though. The Mighty One had never promised an easy road through life, only his love and favour. In the shelter of her Valley home, she had never known the dangers that lurked in other parts of the Realm. Now she knew, and she prayed for strength not to succumb again to the clutches of despair. No, she would fight Dargan in any way possible if the opportunity presented itself. Unfortunately, there didn't seem to be any such opportunity at the moment.

Her thoughts drifted to Kess; to Merric. She wondered if they thought of her, then smiled. In her heart she knew they would be thinking of her constantly, trying desperately to find her. At any moment they might appear with the others: Valor, bravely brandishing his sword; Athennar taking immediate command of the situation. She only wished they would hurry; she had a feeling that Dargan would not be leaving her alone for much longer.

As if in answer to her thoughts, the cell door was dramatically flung open. Dargan stood in the entrance, gazing down with his usual sneer. 'Hello, my sweet. I trust you are enjoying my hospitality? I thought it was time you sampled some of the other delights of my humble little kingdom.' He snapped his fingers and the Zorg jailer came in and pulled her roughly from the bed.

'All right, I'm coming anyway. It's hardly as if I had any choice,' she said.

Dargan signalled and the Zorg released her. She edged away from him; a foul staleness hung over the brute like a shroud.

'Very well,' replied Dargan. 'Follow me, if you would be so kind.' He walked off briskly and the Zorg prodded her into action.

Reluctantly, she followed the retreating figure down two passages until they reached a heavy oak door. It swung open easily under the touch of the Dark Master's fingers.

Linnil paused for a moment, but the Zorg jailer pushed her roughly inside, then closed the door. Dimly, she heard his footsteps receding down the corridor. For some reason, she felt even less safe now the Zorg had gone.

The room was similar to the one Dargan had occupied in his old stronghold. The walls were lined with row upon row of books, many of them old and tattered. Indeed, a fusty smell of age hung over the whole room. Heavily scarred desks supported piles of weathered parchments or collections of bottles, most of which held items that Linnil tried to avoid looking at too closely.

Although the room was obviously well used, it also had an air of neglect. Thick cobwebs draped across the corners between walls and ceiling. In one corner lay a lute coated in thick dust. The thought that Dargan had perhaps once enjoyed music came as a shock to Linnil.

'Welcome to my room, my sweet,' chuckled Dargan. 'Perhaps you would care to sit over there.' He pointed to a tall padded chair over to one side.

Linnil was about to protest when she felt Dargan's mind grip her own. Instantly, to her dismay, she found herself walking to the chair and sitting down.

'Excellent, my dear. Now, I'm afraid I must tie you up for the time being, then I will release my control—unless you start to do something silly, like complain endlessly, of course.' He bound her wrists firmly to the arms of the chair, and her ankles likewise to its legs.

'Now that I have your undivided attention, I have to tell you that I brought you here to, er, assist me in a little experiment. You have already experienced my considerable powers over your mind; particularly over "persuading" you to obey me. However, forcing you to obey my will is one thing—it is quite another to be able to change your personality; to control your feelings. My powers usually work by subduing feelings; by using your own feelings of animosity and channelling them into obedience instead. This new work is far more exciting.' He chuckled once more.

Moving over to a corner of the room, he picked up a long staff. As he brought it nearer, Linnil could see it was the Sceptre. If only she could get hold of it ... She struggled with her bonds, but it was hopeless.

As she watched, Dargan sat in a chair, cradling the staff almost lovingly. He closed his eyes and a strange look—almost of peace—flitted across his face. For a short while he mumbled softly to himself, then his eyes opened again. Their surrounds had become a deeper black and the pupils a brighter white.

Rising to his feet, Dargan smiled briefly. 'Allow me first to demonstrate something of my new-found powers,' he said.

He carried a large flower over to a table beside her. When Linnil looked at it closely, she could see that it was colourless, almost transparent.

'Soon this will fade and disappear completely,' Dargan told her. 'It is just a tiny example of my new abilities.'

'Huh! It's just another illusion,' replied Linnil scornfully, more bravely than she felt.

'You will soon learn differently,' barked Dargan harshly as he took the plant away and then returned.

Linnil shivered as the Dark Master approached her. She wanted to look away, but she found that she couldn't. He was staring at her with that awful gaze. It was compelling, forceful. As if from another room, she heard a voice, insistent, asking her, 'What do you think of me? Do you feel for me?'

Realising he had started his experiment—on her—she struggled, but this time it was a mental struggle. Invisible tendrils already sought to bind her emotions. 'No!' she cried. 'I will not be manipulated. I despise you.'

The gaze withdrew for a moment, as if surprised by such resistance. Linnil found herself back in the room.

Dargan was clenching his teeth. 'So, you resist, do you? Good! It will prove an interesting challenge to my powers.' He glared at her, and once again she found herself drawn to his gaze.

Once more the voice nagged at the fringes of consciousness, and once more she resisted. Images barged their way into her thoughts: Dargan smiling at her, a benign expression on his face. His features somehow seemed more attractive as she studied them.

No! She rejected the images, knowing them to be false. She did not love him, could not. She despised him. But the images didn't fade; they became stronger. The voice became more insistent.

Again, she shrugged it off, but this time with slightly more difficulty. The battle continued: persuasion, denial; insistence, rejection. Linnil was becoming very weary, tired of fighting. She just wanted to be left to sleep.

Sensing victory, the efforts of the voice and the images intensified. She saw the Dark Master as a young man—strong, handsome, a peace-seeker. Something tugged at the corners of her mind, warning her that it was another illusion, a trick, but she was too exhausted to resist for much longer.

The voice came again, clearer than before. 'What do you feel for me? Could you care for me?'

Linnil sat in silence, trying desperately to withdraw.

Again, the voice taunted her: 'What do you feel for me?' The images returned; he stood there smiling again, his arms open wide. It would be so good just to fall into their welcoming embrace.

'What do you feel for me?' he asked softly.

'Leave me alone!' she sobbed desperately. But the questioning became stronger, even more insistent.

'Stop it!' she shrieked, her hands wrestling with their bonds, her mind trying to stop the flow of foreign thoughts ...

But why stop them? The young man who stood before her seemed so kind, so loving.

'What do you feel for me?' repeated the voice, soothing and gentle. 'Do you care?'

'I don't know ... Yes,' she whispered. 'I care for you I think I love you.' A final strand in her mind seemed to snap, and she slumped into a deep sleep.

Dargan threw his head back and laughed. It had been a struggle, but he had triumphed. And this was just a trace of the power that would soon be available to him. In time, he would dominate groups of people, whole lands full of people. They would all be under his control.

Meanwhile, he had an idea for revenge on those meddling fools who had driven him out of his old stronghold. He would teach them a lesson they would be unable to forget; he would show them that he was not to be trifled with. A few more hours' work on the girl and he would be ready. Then he would send her back to them—but they would weep instead of rejoice. And they would learn something else—lessons that the girl had already absorbed. They would learn true fear and despair.

29

Reunions

The line of thunder goblins continued steadily upwards. Gatera realised that he would be able to stop four, maybe five, of the creatures before he was overwhelmed. The pointlessness of it all; the anger at what they had done to Rrum; his pain at the thought of not seeing his family again—all of it welled up inside him. He let forth an enormous bellow of rage that boomed around the mountainside, and shook his mighty fists in the air. Then, taking his staff, he swung it menacingly around.

The goblins paused, unsettled and fearful. 'C'mon, you gibbering wrecks! He's just one man against all of us!' cried Ganniwaggik.

At that moment, Gatera's shout was answered by a battle cry from the valley below. Four horsemen rode into view, waving their swords in the air.

The nerve of the thunder goblins broke at the sight of the riders pounding towards them. Scuttling back down the hill, they scrambled into the stream entrance and were gone.

Gatera's puzzled frown gave way to a sigh of relief as he recognised the riders. He rushed down the slope to meet them. 'Valor! That battle cry was the sweetest sound I've ever heard. It's good to see you all.'

Athennar, Valor, Vallel and Hesteron dismounted
and surrounded the big man, bombarding him with
questions. Gatera held up his hand to appeal for
quiet. As his friends fell silent, he said, 'Rrum has
been hurt—perhaps even killed—in a battle with
those creatures. I must get back to him. He's in the
cave behind that bush.' He started back up the
hillside.

Hesteron ran lightly past him, anxious to see if he
could help.

Athennar joined Gatera and gripped his arm. 'If
we can save him, we will,' he said simply.

'I know, I know,' muttered Gatera huskily.

A figure emerged from behind the bush, the rays
of the sun seeming to stream through her golden
hair. Her dress fluttered around her in the slight
breeze. She looked like a free spirit about to float
away across the skies. The effect of this wondrous
vision upon Athennar was startling.

'Melinya!' he shouted, his lungs almost bursting
and his heart pounding.

'Athennar!' She gazed down with equal surprise,
and then was running, running, running into his
arms. He caught and held her, spinning her round
and kissing her. Then he held her tightly again, as
if he would never let her go. 'Melinya ... how ...
where ...?'

She laughed, a sound that rippled across the
hillside like a happy song. 'Your big friend here saved
me.' Then she became more serious. 'And the other
one—the small one ...'

Nodding in understanding, Athennar led her back
to the cave.

Hesteron greeted them at the entrance. 'He is still
alive—just,' he said.

'Will he ... is he ... can he be carried?' asked Gatera.

'I am sure that if I can get him back to Kravos, our healers will be able to cure him. Being Land Crafters, they more than anyone will know what is most likely to help him. They understand some of the needs of the Rrokki people, especially their need of rock minerals.'

Hesteron hesitated, then said, 'You are right. He must be carried, but gently. A horse ride would be too rough. Will you be able to manage it, Gatera? It's a long way to Kravos, even for one of your strength. We'll be able to give some help, but won't be able to cover the ground as rapidly as you.'

'I would carry him to the southernmost tip of the Southlands if it meant there was a chance that he might live,' the Land Crafter replied earnestly.

'I will tend him as best I can with my herbs,' Hesteron said. 'Although it is dangerous, we should rest here tonight, and then start out at first light tomorrow.'

Athennar said, 'We can light a fire in the entrance later and mount a watch. I have a feeling our little friends are unlikely to return—unless they've gone back for reinforcements.'

Gatera shook his head. 'No, that was all of them.' He gave a faint smile to Melinya and offered his huge hand to shake. 'I'm sorry I didn't have time to introduce myself earlier. I'm Gatera, and that little hero—' he pointed to the unconscious rock man '—is Rrum of the Rrokki.'

Melinya smiled gently in return. 'I am truly grateful to you, Gatera, though I would never have wished to have been the cause of this grief.'

Valor and Vallel arrived in the cave, leading the horses, and joined in the conversation.

'But what in the Realm are you doing here, Gatera?' asked Valor. 'I thought you'd be back at the fortress by now.'

The Land Crafter shook his head and recounted his story. Athennar, still holding Melinya, then explained their exploits in the Ice Kingdom, including the arrival of Fashag and the downfall of Zendos.

After leaving the kingdom, Athennar, Valor, Hesteron and Vallel had found their horses and dressed again in their riding clothes. They had offered to take the Fire Crafter with them, but he had preferred to find his own way home. After an abrupt, gruff farewell, he had left.

As they set off southwards, the company's journey had fortunately taken them past the mountain …

'… where we heard your mighty roar, Gatera,' Athennar finished.

'A sweet answer from Elsinoth,' said Melinya.

Gatera gazed at the still form of Rrum. 'Aye, but what of our little friend?' he said.

Melinya said, 'We are never guaranteed immunity from danger, Gatera—just Elsinoth's help in overcoming the wrong in our own lives, and strength against the evil wishes of others.'

'Were you well treated by the goblins?' Athennar asked her. 'If they did you any harm …'

'I'm all right, my love.' The gentle smile had returned. 'I suffered far more from the pain of being separated from you than from anything that Zendos or his minions could inflict upon me.'

'I've searched so long for you,' replied Athennar. 'It tore me in two when we were at Dargan's stronghold and we couldn't search further for you. I thought my heart would break.'

'That was a cold, hard time.' Melinya shuddered. 'I saw no one but my jailer for weeks on end. Occasionally Zendos would come and gloat over the fact that he had captured me and that you would never have me back. He tried again and again to make me confess that I loved him, but I never did. I built an inner barrier of defiance that must have helped me to survive those cruel days.

'Then he came for me one day. He told me that you had been within the stronghold, and claimed that he had defeated you. I wouldn't believe him. Then he took me to one of those horrible Tarks—he must have drugged me in some way. I remember gazing down from a great height at the stronghold below. The courtyard was empty except for bodies. I was sure then that he hadn't defeated you, or why would he be fleeing? Then he brought me here. He said he was going somewhere without me for a while, but that he would return for me. Then Gatera and Rrum arrived. You know the rest.' She subsided into silence.

Athennar gave her a hug and kissed her. 'You must be tired now. Have some rest while we prepare some food.' He passed her a rolled-up blanket as a pillow.

Gatera moved away to see if there was any change in Rrum's condition. Hesteron, Vallel and Valor went to unload the provisions. Athennar was about to move away as well when Melinya caught his sleeve. He looked at her questioningly.

'I love you,' she whispered.

He kissed her again. 'And I love you,' he said. 'I will never let anyone take you away again.'

Early the following day, the silver fingers of dawn crept softly into the cave, awaking the company. The night had passed peacefully with no further sign of the thunder goblins.

As the friends huddled around the fire eating breakfast, Valor leaned over to speak to Gatera. 'Shouldn't we go back inside the mountain and set the Ancients free?' he asked.

His question was overheard by Athennar. 'You're right. We can hardly leave such a people captive.'

Gatera shook his head sadly. 'They don't want to be free,' he replied. 'I tried my best to persuade them, but their spokesman—it's funny, but I never even learned his name—wasn't interested. It seems that people can lose hold of the idea of freedom. The Ancients no longer realise what it means, how important it is. But to force them to be free against their will would be wrong. They prefer to stay as they are because that way they don't have to face up to the past.

'What they don't seem to realise is that they are still bound by the cords of guilt and fear. When we arrived in their cavern, they were afraid that we had come to punish them for things they had done long ago. I'm afraid that if you tried to free them now, it would probably tip them over the edge, into madness.'

Athennar chewed thoughtfully on a piece of bread. 'Perhaps you're right. It would take a long time to break down such barriers, and time is the one thing we don't have at the moment. However, if we can somehow find Dargan and Linnil—however unlikely that may seem at the moment—and remove the threat of the Dark Master, then I'll come back here one day and deal with the thunder goblins. Perhaps we will then be able to help the Ancients, or at least assist them to understand that they are still loved by Elsinoth.'

'By that time it might be too late,' said Gatera drily.

Hesteron joined in the conversation, gloomily saying, 'It will be too late for all of us if we can't find Dargan.'

'Well, it's no use sitting around here moping,' Vallel said. 'Let's get cleared up and start the journey back to the fortress. Who knows, there may be some good news by now.'

'I doubt it!' snorted Valor.

The travellers made their way wearily across the slopes of the Mountains of Kravos. The journey had seemed long and uncomfortable, and most of them felt dispirited. Only Athennar and Melinya refused to be downcast. Athennar's joy at being reunited with his love had increased his resolve and his trust in Elsinoth.

For the others, it had not been so easy. Valor worried about Kess and about Linnil; Hesteron and Vallel feared for the future of the Realm, and wondered if they would ever know a time of peace together; and Gatera grieved over Rrum, who had shown no signs of improvement. The big Land Crafter was beginning to feel the tightening tendrils of defeat: the struggle against evil seemed so hard at times.

When he realised how near he was to giving up—just as the Ancients had—he gritted his teeth and knew that he could not follow that road. If nothing else, he owed it to Rrum and to his family to continue with the battle. He had carried the little Rrokki tirelessly during the journey, refusing even to let any of the others take the burden for a while. To Gatera, Rrum was no burden; he was a dear friend.

Presently they arrived at the Land Crafters' dell. Mardilla had seen them coming and was preparing a hot meal, both helped and hindered by the children. She greeted her husband warmly, but the warmth turned to concern as Gatera carried Rrum to a nearby cave and laid him gently on a pallet.

'Will you be able to stay with us for a few days?' she asked Athennar as she passed him some food.

'I'm afraid not. We must report back to the fortress and find out what has been happening in our absence. We have already been away far too long.'

Mardilla looked across to the cave. 'Rrum—will he—recover?'

Pausing for a moment, Athennar looked at the heavily-built woman. Anxiety traced its deep furrows across her rough features. 'I don't know,' he said gently. 'The only thing I can say is that he will have more chance of recovering here—with the true loving care of friends such as you—than anywhere else in the Northlands.'

Mardilla nodded in understanding and looked towards the cave where her husband was still tending the Rrokki.

Gatera, unaware of her gaze, looked down upon his friend. 'It's up to you now,' he whispered. Then suddenly he called out, not caring who would hear: 'Don't let him die, Elsinoth; please, don't let him die!' Bending his head with the grief that had been locked up inside, he began to weep great tears that ran slowly down his weather-beaten cheeks.

30

The Jewelled Forest

After several days of travelling, Kess, Whisper and Tolledon's two trusted men—Marason and Callenor—arrived at the Jewelled Forest. It was a wonderful sight, even from a distance. The dark green trees twinkled with a variety of small, round and highly colourful fruits that seemed like jewels when viewed from afar. Bright reds, rich blues, vibrant oranges and striking yellows all contributed to the effect.

The journey had taken them across the plains and over the River Froster, reminding Kess of the time when the company had been attacked by Zorgs and Merric had nearly died. *Merric*! He could still see the elf prince's sad face peering down from the battlements as they had left the fortress. Some streak of stubbornness had stopped Kess from leaping off his horse and racing up to Merric to apologise for his harsh words. The troubadour's friendship was important to him, yet he had felt slighted by his doubts about Whisper. He had tried to bury his own unease about her, convincing himself that her reticence was due to the hard times she had endured in the mists.

Once or twice on the journey he had tried to

question Whisper about her past. Each time, she had become sullen and withdrawn, and he hadn't pursued the matter any further. He wished she would trust him, confide in him. Until such a time, he would have to be patient.

Kess also resented the fact that Marason and Callenor were keeping a close watch on Whisper. At first he had thought that he was imagining it, but once, when Whisper had become angry with his questions, he had noticed Marason's hand slip to the pommel of his sword.

But apart from her short periods of sulking, Whisper had been very lively. She was excited to be travelling through the Realm again. Like a young child, she kept pointing out new wonders, even now: trees, hills, colours she hadn't seen since being held captive by the Mist Mistress. However, as time passed, Kess noticed that she was beginning to show signs of tiredness. He had nightmares in which she disintegrated before his eyes. It was a great relief to him when they approached the forest. Soon they might be able to find the potion that would cure her.

'Don't eat the fruit,' warned Marason as they reached the outskirts of the wood. 'It may look attractive, but it is deadly. One bite and you would be writhing in agony; two bites and you would die instantly.'

Passing under the branches of the outermost trees, Kess' relief changed to an uneasy wariness. Meltizoc had warned that it was a strange place and he had been right. Although the sun was shining above, the air in the forest was cold and cheerless. Even the brightly coloured fruit now seemed dull as they rode beneath the heavily laden trees. He noticed another thing, too: there was little sign of life. No birds chattered merrily among the leaves, no rustlings of burrowing creatures came from the undergrowth. It was a strange silence; not so much threatening as just empty. None of the small company felt like talking, and all of them kept glancing around, feeling as if they were being watched.

Only one thing relieved the atmosphere of the wood: the jocale trees that bore the fruit also produced a fresh, clean, leafy smell that helped to counteract the overall mustiness of the forest.

Moving onwards, the travellers headed into the heart of the wood, searching for the area of red clay mentioned by Tolledon. The soil underfoot was greyish, though mostly covered by a thick layer of leaves.

Soon the trees became too dense for them to ride farther. Finding a little grassy clearing, they tethered the horses loosely to a stand of low trees, after ensuring that none of the poisonous jocale fruit was within reach. Then, proceeding on foot, they followed a track that led from the clearing into a dark section of the forest.

The path wound its way purposefully through the trees. Kess wondered what had made it. There had certainly been no sign of any animal life so far. Perhaps it had been created by nocturnal creatures.

A little light filtered through from above, relieving the gloom. They had only walked a short distance when a creature shot out of the undergrowth some way ahead and stopped in the centre of the path.

'A simbrel!' gasped Callenor in surprise.

The animal stood quietly for a moment, regarding them and trembling slightly.

'What's a simbrel?' whispered Kess.

'It's a creature that only lives in the Jewelled Forest, feeding off the fruit of the jocale trees, apparently without coming to any harm. It is a rare sight. There are supposedly very few of them and they seldom come into the open.'

'It's beautiful,' breathed Whisper.

The creature was like a very small, sleek horse, with a golden mane that continued all the way down to its flowing tail. Snorting suddenly, it wheeled and trotted off down the path.

'I must get closer to it,' Whisper said, and started running lightly after the animal.

'Whisper! No!' called Kess.

Ignoring his cries, she ran on up the path.

The two Hallion men looked at each other. 'We'd better follow her,' sighed Marason. They started running along the track and Kess quickly followed before he was left behind.

The track led upwards. Whisper just managed to keep the simbrel in sight—it almost seemed at times as if it was waiting for her. For some reason it kept to the path and didn't move off into the thicker vegetation. Entranced by it, she had temporarily forgotten the reason they were in the forest.

The simbrel reached a clump of great trees at the top of the hill. Weaving suddenly, it darted between two of them and disappeared.

Whisper sighed as she realised that the creature had escaped.

'Just what do you think you're doing?' demanded Marason, as the others caught up with her. He had been astonished by the speed and lightness of her feet. 'We're in a strange wood, on a serious task, and you dash off after an animal!'

'I'm sorry,' she replied, still gazing into the trees. 'I don't know what came over me.'

'Never mind,' said Kess. 'Let's have a rest. I'm exhausted—and hungry.' He sat down on the grass and started looking through his backpack for something to chew.

Marason and Callenor sat down with their backs
against two of the huge trees, while Whisper wandered to and fro, still trying to catch a glimpse of the
elusive simbrel.

Suddenly there was an angry shout from Marason.
Kess looked up in time to see long tendrils of a sickly
pink creeper wrapping themselves around the Hallion man's body. Another creeper twisted around
Callenor's arm. He struggled valiantly to release
himself. Kess leaped across, pulling his sword and
swinging wildly at the fleshy stems. The ferocity of
the attack caused the plant to lose its grip. Callenor
sprang free. Then he and Kess ran across to help
Marason, who was already completely encased in
writhing stems. Hacking viciously at the creeper, they
fought desperately to set him free. Marason's face was
turning a deeper red as the plant slowly began to
squeeze out his life. Its tendrils were so fleshy that
their swords made little impact and it took several
blows to sever each stem. Then suddenly, even as they
kept attacking it, the creeper started to withdraw into
the branches above. It took its now unmoving victim
with it.

'No!' shouted Kess, renewing his efforts.

It was useless. Within moments the plant was out of
his reach. Marason's sword dropped from his lifeless
hand as his body disappeared among the leaves.

Whisper knelt transfixed, in a state of shock. 'What
have I done?' she kept repeating. 'What have I done?'

White-faced, Callenor stood staring up into the
tree. Kess, meanwhile, collapsed on the ground,
pounding the earth in a mixture of anger and grief.
'Why?' he shouted. 'Why?'

Callenor swung around and gently helped him up.
'It seems a senseless way to die after a life of loyal
service,' he said softly, 'yet none of us knows when or

in what manner our lives might end. He was a good man; a good friend.'

After a few moments of silence, Callenor looked over towards Whisper. 'We must continue our search for the chest,' he said. 'There will be time enough to grieve later.' Picking up Marason's sword, he offered it to Whisper. 'It is best that you take this rather than travel unguarded. Do not betray my trust, or I will see that you regret it.'

'Th-thank you,' she replied, trembling slightly.

Kess, his face strained, went over and put his arm around her. 'Don't blame yourself. You couldn't have known.'

'How can I help but blame myself?' she blurted out. 'If I hadn't gone rushing headlong up this hill, none of this would have happened.'

Callenor, who had been watching with a grim expression, relented a little when he saw how upset the woman was. 'There are many legends that surround the simbrel,' he said quietly. 'One is that it enchants some who see it, and leads them to their deaths. Perhaps it works in some kind of unholy alliance with these creepers; or perhaps it was mere misfortune that Marason was ensnared. It wasn't your fault.'

She looked up gratefully, though still a little shaky. 'Thank you,' she whispered again.

They soon found another track leading across the hill and followed it as it seemed to be heading into the heart of the forest. Whisper was now leaning heavily upon Kess. Although the chase after the simbrel had exhausted her, the roots of this tiredness went much deeper. It was as if something was slowly sucking the energy from her, draining her resources.

'Do you want to stop?' asked Kess after a while.

She nodded, and Kess looked at Callenor, who

appeared sceptical but shrugged his shoulders. 'Very well,' he said, 'but you'd better sit in the middle of the path. I wouldn't advise leaning against any more tree trunks. I'll keep a lookout as you never know what might happen around here.' He gave a slight smile, softening the grim warning.

Whisper sank gratefully onto the leafy path. Kess sat as well, cradling her gently in his arms. His pulse raced as her soft black hair brushed against his lips. As if aware of his mood, Whisper turned slightly to look at him. Her eyes were only inches away from his. Their smooth greyness had become mottled with white blotches, a further sign of her weakness. They still seemed magical to Kess, however, as he gazed into their depths, and he imagined all kinds of secret promises veiled within them.

'It's a comfort to have a friend like you,' she whispered. He felt her soft hand touch his as if pleading for understanding. 'I know I've perhaps not told you everything I might have, but please trust me.'

Kess squeezed her hand in response. Deep in thought, he held her in his arms and gazed unseeing into the forest.

'It's time to move on.' Callenor's voice jolted Kess. 'The sooner we are able to find this chest—if it exists—the better.'

Kess looked down at Whisper. She had fallen asleep in his arms. He prodded her gently. Startled, she awoke and glanced around in fear for a moment. Kess was surprised by her reaction, and wondered if, during her period of captivity with the Mist Mistress, she had woken each morning in such a state. The look passed almost immediately, however, and Whisper smiled at him, banishing the memory.

'Are you feeling better?' he asked her.

'Yes,' she replied softly, 'but I don't think I'll ever feel fully strong again unless our search is successful.'

Callenor waited patiently and then led them along the trail. Tall, russet-leaved trees began to take the place of the jocales, and a fresh, nutty smell wafted downwards. It was a welcome change even from the pleasant fragrance of the fruit trees.

Within minutes, the three companions arrived at a little river, flowing silently as if on a secret quest. The trail they had been following met a new path that traced its way alongside the river. On the opposite side, the river bank was draped with dense foliage.

'What makes these paths, Callenor?' asked Kess curiously.

'I'm not sure. Apparently some isolated groups of elves live in parts of the forest; Hinno-val comes here occasionally to gather information from them. Perhaps they made the tracks originally, although I believe that most of them now live over on the other side of the wood. Anyway, our main problem lies in deciding which direction to take: whether to follow the path upstream or downstream.'

Whisper bent down to splash some of the cool river water on her face. It felt very refreshing. As she scooped up another handful, however, she noticed something strange about it. 'Look!' she called to the two men, pointing into the river. Pale streaks of red swirled around in the water. 'It's traces of red clay,' she explained to the two bewildered men. 'Don't you remember the part of the rhyme that refers to the chest being stained with blood?'

Kneeling down, Kess grabbed a nearby stick and raked away the dead leaves and grass lying across the path. Underneath was a deep red clay soil. 'You're right!' he said. 'But what about the rest of the rhyme—especially the part about: 'When all that has lain quiet comes crashing, tumbling down/Then in the centre, deep inside, the source of wisdom's found'?

Whisper shrugged, but Callenor pondered for a while. 'The whole of this forest is quiet,' he began. 'So much so, it's unnerving. Even the water makes no sounds. I haven't yet seen any signs of rocks or cliffs, even though we have risen a fair height …' Suddenly he stopped and pounded his fist into his open palm. 'Of course! Coming from Hallion, I of all people should have known the answer to the riddle. It's so obvious when you think about it.'

Kess and Whisper looked at him blankly. 'Are you going to tell us?' asked the Valley man.

'Yes,' chuckled Callenor. 'I almost gave you the answer just now when I said the water was quiet. What causes water to come "crashing, tumbling down"?'

'A waterfall,' said Kess triumphantly.

'Yes! And if I'm not mistaken, if we listen carefully we may even be able to hear it.'

They fell silent, straining to hear the sounds. Kess' keen ears heard it first, the unmistakeable noise of water spilling down from a great height. Perhaps at last the chest was within reach.

31
An Unexpected Arrival

Athennar's craggy features broke into a warm smile as Melinya glided across the courtyard towards him. He was beginning to relax at last after their long journey. The company had arrived back at the fortress two days previously, having left Rrum in the tender care of Mardilla and Gatera. The little Rrokki was still unconscious, and the friends were all worried about him. However, there was little that the rest of them could do. The journey back—by way of Hallion—had worn them out, as they had all wanted to press on and reach the fortress as quickly as possible, anxious for any news of Linnil—and of Kess and Whisper.

To their disappointment, little news awaited them. Tolledon and Meltizoc voiced their fear for Kess, while Merric stayed strangely silent. The troubadour had warmly welcomed the companions on their arrival, but Athennar's reunion with Melinya only served to heighten his awareness of how much he longed for Linnil's safe return. Although Athennar knew this, he could do little about it other than encourage Valor to spend some time with the minstrel. The Mountain Guard was only too pleased to oblige, and Merric soon became more talkative.

With Melinya at his side, Athennar wandered over towards the south battlements. He was rediscovering old emotions; ones that had been buried for too long. Whenever she was near, a soft warmth seemed to seep through him; a new sense of awareness of life. Even his friends had noticed how easily a smile came to his lips whenever Melinya appeared.

Almost without thinking, the couple mounted the steps that led to the battlements, exchanging greetings with one of the elf guards. Standing arm-in-arm, they gazed out onto the empty vista of the Southlands, stretching away before them.

'I hope we can find Linnil soon,' sighed Melinya. 'Merric may put on a brave face, but he is hurting deep inside.'

'I know,' replied Athennar, 'but I'm afraid the reasons for finding her are much more important than that. With every day that passes, Dargan must be out there, somewhere, growing in strength. At some point he will become too powerful for us to defeat. But what more can we do? Our scouts range far and wide, yet none has found any clues to his whereabouts. Zendos was our only real hope of finding Dargan, and Zendos is dead. We can only wait now, and that is the hardest task of all. Waiting and praying.'

Melinya wrapped her arm around his waist and cuddled up close to him. 'We must never lose faith,' she said. 'Against all the odds, we are together again. Elsinoth will not allow his world to be so easily taken over; not while there are still those who are ready to trust and do his will.'

'But what is his will?' asked Athennar. 'Sometimes it seems like peering into murky waters, trying to see the pebbles far below.'

'I don't know,' she replied. 'Perhaps it's just being

ready to act when the time is right, and not giving in, however hopeless things may seem.' She smiled at him. 'Who knows what the future holds?'

They were just about to leave the battlements when the sentry gave a cry. 'Sire! Look! A Tark!'

Athennar peered into the pale blue sky. Far up and still some distance away, a dark blob was winging its way steadily towards the fortress. 'Alert the archers,' he shouted to the young elf. 'Then fetch my father and Meltizoc.'

The elf saluted and rushed away.

Barely moments later, it seemed, Tolledon came rushing up the steps with Meltizoc's portly figure puffing along behind him. 'We were in the courtyard,' said Tolledon, 'when we heard the cry.' He looked up at the Tark which was growing larger every minute. 'What do you think's happening, old friend? Is it some message from Dargan? Or perhaps the Dark Master himself, coming to test his power?'

Meltizoc watched carefully as the creature drew nearer, but didn't reply.

'It seems to have a passenger, sire,' said one of the elf sentries.

Tolledon nodded in agreement as the Tark began to circle high over the fortress.

By this time, the elven archers had reached the battlements, but the creature was still out of reach of their arrows. Slowly, it glided down, then flapped its wings lazily before settling on the ground some distance from the fortress gates. A crumpled figure staggered from its back, then collapsed on the ground. Immediately the Tark rose slowly, circled over the fortress again as if mocking the archers, then wheeled and flew off southwards.

'Can you tell who it is?' Tolledon asked one of the most sharp-sighted elves.

'No sire, it's too far away and partially covered by some kind of cloak.'

'It could be a trap,' warned Meltizoc.

'I'm aware of that, old friend,' said Tolledon. He looked around. 'I want four volunteers.'

All the elves' hands shot up. Tolledon selected four, and then said, 'When you reach the halfway point between the fortress and the figure, one of you proceed alone. The other three can cover him; the figure should be well within range. The rest of you up here can cover the three in case they need it.'

Meltizoc nodded his approval of this caution. Meanwhile, the elves ran lightly down the steps towards the gates. At that moment, Merric and Valor arrived to find out what was happening.

They watched the elves below as they moved rapidly across the ground beyond the gates. Halfway to the slumped form, three of them stopped while the fourth continued cautiously forward. He stooped over the figure, and then shouted back to the other three. One of them called up to the watchers on the battlements. 'It's a woman!'

'Linnil! It must be!' cried Merric, leaping down the steps two at a time.

'Take care!' cautioned Tolledon as Athennar ran after him.

The troubadour was already out of the gates before Athennar reached the bottom step. He raced across the field and past the first group of elves. His heart was bursting, dreading what he might find; hoping desperately that it was Linnil, yet also fearful of what that might mean.

Reaching the young elf who was guarding the motionless figure, he kneeled down, gazing speechlessly at the face framed within a grey hood. *Linnil*! Noticing a slight rise and fall in her body, he breathed a sigh of relief—she was alive! Very gently, he scooped her up in his arms, ignoring the young elf's half-stammered protests.

At that moment, Athennar arrived. 'Linnil! Is she …?'

'She still lives. Beyond that, I know not. I will carry her back to the fortress. Could you find Hesteron and any other healers who are available?'

Athennar nodded grimly and raced off as Merric moved slowly back to the open gates. As he walked, he gazed down at the face he had dreamed of, thought of, longed to see over the past few weeks. Linnil looked drained, as if she had spent her days in one long battle. Her face was pale and creased with hidden fears. What had the Dark Master done?

The minstrel felt a cold fury surge up inside him. First his parents, murdered by the deviousness of Dargan—now Linnil. Such evil was beyond his understanding: why should men want to hurt or control others who had never done them any harm? He shook his head. He had no answers.

An hour later, Tolledon, Meltizoc, Athennar, Melinya and Vallel met together in one of the castle's rooms. A Hallion man brought in some lunch, although none of them really wanted food. Hesteron, Merric and Valor were with Linnil, who was still in a swoon.

'What's it all about?' asked Vallel. 'Why did Dargan send Linnil back? I would have expected him to kill her rather than let her go free.'

'We will find the answer to that when—or perhaps I should say "if"—she regains full consciousness,' replied Meltizoc.

'Perhaps it's his way of saying that it is futile trying to fight him; he is already too powerful and our future is in his control,' suggested Tolledon.

'Or perhaps he has poisoned her, and is just allowing her to die slowly while we watch,' said Athennar grimly.

Melinya squeezed his arm. 'The few times I met Dargan at the stronghold, I always felt that he was treading the borders of madness,' she said. 'Could he have slipped over that narrow line? Might he have freed Linnil without knowing what he was doing?'

Meltizoc replied, 'You can be sure of this, I'm afraid: he knew exactly what he was doing when he sent her here. The Tark wouldn't have come all this way without clear commands from Dargan. No, I'm sure there is something more sinister behind this; but all we can do is wait.'

'Wait!' muttered Tolledon. 'That seems to sum up the whole of the past few weeks.'

Meltizoc patted him sympathetically on the shoulder. 'Patience, old friend. It may not be too long before we find an answer.'

In one of the other castle rooms, Hesteron placed his hand on Linnil's brow. 'It is strange,' he commented, 'that she shows no signs of fever, nor of illness or a fall, and yet she sleeps as if drugged. Yet if she was drugged, how did she stay on the Tark's back? It seems from what Athennar said that she was conscious until the Tark landed, and then it was as if some mental trigger clicked and turned off her thoughts.'

'The trickery and deceit of our old enemy is somehow at work here,' murmured Merric. 'Yet is it possible for him to control her mind from such a distance?' A cold shudder ran down his back. 'Is there no end to his power?'

Hesteron scowled. 'Whatever he's done, it is beyond my power to heal. I've tried all the remedies I know—but I think I may be trying to cure something that is not a bodily ailment.'

'But you can't give up,' protested Valor. 'Try something else—anything!'

'I'm sorry,' said Hesteron, gently but firmly. 'If she's going to come out of it, she'll come out of it by herself. There's nothing more we can do.'

'It is best that you both leave,' said Merric disconsolately. 'You must eat. I will keep watch over Linnil lest there be any change.'

Valor started to protest again, but Hesteron steered him quietly out of the door. 'Can't you see he wants to be alone with her?' he whispered as they went into the corridor.

Valor's face sagged with sudden understanding. He felt worn out and hopeless. 'Oh—I'm sorry—I wasn't thinking. I'm just so worried about Linnil.'

'I know. We all are. Perhaps Merric will be able to succeed where I've failed; remember that it was Linnil who pulled him out of his trance in Dargan's dungeons. He might just be able to do something similar for her. We must never underestimate the power of love. Perhaps that is something Dargan would never take into account.'

Merric sat on the bed some time later, gently stroking Linnil's auburn curls. 'Come back to me,' he whispered softly to her. 'I love you, Linnil.'

If she heard, she gave no response.

He took her hand in his. It was pale and cold, like her face. 'Fight, Linnil, fight! Whatever ails you, we can defeat it together. You must not give up!' The troubadour kissed her forehead, but it was like kissing a corpse. His head bowed in grief, and his fist clenched and unclenched in frustration. *There must be some way to bring her back*!

Wearily, he arose and paced the room for a while, trying to think of new ways to reach her. Another idea came to his mind: music had helped when they were captives in Dargan's stronghold. Perhaps it would help now.

Quickly, he rushed to his room to fetch his lute. It was propped in one corner, as if awaiting him. Racing back to Linnil's room, he sat down and began to pick out a slow, melodic tune.

This was no good. The notes hung in the air more like a funeral dirge than anything. He needed to play something that would remind Linnil of life; that would give her a reason to live. Immediately, he struck up a bright, vibrant melody—an old favourite of his; a dancing tune that sang of open spaces, fresh air, vitality. He could almost feel his own hopes rising as he played.

Linnil, however, remained unmoved.

Merric tried several other tunes, but none of them had any effect. Finally, he laid down the instrument and sat beside her again. 'Wake up, Linnil!' he urged her again. 'I need you. Please wake up!'

There was not the slightest change in her breathing, nor any colouring in her pallid features.

'What has he done to you?' he asked. 'What has he done, that even my love cannot break through?' The frustration, the anger, the pain of being unable to help his loved one, all clawed at him, gnawed at his mind.

'What have you done, Dargan?' he shouted at the walls, getting up and waving his fists.

No sooner had he said the Dark Master's name than Linnil stirred, as if something had been instantly unlocked. Merric rushed to her side. He could feel the warmth surging back into her body, sense the pulse in her veins strengthening. Somehow he had done it— somehow he had broken through to her.

After a few moments, Linnil's eyelids flickered. She opened her eyes as if in a daze. 'Wh—where am I?' she croaked.

'You are safe,' Merric reassured her. 'You are at the fortress with friends. Oh, it is such a relief to hear your voice again. I seem to have waited for this moment for ever. I knew our love would win through in the end. I do love you, Linnil.' Tears of joy ran down his face.

Linnil looked confused. 'Love?' she said quietly, as if trying to remember something. Then she looked around the room and spoke urgently. 'Dargan—where is he?'

'You are safe now,' repeated Merric. 'He is far away. You are back with your friends.'

'Friends?' said Linnil weakly. 'But I want to be with Dargan—I love him.'

32

The Secret of the Falls

They followed the path for quite some way, and it gradually became slippery as spray from the waterfall drifted through the air and dampened the clay soil. Then suddenly the wood gave way to rocks. Climbing across them, they came to a breathtaking sight. Kess, Whisper and Callenor gazed in awe at the scene before them. The ground fell away and the river cascaded in a great curtain of shining pearls down to the plains below. The air was filled with noise: a symphony, celebrating the majesty of the falls. Even Callenor, who was used to the waterfall that guarded the entrance to Hallion, was impressed. A double rainbow hung over the waterfall, a fitting crown to its beauty.

Whisper held tightly to Kess, her tiredness temporarily forgotten. 'It's magnificent!' she breathed. Kess could only just hear her, but smiled in mute agreement. Their clothes were becoming drenched from the spray, but it was a wonderful feeling.

Moving over to the edge of the rocks, Callenor peered downwards. 'We should be able to scramble down,' he shouted, pointing towards the base of the waterfall.

Kess nodded and reluctantly turned away from the

view. Guiding Whisper carefully over to Callenor's side, he looked down as well. It would be a difficult descent among the rocks on the steep slope, especially for Whisper, but there was no alternative.

Callenor moved over to a crack between two rocks and started picking his way downwards. Kess motioned to Whisper to stay slightly above him so he could catch her if she fell, and then he followed the tall Hallion man.

At first, the going wasn't as difficult as he had expected. Natural gaps between the huge rocks enabled them to descend slowly, holding on to the sides of the boulders to steady themselves. Halfway down, however, the rocks became very slippery. At one particularly tricky stage, Whisper lost her footing. Kess was immediately at her side.

'Are you hurt?' he shouted, his words being drowned by the sound of the falls even as they left his lips.

Whisper winced, but called back, 'I think I'm rather bruised, but it's probably my pride that's hurt as much as anything. I feel so clumsy.'

Callenor climbed back up to join them, just as Kess helped her back to her feet. She clung wearily to Kess for a moment, then signalled them to carry on. Half-climbing, half-slipping, they somehow made their way down to the base of the slope. Soaked, aching and sore, they sat down on a large flat rock while they decided what to do next.

'There must be a cave or something near these falls,' shouted Callenor. 'Isn't that what you thought the rhyme meant?'

'"Tho' hollowed heart be covered, your chest is stained in blood," Kess muttered to himself.

Whisper suddenly rose to her feet, impatient to continue the search. Kess, watching, realised the reason behind her urgency: she needed to find the chest before her strength faded completely. None of them knew how long it would be before she started to 'dissolve'—her sudden weakness had been unexpected; he had half-believed that nothing would happen to her. Now it was happening and time was running out.

Kess arose and, joined by Callenor, the trio set their faces against the lashing of the water and clambered as carefully as they could over the rocks towards the base of the falls. Suddenly, Callenor stopped and pointed. 'Over there!' he shouted. To one side of the sheet of falling water they could see a dark hole.

Flicking his wet hair out of his eyes, and trying to blink the water drops from his eyelashes, Kess guided Whisper towards the cave. Callenor went ahead and disappeared into the black mouth of the cavern. When Kess and Whisper reached it, he was a little way inside the entrance, unpacking his backpack.

Although the waterfall was only a few feet away, its sounds were strangely muffled inside the cave, echoing hollowly around the walls. The companions found they could hear one another again without having to shout too loudly.

Callenor produced a torch that had been wrapped up tightly inside his waterproof backpack. Even so, some of the dampness from the falls seemed to have seeped through to it, as it was reluctant to light at first. Finally it burst into flame, and they all breathed a sigh of relief.

The cave was long and narrow, and they made their way carefully along, examining the floor and sides for any sign of somewhere that might hide a chest. Eventually they reached the rough end wall.

'Nothing,' said Callenor grimly. 'If the chest ever was here, someone must have found it and taken it away.'

Whisper collapsed into Kess' arms, great sobs of disappointment shaking her. After a few minutes, the tears subsided and, exhausted, she drifted into sleep. Picking her up, Kess carried her carefully back towards the cave entrance. 'It *can't* have gone,' he muttered. 'It must be here somewhere.'

Callenor just shook his head sympathetically. 'I'm sorry. There's not even a crack we haven't investigated.'

Kess gently lowered Whisper so that she was propped up against the cave wall, and went to stand in the entrance. He needed time to think. Who could have taken the chest, and where would they have taken it? The longer he thought about it, the stranger it seemed that such an important article should have been left lying where anyone might stumble upon it. But surely this is what the rhyme meant? He gazed over at the waterfall as if willing it to give up its secrets. Suddenly, there was a slight break in the spray as it was blown by a gust of wind. Behind the curtain of water he glimpsed something. ...

'Of course!' he said to himself. 'The cave hinted at in the rhyme must be behind the waterfall, just like the passage leading to Hallion.' Rushing back to Callenor, he told him about his idea.

Callenor mused slowly over his suggestion. 'You may be right,' he said. 'It would certainly be a logical place to hide something valuable. It would also be somewhere that would only occur to someone who was aware of the underground passage to Hallion. Somewhere that a Guardian of the Realm, for instance, might think would be a fitting hiding place.'

Kneeling beside Whisper, Kess touched her arm. Her eyelids flickered open and she managed a weak smile. He explained his idea, and with great effort she nodded. 'You go and look. I must rest. Hurry back!'

Trying to appear confident, Kess returned the smile and went over to Callenor, who had doused the torch and returned it to his backpack, ready for use again later. Together they left the cave and started scrambling across the slippery rocks. They were right at the edge of the falling water. A thin veil spattered in front of them, but they passed through it without any difficulty and found themselves behind the falls. It was a fascinating feeling being separated from the outer world by a shifting, changing barrier. The cliff was cut away at the base of the falls, and towards the centre was the dark mouth of a large hole. Picking his way across to it, Kess breathed a sigh of relief. Callenor unpacked his torch and relit it.

The hole was actually the entrance to a narrow tunnel. As they made their way forwards, it bent slightly and the sound of the waterfall receded behind them. The tunnel floor was damp and Kess was surprised to see patches of the red clay showing through. He looked nervously at the roof of the passage, but it looked solid enough. Then, abruptly, the tunnel ended in a small cavern, pockmarked with small holes and ledges, and with muddy red puddles on the floor.

Kess followed Callenor as he poked into every recess, looking for anything that might resemble a chest. Gradually they worked their way all around the cave, but with no success.

'I can't believe it's not here either,' said Kess gloomily.

'Let me think,' said Callenor. 'What was that line in the middle of the rhyme again?'

'"Tho' hollow heart be covered, your chest is stained with blood."'

'To be stained with blood, it's unlikely to be on any of the ledges or in holes in the cave wall,' said

Callenor, 'as it wouldn't be touching any clay. Perhaps there's a crack or depression at the base of the wall.'

'No,' replied Kess, 'I looked carefully.' Then he snapped his fingers. '"Tho' hollow heart be covered"! We assumed that meant the cave—covered by the waterfall—but it could also refer to the actual hiding place of the chest. If it's covered and stained with blood, it's …'

'In the ground!' Callenor completed his sentence.

Kess was standing next to the largest puddle in the cave. He knelt down beside it, and plunging his hand into it, he felt down carefully. This wasn't a puddle—it was a small, deep pool! His arm sank down into the red water as he felt around. Suddenly his fingers touched something strange. He grasped hold of it and heaved. With a reluctant sucking noise, it plopped up out of the water.

'The chest!' exclaimed Callenor, gasping with surprise.

Kess looked at it, equally surprised that they had at last found it. 'Surely it's ruined, having been under water all these years?' he said.

Callenor wiped away some of the clay with his sleeve. 'No, this is a special wood we sometimes use at Hallion. It's completely unaffected by water. Look—it hasn't faded or warped at all.'

'If it's Hallion wood, it must be the Guardian's chest!' cried Kess triumphantly.

'Let's open it and see,' suggested Callenor. 'Have you got the key?'

Kess shook his head. 'No, Whisper keeps it on a thong around her neck.'

'Then I think we'd better get back to her.'

Kess picked up the chest and followed Callenor back along the tunnel.

When they arrived back at the other cave, they

found Whisper asleep. Kess nudged her and she
stirred uneasily before opening her eyes. When she
saw the chest, some of her old vitality returned.
'You've found it! You've really found it!'

Fumbling in her haste, she untied the thong from
around her neck and pulled off the key. Kess put the
chest on the floor in front of her as Callenor looked
on. Trembling, she passed him the key. 'Open it for
me,' she pleaded, as if afraid of what might happen.

Kess obediently slipped the key into the lock and
turned it. There was a slight click and the chest
opened. Tucked neatly inside was a thick, medium-
sized book, a rolled-up map and two small phials; one
green and one brown. Very carefully, he lifted them
out. They were labelled with faded, spidery writing,
but he could just make it out. The brown bottle said
'Healing of the body' and the green one 'Healing of
the mind'. He showed them to Whisper, who grabbed
the brown phial and pulled out the stopper.

'Careful!' cautioned Kess. 'We don't even know if it
will work. You said that even Gwindirpha wasn't sure.
Besides, it doesn't say how much to take—you may
only need a drop. The bottle's contents may be
sufficient to heal many people.'

'I haven't come all this way to give up at the last
hurdle. It's all or nothing!' So saying, Whisper tipped
her head back and swallowed all the liquid before
Kess could stop her. Her eyes widened in surprise,
and she let out a strangled cry. Kess took a step back,
alarmed. In the next instant, Whisper sprang to her
feet, her whole body shaking violently. Rivulets of
sweat trickled down her face and she looked as if she
would collapse. Suddenly, however, the shaking stopped. She clenched her fists, leaped into the air and
gave a great cry of exultation: 'Yes! Yes! It's working!
I can feel it!'

Kess and Callenor watched in astonishment. The slim, trim, almost wispy figure they had known was becoming firm and strong; she reminded Callenor of a female warrior. Whisper's hair became a deeper, glossier black and her face showed outwardly the signs of strength that they had only glimpsed before. Kess also noticed that her eyes were changed: no longer were they mottled or even grey, but they were now a pure silver colour.

Turning suddenly, Whisper raced out of the cave, running sure-footed across the wet and slippery rocks. Kess was about to follow her, but Callenor held him back. 'Let her go,' he counselled. 'She's like a young filly with her new strength; she needs to test it before she settles down. If you try to follow her at the pace she's going, you're liable to break your neck.'

Kess subsided and looked again at the chest. One of the arguments Whisper had used to persuade him to come on this quest was that the book might help in the search for Linnil. He pulled it from the chest and examined it closely. To his dismay, he couldn't understand the lettering on the cover, nor any of the words on the pages inside.

As he was glancing through it, Whisper returned, smiling broadly. 'I feel wonderful,' she said.

Kess smiled nervously, not completely sure that he liked the new, strong, self-confident Whisper. He had preferred her as she was. Still, at least she was alive. 'I can't read this book,' he said. 'I don't think it's going to be much use in finding Linnil.'

'Oh, I'm not surprised,' replied Whisper airily. 'But at least we found the phial.'

'You mean you never really thought we'd find something that could help Linnil?'

'I... I didn't know—but would you have been

persuaded to come along otherwise? I needed your
help. Surely you can understand that?'

'I suppose so,' said Kess wearily, too tired to argue.
'But even Meltizoc thought we might find the Great
Tome of Neldra—and this book is hardly big enough
to warrant such a title.'

'It's time we were getting back to the horses,'
interrupted Callenor. 'I hope we can still get out of
this forest before nightfall.'

Nodding, feeling dazed, Kess put the book and the
two phials—one now empty—back into the chest.
Callenor picked it up, and the three companions set
off on the long trek back through the forest.

33
Fading Hopes

Merric gasped as if a thunderbolt had struck him. 'What do you mean, you love him?' he asked, dumbfounded. 'He is evil....'

'Dargan, where are you?' pleaded Linnil, ignoring him. 'I love you. Don't leave me alone—please!'

Merric's tears of joy turned to grief. So this is what Dargan had done. He had spent his time practising his mind-games on Linnil. Merric had few illusions about what had happened. He knew Linnil well enough to know that she could never voluntarily succumb to the Dark Master—and could certainly not have fallen in love with him, whatever words she might have been taught to repeat. But how could he release her from this trap? 'Linnil, it is I—Merric. I love you. You told me that you love me too. Have you forgotten?'

She refused to answer, as if she couldn't see or hear him. 'I love you, Dargan,' she whispered over and over again, until Merric thought that his heart would break.

'Stop it!' he shouted. Linnil still didn't look at him, but she stopped speaking. 'Linnil, I know that some-where inside you there is a corner unreached by Dargan. Hold onto our love somehow—I will find a way to reach you. Hold on!'

He picked up his lute again and tried to play, but he couldn't summon up the enthusiasm. It would take more than music to unlock Dargan's hold upon her mind. Until they found a cure, he would have to be patient. Meanwhile, he would tend her and help her to build up her strength again. She would need it if she was ever going to break free.

A few hours later, the friends were all gathered around Linnil's bed. There had been little change in her condition—she didn't respond to any questions. Occasionally, if Dargan's name was mentioned, she would start her litany of 'I love you, Dargan!', though she would stop again when commanded. It was only small comfort to Merric that if Dargan had intended her to behave fairly normally, merely changing her allegiances, he had failed. Her reactions were automatic, almost mindless. If she was offered food, she would eat it, but always with the same blank look in her eyes.

'So this is Dargan's plan,' said Meltizoc. 'He's mocking us. He's flexing his powerful new mental "muscles", showing us how much in control he is. Such power! He must have managed to find a way of tapping the resources of the Sceptre, twisting them to his own use. I'm afraid that is not a good sign for the future of the Realm.'

'If only we could get through to her,' said Valor bitterly. 'Perhaps when Kess comes back he will be able to....'

'Dargan knew that we wouldn't be able to unlock his control,' replied Meltizoc, 'otherwise he wouldn't have let her from his sight. No, I'm afraid that if Merric was unable to draw her out, it is unlikely Kess will be successful. The Dark Master has sent her here to taunt us, to show us that it's hopeless to resist him, to feed our hopes but then dash them.'

'He succeeds, then,' muttered Merric.

'He mustn't,' replied the wise man. 'We are the only hope for the Realm. We can't give up now, however difficult things may seem. We have to keep trying to help Linnil. Dargan is playing a more dangerous game than perhaps he realises because even if we were unable to unlock her mind, she might be able to give us some clues to his whereabouts.'

'And perhaps garrids could sprout wings and fly,' said Valor scornfully. 'Instead of standing here talking, we should be out and about, searching the Southlands.'

'We have many scouts covering that land already,' interrupted Tolledon. 'I need you all here.'

'Why?'

'Because if we can discover where Dargan is, you will be needed to search him out. You have all seen him before, and I believe you still all have your parts to play before this saga is ended.'

Merric, who had been brooding silently, suddenly gave a hoarse whisper. 'Meltizoc! Look at her hands!' He picked up Linnil's left hand gently and held it up to the light. 'Her fingertips are becoming translucent.'

Meltizoc inspected the hand closely and then shook his head slowly.

'What is it? What is happening to her?' the minstrel demanded.

'I'm not sure, but it seems that Dargan's control is somehow physical as well as mental. It's as if her life-force is being gradually drained away in tiny amounts.'

Valor looked sharply at him. 'What do you mean, "being drained away"? Are you saying that she might die soon?'

Meltizoc paused for a moment, glancing at Merric.

'Not exactly. Something far more sinister in a way. It seems that she is beginning to fade.'

'Fade?' said Hesteron incredulously.

'Yes. I have read about such things in ancient times, but I've never seen it happen before. Unless we can help her, she will gradually become more and more transparent. One day we will be here and she will just—disappear.' His voice echoed with weariness as he rose to his feet. 'I must investigate further. Somewhere, in one of my books, I may find an answer. It is unlikely, but I must try.'

'Is there any way we can help?' asked Athennar, who had been silent until now.

'Only by hoping—by clinging on to the fact that Elsinoth will not desert us, and by continuing to seek his help.'

'He's already deserted us!' exploded Valor. 'How can you stand there and talk about Elsinoth's help? What help has he been to Linnil? Where is he when he is needed?'

'He is here,' replied Meltizoc gently. 'He is with each one of us. He grieves, also.'

Athennar and Melinya walked quietly together down a deserted corridor. 'Athennar, I fear for our friends. My faith is strong; even when I was parted from you for so long, I always believed we would be together again one day. But someone like Valor, for instance, who is still so young, doesn't yet understand Elsinoth's ways. He seems to think there should be instant answers, and some kind of magical protection.'

'I know,' Athennar replied. 'I myself am only just learning to trust. But Valor has hidden strengths. Although he may be very enthusiastic one day and despair the next, he has an inner courage which will see him through yet. As you say, he just needs to understand as well. That only comes gradually, I fear. We must just hope that he takes time to think things through. It is difficult, though. Strangely, I see much in him that I can remember in myself when I was younger.'

'You poor old thing,' she teased, then grew serious again. 'But what of the others?'

'Vallel and Hesteron are a great source of strength to each other. It is Merric that I am most concerned about. He has seen the one person he loves above all others returned to him—yet she is unable to recognise him or talk to him—except to speak of her love for someone else.'

'We must support him, however we can.'

'Unfortunately, we probably remind him of the happiness he is denied. Watching his reactions as he tends Linnil makes me wonder what I would have done had you been returned to me in a similar state.'

'Shhh!' she whispered. 'Don't even think of such things.'

Meanwhile, Hesteron and Vallel were talking quietly together in one corner of the dining hall. A slight breeze ruffled the Air Crafter's hair as he spoke. 'When this is all over, I would like to visit Tarrelford. Do you think your fellow Crafters would mind?'

Vallel laughed and brushed back her own flowing hair. 'I'm not sure. They've never really approved of my wild ways, and once they knew I'd become friendly with an Air Crafter ...' A familiar look twinkled in her eyes. 'But I'm sure you'd soon win them over. Don't expect them to become Air Crafters, though!'

'No, I wouldn't expect them to do anything that sensible. They are Water Crafters, after all,' he countered, and was rewarded by a gentle punch.

'Enough!' he laughed. 'Being serious for a moment—I hope we get the opportunity. If Dargan isn't defeated, I fear the Realm will soon begin to suffer. He's unlikely to care much about the streams or rivers. After all, he was the one who poisoned the stream flowing into Merric's homeland.'

Vallel agreed. 'We must stop him if we get the chance,' she said. 'I was hoping that when we returned from the Ice Kingdom, I would be able to go back to Tarrelford for a while. Oh, how I miss the waterfalls and the river. This place is so grim and lifeless. I know now, though, that we must complete this quest before we can hope to go back. I only hope we get the chance; there is so much that I want to show you.'

'Likewise,' Hesteron said, smiling slightly. 'I want to show you the secret places of Winderswood, the parts of the forest where you can hear the breeze singing in the trees. Meanwhile, we must hold on to such memories.'''

Vallel returned his smile and squeezed his hand. Closing her eyes, she imagined that she was already in Tarrelford, lying beside a cool stream ....

Linnil put the glass of water back on the long tray and leaned back against the pillow. Taking the tray from her lap, Merric set it to one side on a little table.

'At least she's eating and drinking,' said Valor, trying to encourage his friend. He didn't like to see him so morose and quiet. It was so unlike him. The young Mountain Guard had calmed down a little, realising that Merric needed his help and support.

'I remember how she looked when I first saw her,' Merric said softly, gazing down at Linnil as she lay quietly on the bed. 'She was so full of life—so beautiful. I was entranced; it was as if she had laid a spell

upon me. Now Dargan has worked his cruel powers
upon her, and it is as if her body is here but her spirit
is elsewhere—like someone who leaves only her
shadow behind. Yet I know she is in there somewhere.
Perhaps she can hear, can understand that I am here.
I hope Meltizoc can discover something that will help
her.'

'How long before … how long do you think …?'

'Before she "fades away"? I know not. It might be
days, possibly weeks. Dargan was doubtless anxious to
prolong the agony for as long as possible.'

'Dargan? Where are you? I love you!' called Linnil,
her voice cold and emotionless.

'Hush, my love.'

The Valley girl subsided into silence again.

'At least the Dark Master's cruelty could play into
our hands,' Merric continued, turning back to Valor.
'By prolonging the process, we are also given more
time to find a cure, though he must be confident that
we will fail. There must be a way, though—there has
to be!' The troubadour, too, lapsed into silence.

'I wonder where Kess and Whisper are?' mused
Valor. 'I wish he would return, if only to be with
Linnil. He would be heart-broken if he knew that she
was here, in this condition, while he searches the
country for a cure for Whisper.'

'Each must do what he feels is right,' replied Merric
wistfully. 'Kess has made his choice; it was not an easy
decision for him. I hope he succeeds, and soon. I too
would like to see him again.'

'There seems little point in saving Whisper if all the
Realm is going to come under Dargan's domination
anyway,' Valor commented sourly.

'You must not think like that. Remember instead—
and I know all too well how difficult it is—all the good
that has happened: how we were saved—twice—from

the Fangers; how Linnil was rescued from the Zorgs; how you all survived the perils of the Whistling Waters and of the Ice Kingdom. It is too easy to remember only that which is bad, and to feel defeated. Far too easy.' He pulled a wry face.

'I know, but ...'

'No "buts"! Toroth has helped us before and he will help again. But he will not work if we do not let him—that is the way it is. He chooses to work through us. We always have the chance to turn our backs on that; to blame him for anything that goes wrong, rather than blame others or our own failings. Believe me, I know how tempting it is to despair when everything fails to go smoothly. But our trust is very weak if we admit defeat as soon as we encounter obstacles, however impossible they may seem.' The minstrel gazed down at Linnil. 'And some of them do seem impossible at times.'

Valor followed his gaze. He knew that Merric was right, and he was determined to show that he wasn't the kind of person to give up. He knew, too, that Elsinoth—or Toroth as the elves called him—was the only hope they had. Sometimes, though, it was a struggle to believe that Elsinoth really cared about them, or that he would act in time. Time was running out—for Linnil and for the Realm.

34

Return to the Fortress

It was a hard climb back up beside the waterfall, and then a long walk to the horses, but Whisper didn't seem to notice. She was like a new person, bursting with vitality. She ran ahead, leaping over obstacles, laughing merrily all the time. 'Oh, isn't life marvellous!' she shouted. 'I feel so good, I could run anywhere, climb anything.'

'Well, don't go running on too far ahead again,' warned Callenor sternly. 'You might remember what happened last time you did that.'

Whisper calmed down for a moment, but nothing could dampen her spirits for long. Soon she was racing up and down again, shouting and singing until Callenor had to quieten her once more.

Kess was rather worried about her and hoped she hadn't taken too much of the liquid from the phial. He wondered if the effect upon her energy was just temporary or permanent. The climb from the waterfall certainly hadn't slowed her at all. Worries about Linnil nagged at him, too, and he was beginning to regret having come so far from the fortress. He wondered if his friends back there had found out yet where she was being held.

Whisper bounced up to him, disrupting his

thoughts. 'Come on, cheer up! I thought you'd be pleased that the potion worked.'

'I am,' he replied, attempting a brave smile. 'I'm just worried about Linnil.'

'She'll be all right. Look, you've saved my life twice now. When we get back to the fortress, I promise I'll help you to search for her.'

'We don't even know where to look.'

'There's that old map in the chest. Perhaps that will give us some clues.'

Kess brightened slightly at the thought. He hadn't looked at the map yet. Perhaps Whisper was right. The sooner they could get back to the fortress and study it the better. Tolledon and Meltizoc might have some useful suggestions to make, and Merric.... He stopped short. He preferred not to think about Merric at the moment: he regretted his harsh words with the troubadour.

Soon they reached the horses, who were happily nibbling the grass in the little clearing near the edge of the forest. Kess felt a great sense of relief as he had half expected them to have been spirited away in their absence. He watched Whisper as she leaped nimbly onto her steed. She had a proud, almost regal, bearing, and had mounted her horse with an expertise that suggested she had spent many of her earlier days riding. Again, he wondered who she really was.

A few yards away, he noticed Callenor watching her warily. The Hallion man had hardly spoken on the journey back through the forest, apart from the occasional warning to Whisper. His normally cheerful features were sombre; he was obviously feeling the loss of Marason. Perhaps, too, the responsibility of getting safely back to the fortress with the chest—and with Whisper in her strange mood—was weighing heavily on him.

The light was fading as they rode out beneath the straggling branches of the jocale trees, but none of them had any desire to spend the night within the forest. Pressing on for a little way in the open air, they eventually found a small copse which would provide some shelter against the cool night breeze.

After a hurried meal, Kess wrapped himself up in his blanket and fell into a deep sleep. It wasn't a peaceful sleep, however. It was disturbed by dark shadows, menacing forms often just out of reach. Strange battle cries floated in the air and water lapped thirstily against a cold shore. A woman's face intruded his tortured thoughts—a face that was at first Linnil's, then Whisper's, then again Linnil's. In the background, he could hear a mocking laugh, which he somehow knew belonged to Dargan. Then swirling grey winds whipped up the sands, the faces, the shadows, tossing them around and discarding them.

The scene cleared and he saw a long beach under dark skies. Fierce people were riding, shouting, bearing down upon others who were fleeing along the beach in panic. With a shock, Kess recognised the leader of the riders. It was Whisper (or was it Linnil?). She savagely rode down an old man, laughing as his face crashed into the sand. He heard cries for help, screams of anguish, and all he could see was Whisper fighting, fighting, fighting....

He awoke with a start. A trickle of sweat ran down his face, and he wiped it away. Suddenly he realised that someone was staring down at him. Whisper!

'Are you all right?' she asked. 'You were tossing and turning, and I thought I heard you call my name.'

'Sorry,' he said, abashed. 'I think I must have been overtired. I had a bad nightmare where you were riding a horse and fighting people.'

Whisper smiled strangely. 'Try and sleep,' she said.

'I wish you both would—then I could as well!' came Callenor's voice out of the darkness.

Kess chuckled and turned over, and this time he sank into a dreamless sleep.

Several days later, saddle-sore and tired, the three travellers arrived back at the Fortress of Fear leading Marason's horse. As they approached the fortress, the huge wooden gates creaked open and Meltizoc and Tolledon came forward to meet them. 'Good meeting! Was your trip successful? Where is Marason?'

'Good meeting,' replied Kess, then guardedly he said, 'I'm sorry. Marason is dead, killed in the Jewelled Forest. We found the chest, and the potion—as you can see—seems to have helped Whisper.'

Tolledon was taken aback by the news of Marason and motioned Callenor to one side to speak to him.

Meltizoc looked at the young woman approvingly. 'You look as if you've been exercising for several months to be in such fine shape,' he commented. She blushed, knowing he still regarded her with some suspicion.

'Has there been any news of Linnil?' Kess asked anxiously.

'Yes,' replied Meltizoc. 'She's here....'

'Why didn't you tell me straight away? I must go and see her.'

'Kess, be patient until we have explained. Linnil is not ... herself. She's somehow under Dargan's power, and we've been unable to break his hold.'

'Dargan!' hissed Kess. 'If he has hurt her, he'll answer for it.' He rode impatiently into the courtyard, not waiting to hear more.

'He has been—worried,' explained Whisper, as she watched Meltizoc's gaze follow the Valley man.

'I know,' he said. 'Unfortunately, he is likely to be even more worried when he sees her.'

Merric sat quietly in the small room, holding Linnil's hand and singing softly to her. She was continuing to fade; slowly, almost unnoticeably to most people, but he could see it. He saw it in the paleness of her hands, the lack of colour in her lips and cheeks. Every day since she had been brought to the room he had sat beside her, either talking or singing to her, desperately trying to think of some way to help her.

The door was suddenly flung open and a lithe figure rushed in. Merric almost drew his sword in surprise, then recognition dawned across his features. 'Kess! Welcome back! Did you find anything?'

Kess ignored him and sat down on the bed beside his sister. 'Linnil!' he called, hugging her. 'It's Kess! Linnil, I'm here!'

There was no response. Linnil lay staring up at the ceiling, oblivious to his calls.

'How long has she been like this?' he asked harshly.

'For several days now,' replied Merric. 'A Tark brought her in, and as soon as it landed, she collapsed. At first she was unmoving, as if unconscious. Then when Dargan's name was mentioned....'

'Dargan, where are you? I love you!'

'Hush, my love.' Merric looked at Kess and ran his hand across his brow. 'That is the only response she gives. I have tried talking to her, singing to her, but to no avail.'

'You haven't tried hard enough, then,' barked Kess.

Merric bit his lip as the words cut cruelly into his heart, but he said nothing.

'Linnil!' Kess cried. 'Dargan isn't here! Listen to me! Dargan is evil—you don't love him. He has tricked you into saying that. Listen to me, Linnil—you don't love Dargan.'

'W-What?' she said. 'Where are you, Dargan? I love you! Please come back to me! I love you, Dargan!'

Merric quietened her again, and then watched as a string of emotions drifted across Kess' face. They were all ones that he himself had experienced many times over the past few days: frustration, grief, despair and worry.

Gritting his teeth, Kess arose from the bed. 'There must be some way to unlock her mind,' he said. 'There has to be.'

Suddenly he remembered the heart's tears pendant he had carved for her at Hallion. It seemed months ago. Rummaging through his backpack, his fingers closed around it. Perhaps this would jolt her memory—the feel of wood, the familiar shape of the flower, the call of his voice.

'Linnil, I have a present for you.' He dangled the pendant enticingly in front of her eyes. 'It's for you, Linnil. Remember the heart's tears? Remember the Valley?'

'Present?' she said huskily. One pale hand reached up weakly and grasped the carving. 'Present,' she said. 'I love you, Dargan!' Then she leaned back, still holding on to the pendant, although she had again fallen silent.

Kess sighed. 'I *will* find an answer,' he said defiantly. ''Even if it takes me all my life.'

'You may not have that long,' said Merric softly. 'Her mental state reflects only a portion of the Dark Master's cruel powers. Look at her hands, her face! She fades, Kess!'

'But ....'

'The only hope is to find an answer soon. Did you locate the book?'

'We found a book, but I don't think it was the right one.'

'Then you are wrong, young man,' said Meltizoc's voice from the doorway. 'That book is a most valuable item—should we ever be able to make use of it. It is indeed the Great Tome of Neldra.'

'But I thought ....'

'Size isn't everything, my friend. Its greatness lies in what it contains, not in its physical dimensions.'

'The phials!' shouted Kess suddenly. 'There were two phials in the chest. Whisper used the one that was labelled "For the healing of the body", but there was another called "For the healing of the mind". That might contain a cure for Linnil.'

Meltizoc looked doubtful, but gave a nod. 'It is worth a try. I fear, however, that the kind of control Dargan exerts will not easily be broken by a potion, however powerful. If there is some of the body-healing fluid left, that may at least help to delay the fading.'

Kess groaned and shook his head. 'Whisper used it all before I could stop her,' he said. 'If she has deprived Linnil of a chance to live ....'

He hadn't finished the sentence when Whisper and Callenor arrived, along with Tolledon, who was carrying the chest under one arm.

Frustrated and uncharacteristically impatient, Kess asked Tolledon for the full phial. As he was handed it, he looked across at Whisper and scowled. 'I hope your selfishness hasn't ruined my sister's chance of recovery,' he snapped.

'What?' she said, taken aback.

'I'll explain later,' Meltizoc interrupted. 'Kess, I think it's best that you concentrate on the task in hand. There will be time enough for your complaints later.'

The Valley man glared at him, and then turned round to tend his sister. Cradling her head in his hand, he gently persuaded her to sip some of the liquid from the green phial. Linnil obediently drank a little and then sank back against her pillow. The others looked on in anticipation, but nothing happened.

'With Whisper, the cure was immediate,' muttered Kess, almost as if to himself. He propped up his sister again and desperately made her swallow all the remaining contents of the bottle. She seemed to smile slightly before leaning back against the pillow once more.

'How will we know if it has worked?' asked Tolledon.

'There is one way,' replied Merric wistfully. Hesitantly, he looked at Linnil's now expressionless face. 'Linnil, do you remember anything?' he asked tentatively. 'Do you remember Dargan?'

She was silent for a moment, and then a smile crept over her face. 'Dargan,' she whispered, 'I love you!'

Merric bowed his head in his hands; Kess let out a shriek of frustration. Their attempt had failed. Linnil was still under Dargan's control.

35
Renewed Hopes

'Get up, you scum-bag! There's someone coming. Perhaps we can make a break for it.' Gur'brak kicked his snoozing companion, who opened his one eye and then closed it again. He was rewarded by a harder kick.

'Aw, give us a break, Gur'brak! What's the point? We've tried twice before, and failed each time.'

'The point is that I don't intend to be stuck in here for ever, even if you do.' He cuffed Bar'drash around the head.

Grumbling, the shorter Zorg staggered to his feet. He could now hear footsteps approaching down the corridor.

'Get ready to rush 'em!' hissed Gur'brak. 'We'll take 'em by surprise.'

The key grated in the lock, and the door creaked open.

'Now!' shouted Gur'brak. He made a rush for the door, followed by his reluctant companion. Abruptly, he found himself grabbed by his waist, swung around through the air and unceremoniously dumped back in the cell. The guard who had opened the cell door chuckled.

A second guard caught Bar'drash by the ear. 'Ow!

Leggo!' squealed the Zorg. He was pushed over to join his companion, and sat down with a bump, rubbing his ear.

A tall figure stepped into the cell and looked down at the two Zorgs. 'Is this any way to repay our hospitality?' he said in an amused tone.

Gur'brak snorted but said nothing.

'I have come to ask for your help,' continued Tolledon. 'I presume that you know Dargan as well as any of us—probably better. Have you any idea where he might be?'

'Why should we help you?' asked Gur'brak.

'Why not?' Tolledon asked in return.

'What's in it for us?' the Zorg demanded.

Tolledon smiled. 'I could perhaps arrange for you to be moved to more comfortable quarters.'

'How about letting us go free?' said Gur'brak.

'Not yet,' replied Tolledon. 'But who knows? We would not be ungrateful if you chose to help us. But enough of this bantering. Where is Dargan?'

The Zorg paused and then shrugged. 'He lives in a huge fortress on an enormous rock in the middle of a wide plain.' He sneered. 'You'll never break into it.'

'You mean his stronghold? No, he escaped from there some time ago.'

Gur'brak looked astonished at the thought of the Dark Master fleeing from anything or anyone. 'I don't believe you,' he said.

'It's the truth, I assure you,' replied Tolledon. He briefly described the stronghold so that the Zorgs would be in no doubt that it had been captured. 'Can you think of anywhere else he might have gone?' he persisted.

Gur'brak shook his head and Bar'drash scowled. 'If he was with a Tark, he could have gone anywhere,' the Zorg captain said. 'You'll never find him.'

It was Tolledon's turn to scowl. Turning abruptly, he left the cell, followed by the guards.

As the door was locked again, Gur'brak looked at his silent companion. 'I wonder what all that was about?' he said.

Bar'drash shrugged, closed his eye, and was soon asleep again.

'It's been a week since I arrived, and still I haven't been able to help her,' fumed Kess, pacing up and down the oak panelled room. The frustration kept bubbling up inside him, ready to erupt with great ferocity at any time.

'You've done all you can,' replied Valor. It troubled him to see his friend so upset. The young Mountain Guard had found himself acting as comforter to Kess, just as he had to Merric. It was a role he had never imagined for himself. He knew just how Kess was feeling. He felt it himself, but refused to let despair get the upper hand any more.

'Meltizoc has been spending a lot of time studying the book you brought back from the Jewelled Forest,' said Hesteron, who was sitting on a bench against the wall with Vallel. 'Perhaps he will find something of help.'

'I hope he hurries,' said Kess sharply. Then, collapsing in a heap, he sighed. 'I'm sorry. I don't mean to be so snappy. It's just that I feel so on edge.'

'We understand,' replied Vallel. 'When Hesteron was wounded, I was desperately worried about him. But don't give up—Toroth will help her.'

'Toroth! Elsinoth! Why doesn't he help us now?' said Kess, disgruntled.

Before Vallel could answer, the door opened and a big beaming face peered round it.

'Gatera!' said Valor and Kess at once.

'Good meeting!' boomed the Land Crafter.

'How's Rrum?' asked Vallel anxiously.

'You can see for yourself,' replied Gatera.

A little stocky figure waddled into the room. 'Good meettingg!'

'Once he awoke fully, he seemed to recover rapidly,' explained Gatera. 'In fact, I nearly had to tie him down to get him to rest and to stop him from coming here straight away.'

The little Rrokki ambled over to Kess and shook his hand gravely. Strangely, Kess realised that Rrum was wordlessly demonstrating that he understood his grief over Linnil. 'It's good to see you,' he said, warmly returning the handshake.

'Yes,' Rrum replied.

'Tolledon told us about Linnil. How is she?' asked Gatera solemnly.

Kess shrugged. 'We've tried everything, but we just can't get through to her.'

Rrum patted his hand sympathetically. 'If we can helpp …' he said.

'I know. I know,' replied Kess. 'I only wish you could. She needs help from somewhere—and soon. But I can no longer see any hope.'

'She is alive, and there is therefore hope,' said Hesteron, 'however slim that hope may seem to be.'

Kess grunted but didn't reply.

The following day, Tolledon called a meeting in the Dining Hall of the fortress. When everyone had arrived and was seated at the table, he looked around at their dismal faces and frowned, wishing he had some good news to report.

'This has been a difficult time for all of us,' he started. 'Unfortunately, I fear that even more difficult times will soon be upon us. Our scouts have failed to find any trace of Dargan's whereabouts, yet there is little question that he is somewhere in the Southlands, plotting the downfall of the Realm. The future of our land lies with us, yet we are still groping around, trying to catch a fly in the mist. Can any of you think of anything at all—however small or seemingly stupid—that we could do to find Dargan and the Sceptre?'

A heavy silence hung in the air for a few moments.

'Perhaps if we could catch a Tark?' suggested Valor. Normally the others would have laughed at such an outrageous suggestion, but one or two heads turned hopefully in Tolledon's direction.

The Guardian shook his head sadly. 'Even if such a thing were possible, and even if somehow we knew where to find the creatures, we have no way of persuading them to divulge such information. Besides, no Tarks have been seen since the one that delivered Linnil.'

'Would there be any clues in the books at Dargan's stronghold?'" asked Kess suddenly.

'They were desttroyed,' Rrum reminded him solemnly.

The room fell quiet again. Athennar stood up and leaned on the table, gazing down to his father at the opposite end. 'We have to do something,' he declared. 'We've been cooped up in this place for too long. At least we could be out in the open air searching for the Dark One.' Several of the assembled company nodded in silent agreement.

Tolledon sat for a while, musing, and then shook his head. 'It would be futile. There must be a better way. But ...'

The door suddenly burst open, and Meltizoc wheezed and puffed his way into the room. 'I have an answer!' he called, triumphantly waving a book. 'You thought you had failed when you brought back this book, Kess—but it may provide the solution we've been seeking. Perhaps your friend's quest wasn't so misguided after all!'

Whisper flushed in confusion while Kess just looked perplexed.

The wise old man sat down, dropping the Great Tome of Neldra on the table. A cloud of dust puffed out from between its covers. 'What is it exactly that Dargan has done to Linnil?' he asked.

'Controlled her mind?' suggested Vallel.

'How?' asked Meltizoc.

'By forcing her to believe lies,' muttered Merric.

'Exactly! And how do you counter lies?'

'With the truth,' replied Kess. 'But we've been trying that, and we haven't got anywhere.'

'No, but I know something that could help us,' said Meltizoc. Smiling at their looks of puzzlement, he continued. 'The Great Tome is written in an ancient language of the Realm. I knew a little of it, but have had to spend much of my time in study to be able to translate it properly. I concentrated on the section that gives the location of the objects made by Elsinoth after he had finished his work of creation—items like the Golden Sceptre.'

'What use is that?' snorted Valor impatiently. 'We already know that it's been stolen.'

'Still speaking before you listen, Valor? You still have much to learn. As I was saying, items like the Golden Sceptre and the Globe of Truth, among others.'

'The Globe of Truth,' whispered Tolledon, sudden understanding dawning in his eyes.

'Precisely. The Realm is founded upon truth, and it is said that no one can willingly tell a lie when holding the globe. Linnil will be forced into recognising the truth about herself.'

'But it could destroy her!' exploded Merric.

'Possibly. But I think not. I suspect she is made of sterner stuff. If we can break Dargan's hold on her mind, not even he would be able to re-establish control over such a distance. Furthermore, Linnil should be able to tell us where he is.'

'It might just work,' breathed Tolledon.

'And it might not!' retorted Kess. 'This is my sister's mind you're meddling with.'

'Do you have any better suggestions?' asked Meltizoc.

Kess muttered to himself, but subsided into silence.

'But where is this globe?' asked Hesteron.

Meltizoc produced the map that had been in the chest. 'This map shows the last known location of all the articles. Unless it has been removed, which is unlikely, it is still here,' he said, pointing to a spot in the centre of the Northlands.

Athennar looked at it closely and then sighed.

'Well?' asked Hesteron.

'The globe is in the Black Caves,' he replied.

'The Black Caves!' exclaimed Kess. 'Why there, of all places?' He was now back in Linnil's room with Valor, Gatera and Rrum. The thought of the Black Caves made him shudder. He remembered finding Rrum there, and hearing of the legends: that few re-urned if they ventured too far into the dark tunnels.

'At least we'll be doing something,' said Valor.

Kess shook his head. 'I must stay here with Linnil,' he replied. 'Somehow I might still be able to get through to her. But I will be grateful to any who go in search of the globe.'

'We will ggo,' said Rrum, looking at Gatera.

The big Land Crafter nodded. 'Aye, we have a

score to settle with those caves. And who better to go than a rock man and a Land Crafter? I have little love of caves and dark passages, but it seems that I am destined to spend my time in them.' He grinned at Kess.

'My thanks. It's good to know that you three have remained my friends. I'm afraid I've lost Merric's friendship for ever by my harsh words.'

'Then you do not know me very well, my friend.' Merric had slipped in through the doorway unnoticed. He walked over to Kess and clasped his shoulder. 'Do you think I fail to understand how you feel? I, too, have been wandering the corridors of this place like a disgruntled Zorg! I would be a poor friend if I deserted you so readily.'

Kess tried to thank him, but failed because of the large lump in his throat.

'I will accompany Gatera, Rrum and Valor, and keep them out of mischief,' continued Merric. 'Indeed, I suggest we leave immediately.'

'But what about Athennar and the others?' Kess managed to croak.

'The fewer the better if we are to venture into the caves!' replied the troubadour. 'And it is best that some remain here, lest we fail.'

'What he means,' boomed Gatera, trying to lighten the mood, 'is that we might need rescuing! But not if I have anything to do with it.'

Kess forced a smile. 'If success depends on friendship,' he said quietly, 'then I would have no fears of your failing.'

His friends smiled and said their goodbyes. After they had gone, Kess turned to Linnil and held her pale hand lightly. 'Perhaps there is still hope,' he whispered, as much to himself as to her.

For a brief moment, he thought he could see her smiling.

The tale is concluded in the final part of the Stories of the Realm trilogy, The Fading Realm.

The Will Of Dargan

by Phil Allcock

Trouble has darkened the skies of the
Realm: the Golden Sceptre crafted by the
hands of Elsinoth the Mighty has been
stolen. Courageous twins, Kess and Linnil,
team up with an assorted company of elves
and crafters—and set out to find it.

Their journey takes them through rugged
mountains, gentle valleys and wild woods to
the grim stronghold of Dargan the Bitter.
Will they win back the Sceptre? The answer
depends on their courage, friendship and
trust.

Phoenix
Published by Kingsway